The screaming continued. Sprocket stood up from the floor and gave me a concerned look. There's nothing worse than a worried poodle, except possibly a worried poodle that comes up to your waist. That's a lot of worried poodle. The screaming went up in pitch.

I shut off the heat under the sauce and rushed to the back door of POPS, which opened into the alleyway that ran behind the shops on Main Street in Grand Lake.

I pushed open the door and felt my heart clench. There was broken glass on the back porch of Coco's shop and the back door was open. The screams were definitely coming from Coco's Cocoas. I ran . . .

Kernel
of Truth

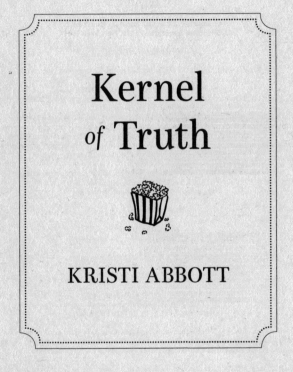

KRISTI ABBOTT

BERKLEY PRIME CRIME, NEW YORK

BERKLEY PRIME CRIME

An imprint of Penguin Random House LLC
375 Hudson Street, New York, New York 10014

KERNEL OF TRUTH

A Berkley Prime Crime Book / published by arrangement with the author

ISBN: 978-0-425-28091-1

PUBLISHING HISTORY
Berkley Prime Crime mass-market edition / March 2016

PRINTED IN THE UNITED STATES OF AMERICA

10 9 8 7 6 5 4 3 2 1

Cover illustration by Catherine Deeter.
Cover design by Sarah Oberrender.
Interior text design by Tiffany Estreicher.

Penguin
Random
House

ACKNOWLEDGMENTS

This book would never have even begun to exist without Leis Pederson. She is inventive, funny, smart, and flexible. In short, she's totally fantastic. That's not a short joke. Although it could be. I'm reasonably certain that anyone who has seen us walking anywhere together would like to make some kind of Mutt and Jeff joke. Go ahead. We don't care. We like it this way.

The recipes in this book would never have worked without Spring Warren. After she got done laughing at me for thinking that marshmallow crème was appropriate in a breakfast bar, she got down to work and made Rebecca's creations a reality. Watching Spring in a kitchen is like watching someone dance: beautiful and breathtaking. Everything started, however, with Barbara Smith's caramel corn recipe. I would have been lost without it. Thank you also to Teddy and Alex Rendahl who happily ate the recipes even when they didn't turn out so hot.

Thank you to my beloved Andy Wallace for blithely coming up with red herrings, plot twists, and endless encouragement.

You continually amaze me. I'd like to thank Deb Van Der List and Helen Raybould for their funny stories about life with poodles. Thank you to my sister Marian although she won't remember what I'm thanking her for or why. I'm not sure I do either, but it's so rare that I don't need to consult her on something medical in the course of writing a book that I thank her by reflex.

There was a moment—possibly a series of moments—when I thought my head might explode while I was writing this book. My sister Diane and my mother, Deborah, stepped in and took troubles off my shoulders. I'm not sure how I could have finished this without them.

One

The caramel sauce was almost three hundred and fifty degrees when the screaming started.

I wasn't proud that my first instinct was to ignore it. The screaming, that is, not the sauce. I was at a critical moment. In a matter of seconds, it would need to be removed from the heat and have the baking soda added. Then it needed to be poured over the freshly popped popcorn and mixed. Leave it on the stove longer and my sauce was going to be bitter. Take it off now and it wasn't going to be ready for the baking soda to create the requisite air bubbles to keep it light.

But screaming, right? Human screaming. Human screaming versus caramel sauce. Sprocket stood up from the floor and gave me a concerned look. There's nothing worse than a worried poodle, except possibly a worried poodle that comes up to your waist. That's a lot of worried poodle. The screaming went up in pitch.

I shut off the heat under the sauce and rushed to the back

door of POPS, which opened into the alleyway that ran behind the shops on Main Street in Grand Lake.

I pushed open the door and felt my heart clench. There was broken glass on the back porch of Coco's shop and the back door was open. The screams were definitely coming from Coco's Cocoas. I ran.

I ran through the back door and through Coco's kitchen toward the sound. It was coming from the office at the front of the renovated house that served as Coco's shop. I screeched to a halt, nearly tripping over Coco's quad cane in the doorway. I picked it up and tossed it aside. Sprocket bumped into me from behind. Jessica James stood in the middle of the office, back to the door, shrieking her tiny, blond shrill head off.

I could see why. Or at least partially why. In the dim light, I could see Coco's feet. They were sticking out from behind the big wooden desk. I knew they were her feet because I recognized her shoes. She hated them. She hated their clunky rubber soles. She hated their boxy shape and their elastic laces. She hated the sensibility of them. She said she wouldn't mind growing old so much if she could grow old in style.

"Jessica," I said. "What happened?"

Jessica whirled around. She probably hadn't heard me come in over her own wailing. Her face was like a mask, white and sort of distorted. Her lips and eyes stood out, too vivid against the pallor of her face, eyes red-rimmed from crying. She reached toward me, her hands shaking.

"I don't know, Rebecca. I don't know. But I think Auntie Coco is dead." She gasped out the words.

I pushed past her to get to Coco and froze. One glance was all it took for me to know it was way too late for me to help Coco. She was crumpled against the credenza, her eyes glassy and open but seeing nothing. She looked like a rag doll discarded by a bratty child. Except rag dolls didn't leave blood smears like Coco had clearly left on the credenza.

Behind me Sprocket began to howl, which set Jessica off again. She launched herself at me. "I should never have left her alone last night. I should have stayed."

I wrapped an arm around her, grabbed the phone off the desk and dialed 911.

I pulled the blanket tighter around myself and tried to get the coffee cup up to my lips, but my teeth still chattered too hard. After calling 911, I'd gotten Jessica and Sprocket and me out of Coco's Cocoas and back to POPS. I'd managed to pour a cup of coffee before the shaking had started. Now it wouldn't stop. I'd been this cold only once before in my life. That had been after a death, too. Then my sister, Haley, and I had huddled together for warmth. Today Sprocket pressed himself into my side, resting his head on my lap. I could barely feel the heat from his body. I curled my fingers into his apricot fur and the shaking slowed a little.

Dan sat across from me in my pretty blue kitchen, our knees almost touching. He tucked a stray lock of my hair back behind my ear. His hands felt warm against my face. "Take your time, Bec. Start at the beginning and tell me what you remember."

Dan, or Sheriff Cooper as most of the town now addressed him, had the clearest, lightest blue eyes I'd ever seen. They were set in a square-jawed face that rested atop a fairly substantial set of shoulders. Instead of answering his question, I leaned forward, put my head on one of those shoulders and sobbed.

Dan patted my back. Dan had been patting my back off

and on since second grade, when I punched him in the nose
for putting a worm in my chocolate milk. We had been best
friends from that point on, so close he was like the brother
I didn't have until he actually became my brother by marrying my sister, Haley, when he moved back to Grand Lake
after college. Which was surprisingly not weird. Go figure.

"Why, Dan? Why? Why would someone do that?" I snuf-
fled onto his brown uniform shirt. Haley was going to be
furious with me for getting snot on it. I didn't care.

"It looks like a burglary gone wrong, Bec. The back
window was bashed in. The cash register was emptied." Dan
kept patting.

"Did Jessica know how much was missing?" It couldn't
have been much. It certainly couldn't have been enough to
warrant killing Coco to get it.

"Jessica is not in any shape to know anything. She's a
mess. She wasn't making any sense. We'll figure it out later.
It doesn't really matter anyway. Coco's still gone whether
they got fifty dollars or five hundred." Dan sounded pained.

I straightened up, grabbed a bunch of tissues out of the
box that had somehow magically appeared at the table in
the kitchen and blew my nose. Hard. I was a very snotty
crier. "Do you think she tried to fight them off?" I wouldn't
put it past her. Coco was nothing if not feisty. I could have
totally seen her taking a swing at an intruder with her quad
cane. Maybe she'd flung it at the intruder. Maybe that's why
it had been in the doorway. Otherwise it was rarely more
than six inches from her right hand.

"We're still piecing all that together. Right now it looks
as if someone shoved her and she lost her balance and stumbled backward. She hit the corner of that credenza with her
head in exactly the worst way possible." Dan drummed his
fingers on his knee.

Coco's balance was terrible. It was some kind of ear thing. That's why she had the cane, an item that she had hated even more than the sensible shoes, in the first place. It wouldn't have taken much of a shove to send her toppling ass-over-teakettle. A child could have done it. "Maybe it was an accident," I whispered. "Maybe she just fell."

"Not with the busted window and missing cash." Dan shook his head. "It still could have been unintentional. A shove that sent her backward harder than intended, but someone did this, Rebecca. Someone's responsible. Can you tell me what you saw?" Dan asked.

"I was making a new caramel sauce, one with Kahlúa in it, for the new popcorn line when I heard Jessica screaming. I looked out the back and saw the glass and the door at Coco's standing open and ran over there." And inside I saw something I was afraid my brain would never be able to erase. It wasn't how I wanted to remember Coco. I started to sniffle again.

"Okay. Good," Dan said. "What time did you get here today?"

I thought about it. "A little before six."

He made a note in his little notebook. "How come you didn't notice the glass and the door when you got here?" He scratched Sprocket behind the ears and got a grateful lick in return.

"Sprocket and I walked, we came in the front. I only come in the back when I drive." It's about two miles from where I live to the shop. I try to walk whenever I can. It's good for Sprocket to walk. It's good for me, too. Caramel sauce doesn't taste itself. Haley and I came from thin people. We were lucky and I knew it, but that didn't mean I could rely on genes alone to keep me in my skinny jeans.

"When was the last time you were out in the alley?"

I wrapped my hands around my coffee mug; I was starting to be able to feel the warmth from it. "I think probably when I took the garbage out yesterday when I was closing up."

"What time would that have been?"

I set the mug down and rubbed at my forehead. My head had started to throb. "Around six thirty. I started winter hours two weeks ago."

Dan nodded and made another note. Grand Lake is a tourist town and we get most of our traffic in the summer months. We still get a little in the fall, but not enough to warrant keeping the shop open past five thirty or six on a weeknight. If people want popcorn for dessert, they've bought it by then. There weren't enough folks strolling up and down Main Street in the evenings to keep the shop open until nine after Labor Day, so I put away my white shoes and switched to winter hours after the first Monday of September.

"You didn't notice anything unusual then?" He wasn't even looking at me.

My shivering stopped. Maybe it was the warmth of indignation. "Do you really think I'd see Coco's back window bashed in and not go check on her?"

He sat back in his chair, looking very directly at me now with those clear blue eyes. "Bec, I need to ask the questions. All of them. Even if they seem stupid or rude to you. There's no telling what could be important later."

I unruffled my proverbial feathers. He was Sheriff Cooper right now, not Dan, my best friend since forever. I shut my eyes and tried to remember exactly what I'd seen or not seen. "Well, the back door was definitely closed and the window was fine. I don't remember there being a light on in back. If there had been, I would have probably knocked to see if Coco wanted me to walk home with her, but her office is in the front of the house. If there was a light on in there, I might not have seen it."

Coco's house was only two blocks away and she prided herself on still walking to and from the shop every day, but I knew once the light started to fade earlier and earlier, curbs and cracks in the sidewalks turned into issues for her. She hated the idea of being cosseted, but if I told her that I needed her advice on something for the shop (and I pretty much always needed her advice on something for the shop), she'd let me walk with her and keep her from missing a step off the curb or tripping over one of the tree roots that humped up the sidewalk better than any earthquake could.

"Are you sure about there not being a light on?" Dan pressed, his head cocked to one side.

I squinched my eyes tight shut, trying to remember it exactly. Had there been a light? Hadn't there been? Would I have noticed? I thought I would, but couldn't be certain. It had still been light out. Maybe she hadn't even needed a light on inside yet. No. That wasn't right. Coco's eyes weren't what they used to be either. She always needed a light. I opened my eyes, blew out a breath and shook my head. "I don't think there was one, but if you're asking if I could swear to it in court, the answer is no." I dropped my head into my hands. What else had I missed? Could I have kept this from happening?

He patted my hand. "It's okay." He looked back down at his notepad. "Did you see anyone else out there? Anyone hanging around? Or even walking through?"

The great thing about routine when you run a shop is it gives you some consistency and reliability. The bad thing is that days tend to run together because they're all the same. It was hard to be sure what I had seen last night or the night before or a night a week ago.

"Well, I didn't see Jasper," I said. "But I left him yesterday's popcorn in a bag by the back porch rather than throw it out."

If you're selling gourmet popcorn, the least you can do is make sure it's fresh. Rather than toss what was left at the end of the day, I gave it to Jasper. Jasper wasn't exactly homeless. He had a place, or so I'd been told, near the south end of town. He did not, however, have a job beyond wandering the streets of Grand Lake and panhandling. He wasn't a raving lunatic, but he was a few old maids shy of a fully popped bowl. Town legend had it that Jasper had been a professor at Oberlin and had lost his mind in pursuit of tenure. Now he wandered the streets of Grand Lake spouting bits and pieces of obscure philosophy and history and conspiracy theories that generally revolved around him and some cabal trying to keep him down.

"And the bag was gone this morning?" Dan sat up a little straighter.

I didn't remember seeing it. "Is it there now?" I asked.

Dan got up and looked out the back door. He came back shaking his head. "There's nothing there now."

"Then he probably came by after I left. Maybe he saw something." Jasper had a tendency to lurk in the shadows and pop out unexpectedly. It was one of his less charming habits, but maybe it could be helpful this time. Maybe he saw who broke into Coco's.

"I'll definitely be asking him," Dan said. "Now, what did you touch while you were in Coco's shop?"

I sighed. I'd already gotten a dirty look from Dan for tramping through the broken glass going in and out of Coco's. Apparently, there was a trail going down the steps and now they weren't sure if it was left by me or whoever had done what they'd done to Coco. "The door, I think. The phone in the office for sure."

"Light switches?"

"Maybe." I thought for a second, then shook my head. "No. I didn't turn on the light. Definitely Coco's dress, though. I touched that."

Dan's eyebrows shot up above his baby blues. "Her dress? Why?"

I blushed. "It was kind of rucked up. I pulled it down. It wasn't . . . dignified." Coco would have been horrified at the thought of all those people seeing her underthings.

Dan set his pad and pen down and stared at me. "Bec, it's a crime scene. You're not supposed to mess with the crime scene."

"I know it was a crime scene. I also know that Coco was the victim. I didn't want to make her into even more of one by letting half the town see her knickers." Men. They understood nothing.

He shook his head and made some notes on his pad. "Fine. Whatever. Have you seen anyone strange hanging around? Someone who shouldn't be here? Or someone you don't know?"

I bit back the snarky remark about men in trench coats twirling pencil-thin mustaches that was on the tip of my tongue. "Not that I remember. It's been quiet now that the season is over."

"I know. It was kind of nice." Dan rubbed his face.

Speaking of quiet, I could no longer hear Jessica shrieking. "Where did Huerta take Jessica?" Glenn Huerta, Dan's deputy, had bundled her off somewhere after Dan and the paramedics arrived.

"Huerta took her over to the urgent care." Dan jotted down something in his notebook.

"Seriously?" That was so Jessica. She had found a way to make Coco's death all about her. Making herself into the victim was like her superpower.

He shrugged. "She couldn't seem to stop screaming."

I rolled my eyes.

"Bec," he said, his tone a warning. "She found her aunt dead on the floor. Look at the reaction you had and you're not even related to Coco." He gestured at my blanket and coffee.

Being related to a person didn't necessarily make you close. I was more connected to Coco than Jessica would ever be in every way that counted except blood, and I wasn't screaming my head off. Instead I shook hard enough that I couldn't lift a coffee cup to my mouth. It was totally more dignified.

Two

I didn't feel like opening POPS for the breakfast crowd like I usually did. I had no idea how much business I was losing. I had quite a few regulars who usually came in for coffee and one of my popcorn breakfast bars. Plus I could have probably made some bank on the Lookie Lous crowding around the yellow-tape lines protecting Coco's Cocoas—ghoulish rubbernecking could work up an appetite—but it didn't feel right. In fact, it felt downright gross.

I didn't particularly want to go home, either. Staring at the walls and trying to get the mental picture of Coco slumped over, hands limp in her lap, legs splayed, blood in her smooth gray chignon, eyes lifeless out of my head was even less appealing than serving blueberry-almond popcorn bars to a bunch of bloodthirsty bystanders.

Besides, I loved my shop. It was a haven for me. I wasn't afraid to brag about it. The house had already been converted into a shop front before I came onboard, but that was about all you could say for it. It didn't have any personality.

It didn't have any style. It didn't have any pizzazz. What did it have? A fan-freaking-tastic location between the chocolate shop and the florist on the main tourist drag.

I knew people had talked when I started remodeling it to suit my purposes. I wasn't an idiot. I knew what it meant when people stopped talking when you walked into a room. They thought I should see if the business would take off first before I started pouring money into it. They thought I was bringing my snooty California design ideas to Main Street U.S.A., where they would not be appreciated. They thought I'd screw it up like I'd screwed up everything else before I left here almost before the strains of "Pomp and Circumstance" died at my high school graduation.

I didn't give a rat's ass.

Okay. Maybe I gave part of a rat's ass. Like part of one rat buttock. It's not easy to come back to a town that you left with a reputation somewhere on the continuum between sketchy and shady. I couldn't expect everyone to respect my choices. I was going to have to prove to everyone that I'd grown up okay. Well, to everyone except Coco and Dan and Haley. It didn't mean I liked it though. I'd had eleven years of no one taking me seriously because I was Antoine's wife. That had been hard enough to take. Now they weren't taking me seriously because they thought I was still high school me.

At any rate, there'd been a lot of "who does she think she is" and "what does she think she's doing" conversations buzzing around as I'd expanded the kitchen space, had the walls painted a smeary textured blue and started putting in glass shelving. There had been a lot of people making up excuses to come in and out of the shop to watch its progress and report back to the folks at Bob's Diner and Winnie's Tavern. From what I'd heard, a verified account of what type of light fixtures I'd had installed was good for a piece of pie or a draft beer. If you knew how much they'd cost, you could get the pie a la mode.

Luckily, my contractor was Carson Jenkins, who was enjoying confounding the local population even more than I was. Carson and I used to smoke cigarettes out behind the high school during passing period. Neither of us smoked anymore, but friends you made while hiding from the vice principal apparently were friends for life.

"I placed an order for two hot tubs," he told me one morning over coffee as we discussed plans. Before I could protest, he held up his hand. "Don't worry. I'll cancel 'em, but let's see how long it takes to get around town that you're putting one hot tub in your shop and another in your sister's garage."

The answer was approximately eighteen hours. Dan had come home the next evening and asked where on his property did I think I was going to be naked hot-tubbing.

I was impressed at the addition of nudity to the rumor. Someone was augmenting the gossip with some special flourishes. "Gossip much?" I'd asked.

"It's kind of my job these days. The more I know about what's going on around town, the more I can keep everyone safe and everyone on an even keel." He'd started using sailing metaphors. He was hanging out with Mayor Thompson way too much.

"And how will my naked hot-tubbing endanger anyone or knock anyone off course?" I enquired, trying to keep my tone as sweet as Coco's Signature Fudge.

"Teenaged boys could fall out of the trees they've climbed to get a glimpse of you in all your glory in the backyard and then break their necks. It would be bad for the town and for my insurance premiums. Double whammy," Dan declared. I was flattered enough that he thought anyone would climb even a step stool to see me naked that I let it go even though

I'd had to give Carson five dollars the next day because it had taken less than twenty-four hours before law enforcement was involved. "Never bet against the house, Rebecca," he'd said as he'd pocketed my money. "It's a lesson well worth a fin."

The lesson was worth a fin and Carson was worth every penny I paid him for the Versailles patterned tile floors, the sky blue walls and the glass cases with their sunny yellow trim. He had been more interested in constructing bongs than conjugating French verbs in eleventh grade, but the construction skills were serving him well these days.

I dumped out my caramel Kahlúa sauce and started over. This time my phone beeped a text message alert when the sauce was at almost three hundred and fifty degrees. Did the universe send out some kind of message to interrupt me right then? I ignored it. A text message wasn't a scream. It was ignore-able. I wasn't throwing out a second batch of caramel sauce for anything that wasn't at least scream-worthy.

I pulled the sauce off the stove as I saw the first wisp of smoke and stirred in the Kahlúa and the baking soda. Then I poured the whole thing over the popcorn and mixed it in. Once I finished making that into balls and set them aside to cool, I washed out my saucepan and started on the chocolate sauce with Irish Cream. I decided on a ganache-like base as my sauce, and for a little while I was focused on making sure it was light but still glossy and spoonable enough to coat the popcorn. Everything else disappeared for a while. It was me and the chocolate and the butter and the heat and the wooden spoon in the heaven-blue kitchen I'd created to be my refuge at POPS.

It was what I'd always loved about cooking. So many of my senses were engaged—sight, smell, taste, feel, even sound as I listened for boiling points and the like—that I could make everything else go away for a bit. Every bit of gossip, every regret, every sorrow disappeared into fragrant steam and spice. Then I started drizzling the raspberry stripes across the chocolate popcorn and the vision of Coco's blood smeared down the credenza behind her popped back into my head, and I had to sit down before I fell.

Coco was gone. She'd been a fixture in my life for so long that it didn't really seem possible. A deep sob clutched in my lungs, burning as it traveled up to the air. I thought about what a mess I'd been as a teenager after my parents died and how Coco had been one of the people to pull me back from the brink. I thought about how thrilled she'd been for me as I left for the Culinary Institute of America in Napa and how she'd given me a candy thermometer for good luck as I left Grand Lake. I thought about how she'd held out the lifeline of helping me start POPS as my marriage had disintegrated and I hadn't known where to go, what to do, how to live.

I thought about our plans. Coco was an amazing chocolatier. She had a touch and a talent far beyond what you'd find in most small-town chocolate shops. She was the equal of anyone I'd met in California and more. She was also a fairly shrewd businesswoman. I don't mean she was the type who started with nothing and ended up dominating the world, buying and selling her way past the competition. But that wasn't her goal. In fact, that was one of the most important things she taught me as I made the plans to open POPS. Identify your goal. Make a plan to reach it. Implement. Sounds easy, but it's not.

Coco might have been seventy-two, but she still had plans. Plans that she and I were going to make happen together. I could have sworn that those plans had put a bit of a spring in her step and roses in her cheeks over the past few weeks. She'd been fretting about how to break the plans to Jessica, but now it looked like that wasn't going to be a problem. Those plans died with Coco.

A knock on the back door startled me out of my reverie. I looked up to see Annie's face peering in. I stood up and unlocked the door and she rushed through and threw her arms around me.

In unison, we said, "God, you smell awesome."

"You smell like chocolate and vanilla and sugar," she said into my hair.

She smelled like roses and lilies and green things growing in clean, fresh dirt. It was exactly what her shop, Blooms, always smelled like, too. Like you'd stumbled into a fairy garden. Annie was in her early forties and had pretty much reverted to some flower-child version of herself that probably had never existed. She had long graying hair that she wore loose, and was rarely seen in anything except peasant skirts with tunic-type tops that generally had some kind of embroidery on them. Sometimes there were little bells sewn onto the hems. Those were my favorites.

She pushed me away to arm's length and looked me up and down. "Are you okay? You found her?"

There was no need to ask what she was talking about. No one was talking about anyone but Coco today. "Not really. Jessica found her. I heard Jessica screaming and went to see what was wrong."

Annie twisted her long graying hair back and tied it in a knot at the base of her neck. From watching her do this before, I knew it would be down again in about two minutes. She said playing with her hair kept her from smoking. It was something to do with her hands. I thought that given that she'd quit smoking twenty-two years ago, she maybe should be over it by now. "But you saw her?" Annie asked.

I nodded. I so wished I hadn't seen her, though. I so wished I hadn't walked around the desk. I wanted the picture of Coco alive and laughing, or tasting a new batch of chocolate truffles, or sipping a glass of red wine in front of her fire on a winter evening back in my head. Not the picture of her on the floor of her office, glassy-eyed and limp.

"I'm so sorry, honey." Annie sat down at the rectangular table that dominated the center of my kitchen, tucking her peasant skirt under her.

I pointed to the coffee carafe and she nodded, so I poured her a cup in a thick white china mug and then one for myself.

"What are those?" she asked, pointing to my morning's work cooling on racks over on the counter.

"Adult popcorn balls."

She arched a brow, cocked her head and looked at them from another angle.

"Alcoholic popcorn balls," I explained further. I was going to have to figure out something to call them that didn't make people think of triple-X movies. Although maybe there was a market for that. I'd have to think about it.

"Sounds like just the ticket," she said, standing and grabbing a chocolate one before returning to the table.

There were worse people to try them out on, so I put one of the caramel Kahlúa ones on a plate in front of her as well and sat down across from her, hooking my feet into the rungs of the ladder-back chair. "Did you hear or see anything last night?"

Annie bit into the chocolate popcorn ball, closed her eyes and moaned a little. "Not a thing," she said after she finished chewing. "I was closed and out of here by a little after six, though."

"Me, too." I turned my coffee mug round and round on the scarred wooden tabletop. "I wonder why Coco wasn't."

Annie shrugged. "You know Coco. Who knows what she was cooking up?"

Knew. I knew Coco, I thought, but didn't have the heart

to say. I also knew how hard it was to start referring to people you loved in the past tense. Then something Annie had said niggled at the back of my brain. "She wasn't cooking, though. She was in the office, not the kitchen."

"There's cooking and then there's cooking, grasshopper. She was up to something, otherwise she would never have closed early," Annie said. Annie and Coco have both been coaching me on the business side of opening a business. I knew how to cook. Figuring out how to sell what I cooked was a whole 'nother ball of popcorn.

"She closed early?" That didn't sound right, either. She hadn't mentioned closing early to me. The only thing she'd mentioned was that she'd been having computer problems. She couldn't get something to print. I'd been supposed to go over this weekend to help. Oh, why hadn't I gone over last night to fix her stupid printer? It probably just needed to be turned off and back on again. She never remembered to try that first.

Annie nodded and ate some more. "Must have. Aaron Woodingham came to Blooms to buy flowers for Delia because Coco was already closed. He wanted to bring her chocolate. He was kind of disappointed. Didn't do much for my ego, I can tell you." She sighed. "I hate being second choice."

Aaron and Delia Woodingham had pretty much the stormiest relationship in Grand Lake. Nothing in their life was executed without high drama. Aaron was a regular customer at all our shops, looking for make-up gifts. I suspected they had fantastic make-up sex and all the drama was an excuse to hit the sack in a state of emotional intensity akin to Vesuvius about to explode. "What did he do now?"

"Something about being late for dinner at her mother's." Annie shrugged and made a face.

I leaned my head on my hands. "I didn't even notice Coco

had closed early. I waltzed out of here without a thought about her. I would have waited and walked home with her if she was still working on something." Maybe if I'd gone in and asked if she wanted me to wait, none of this would have happened. Coco would still be alive and her blood wouldn't be smeared down the credenza she'd inherited from her mother.

Annie dropped her head as well. "I could have, too. I stopped by before I left to drop off those sachets she wanted. I dropped them by the back door without a second thought." She sat up again. "We absolutely cannot blame ourselves for this. Some stupid crackhead broke into her shop and she was at the wrong place at the wrong time. Neither of us could have known that anything was going on." Annie held up what was left of the caramel Kahlúa popcorn ball. "These are amazing, by the way."

"Thanks." I knew I should be more excited. I'd been toying with the recipes for a couple of weeks. I'd been planning on running them by Coco next week if they finally turned out how I wanted. Somehow I didn't have it in me to get enthusiastic now. "I'm not sure what the point is. I'm not sure how I'm going to keep going forward without Coco."

Annie sat up straight in her chair. "What is that supposed to mean?"

I gestured around the kitchen. "This. I don't know how I'm going to make this all work without her."

"You're already making it work. The only reason the shop isn't packed with customers right now is because you didn't open," Annie said.

I shook my head. "You know there's more to it than that. She was my guiding light. She was the one who was helping me see how to rebuild my life into something worthwhile."

Annie rolled her eyes. "As if your life wasn't already successful. You have your own business. You have family and friends who love you. What more do you need to feel successful?"

I had a lot of potential answers to that one, but my phone beeped again. I'd forgotten all about the text earlier. Now there were two, both from the same number.

The first one read: **How are you today, gorgeous?**

The second one: **U ok?**

And he would keep texting until I answered. "Sorry," I said to Annie as I texted back that I was fine, but busy.

"Antoine?" Annie asked, one eyebrow raised.

I nodded.

"What does he say?" She leaned forward and licked her lips.

I set the phone on the table and shoved it across so she could read it for herself. She shook her head, making the knot of hair come loose and fall around her shoulders, then she laughed. "Do you know how many women in America would get their crème brûlées in a bunch to get a text like that from Antoine Belanger?"

I did know. I knew it all too well. My ex was the hot chef of the moment all across America, and by hot I don't just mean popular. I also knew exactly what it meant to be with Antoine. The Belanger Bunnies, as his legions of fans were known, had clearly never had his Hasenpfeffer. They'd have another think coming if they had.

If I were being brutally honest with myself (which is a terrible thing to do but something I was prone to in the way moths are prone to flying into porch lights on summer evenings), I'd have to admit it still got my crème brûlée in a bunch when Antoine said things like that to me. He was handsome as all get-out. Eyes as blue as the Mediterranean Sea. Hair the honey-kissed blond of waving wheat fields, with the slightest kiss of gray at the temples. Broad shoulders. Strong chin. And those hands. Those strong square fingers that could make a pastry so light it practically floated. He had charisma so powerful it sucked all the air out of the room. I'd seen women actually faint when he walked into a room. Actually literally faint. Then he had that French accent. His words flowed around you, soft and warm and sweet as the first bite of a freshly baked brioche. I didn't leave him because I didn't find him attractive anymore. When I heard his voice or remembered the feel of his hands on my skin, sometimes I wondered why I did leave him.

Annie finished off the chocolate popcorn ball with one last bite and brushed off her hands. "Do you have plans for tonight? I don't think you should be alone."

"I'm supposed to have dinner at my sister's. I'm going to bring those for dessert." I nodded my head toward the popcorn balls.

"Good." She stood up and dusted off her hands over the sink. "I'm going to go open Blooms. Call me if you need anything, okay?"

I nodded.

If Coco was the one who got me to move back to Grand Lake, Annie was one of the main reasons I stayed. We'd gotten to be friends. It was nice to have someone to hang out with besides my sister, nephew, and brother-in-law. Annie was ten years older than me and ten years farther down the path of getting divorced and starting her own business, and possibly ten years lonelier than I was, which could be pretty darn lonely. Unfortunately, I was also all too well aware of how lonely someone could be even when she was in a relationship.

I was lucky to have Annie around. Our shops kept us busy. Our friendship kept us sane.

Three

I eventually opened POPS around noon despite my misgivings. Serving popcorn to ghouls was better than staring at the walls. Besides, Friday afternoons were my busiest time and I had dozens of special orders to get ready. Thank goodness Susanna would be in by three thirty. I was in no shape to smile and make nice with the public as they came by to pick up their variety packs for movie nights and parties and whatever other fun things they had planned that Coco would never be able to attend again.

Susanna Villanueva was seventeen and a bit of a bombshell. Luckily, she was too much of a jock to know it. Tall and willowy with jet-black hair as straight as a board, she didn't just turn heads walking down the street. She caused traffic accidents. She also worked damn hard at everything she did. She'd started with me this summer and I honestly didn't know how I would have gotten POPS off the ground without her help. She was playing in a fall lacrosse league, so I'd lost her help for some afternoons but still had her every Friday. It would be worse in spring when her season got serious. For now, however, I was grateful to have her help whenever I could get it.

She breezed into the shop at half past three, her usual bubbly demeanor significantly dampened. "I heard," she said as I looked up, trying to figure out how to break the news of Coco's death to her.

"How?"

She shrugged. "The usual way. Someone at school saw it on the Internet and posted it on Facebook. Are you okay?"

So that was the usual way now. I shook my head. I wasn't okay. I didn't see any point in lying about it. It was going to be a long time before I was okay.

"Miss Jessica must be devastated." Susanna grabbed an apron and wrapped it around her waist.

A vision of Jessica's white face and red-rimmed eyes swam before me and the sound of her screams echoed in my ears. "She is. They had to take her to the doctor to get something to calm her down."

Susanna smoothed her hair back into a ponytail. "I can see that. She's kind of jumpy in the first place. You should have seen her last night at the Make Your Own Sundae Bar at the church."

"I'm betting we'll all be a little jumpy until Dan figures out who did this." I headed toward the kitchen. "I'm going to start packaging up the special orders. Can you cover the front?"

"You got it, Ms. Rebecca." Susanna nodded and turned to face the front of the shop like a soldier facing a firing squad.

I stayed in the back, focusing on presentation and packaging, and the afternoon flew by. I closed up at about five thirty. I sent Susanna home and took the trash out back to the Dumpsters like I did every night. Like I had the night before. Like I'd probably do the next night. I stood for a second staring at the backs of the shops. Blooms, POPS, Coco's Cocoas, and then Betty's Boutique and Lake Erie Collectables next to that. I shuddered thinking about some stranger lurking back here, deciding which store to break into. What had made Coco's the target of whoever had bashed in that window and then bashed in Coco's sweet little white-haired head? What incredibly craptastic piece of luck had led the rat bastard to pick the chocolate shop over all the other empty shops to break into? Annie and I had both been gone. Betty probably had been, too, and the collectables shop closed earlier than all of us. It didn't make any sense. None. At least none from where I stood out by the Dumpster. There was nothing to distinguish Coco's back porch from mine or Annie's.

In fact, why break into any of the shops on our block at all? If I were a thief, I'd have chosen the diner two blocks down. They did way more of a cash business than any of the little shops on this block. As Dan often pointed out, though, most criminals commit crimes because they're too stupid to figure out how to earn a living doing something legal. Very few of them are Lex Luthor.

I shook myself out of it, and Sprocket and I walked home a few minutes later. Sometimes I still couldn't believe I was walking these same tree-lined sidewalks again. I felt like I knew every inch of their cracked and humped-up surfaces. When I'd left here after high school graduation, I would have as soon taken a sledgehammer to them than move back and walk to work over them every day. Then I thought of Grand

Lake as a prison I was breaking out of. Now it seemed like a safe harbor. I was as surprised as anyone else by it.

Then again, life is full of surprises, few of them good. Haley and I had learned that when the police officers showed up at our door to tell us our parents had been in an accident. I'd been sixteen. Haley had been eighteen. I don't think I've enjoyed a surprise since. I doubt Haley has either.

I waved to Mr. and Mrs. Winthrop as I walked past their house. They were sitting on their front porch sipping lemonade. That was the kind of town Grand Lake was. Sprocket stopped to sniff the edge of their property. I tugged on Sprocket's leash to keep him from relieving himself on their white picket fence while they watched. Mr. Winthrop lumbered down off the porch, his legs as bandy as if he'd been a cowpoke instead of a dock master at the marina for thirty-five years. He had to be in his seventies now. There were about two hairs on his head and they were both coming out of his ears. His pants were belted low under his substantial paunch, which strained at his plaid shirt.

"I heard about Coco," he said, leaning down to give Sprocket a pat. "Terrible shame."

I nodded. I decided to only award Mr. Winthrop with the Understatement of the Week Award in my head. I'd learned that Mr. Winthrop didn't get sarcasm when I was a teenager and got caught trying to steal a motorboat at the marina for a joyride. The man had zero sense of humor. Zero.

"Any word on who's responsible?" he asked.

This was also the kind of town Grand Lake was. The kind of town that ran on gossip.

I shook my head. Coco's death might end up being fodder for a million late-night conversations at Winnie's Tavern and Bob's Diner, but the information swapped wasn't going to come from me.

"I heard it looked like someone might have broken in," Mr. Winthrop said, pulling out the last syllable as if it might get me to jump into the conversation.

I couldn't stand being mute anymore. "I don't know what happened, Mr. Winthrop. I just know that someone dear to me is gone too soon. Again." I pulled Sprocket's leash and we walked away.

I heard him say, "Those Anderson girls are mighty touchy," to his wife as he lumbered back up his porch.

Whatever. "I'd rather be touchy than be a big fat loud-mouth who can't get a joke," I said under my breath to Sprocket. Sprocket stopped, cocked his head and gave me a look. "Okay, fine," I said. "He's not fat." Sprocket snorted and we walked on.

We turned right on Tulip Lane and followed it until we hit the river, then turned left on Marina Road and continued on until we got to the Grand Lake Lighthouse. Sunset was hours away yet, but the sun was lowering and the light turned golden as it hit the water. The lighthouse glowed white against the still blue sky. Olive Hicks carried a package into the lighthouse. It must be time for the meeting of the historical preservation society. Sprocket sat, leaning against my leg, his fur golden in the raking light. I took in a deep lungful of air, briny and sharp. I'm not sure how long we would have stood there staring if a big black SUV hadn't roared up Marina Road, making both Sprocket and me jump.

"Whoever that was was in a hurry," I observed as we turned and started walking toward home.

Sprocket harrumphed in response.

I lived in the granny flat over the garage of the house I grew up in. If this sounded pathetic, there was a reason. It was pathetic. When I left Antoine and moved back to Grand Lake, I hadn't wanted to take any of Antoine's money. I hadn't wanted anything of Antoine's at all. Not even a wooden spoon. I still didn't. He occasionally sent me checks anyway, which I then ripped up into little tiny pieces and sent back to him. At any rate, I didn't exactly have a lot of cash to spend and what I did have needed to go into POPS. Haley had been using the rooms above the garage for storage. She offered them to me rent-free. She felt a little guilty about living in the two-story Craftsman bungalow we'd grown up in for all these years. She shouldn't have. I couldn't wait to get out of it when I left Grand Lake at eighteen and I really didn't want to move back into it now. Somehow the granny flat seemed different enough from moving back into the room I had as a child to only be a small plate of pathetic and not an entire entrée of loserdom. Not that I would have been able to have that room even if I had wanted it.

My room was now Evan's room. The very Evan who was driving his Big Wheel in a wild figure-eight pattern around a toy fire truck and a stack of blocks in the driveway as Sprocket and I walked up. He paused for a second to give a tip of the batting helmet he was wearing to us, then took off again as fast as he could, Batman cape sailing behind him. He was also wearing galoshes. He was three and about the most glorious three-year-old on the planet. I was his aunt and I was completely unbiased on the topic.

I cut across the lawn and sat down on the front steps to the wide front porch next to Haley, who was shucking peas into a bowl balanced precariously on the very tips of her knees, pushed there by her very pregnant belly. I leaned against her and she slipped an arm around me. "You okay, Bec?"

"Not so much, Leelee. Not so much." Sprocket sat down on the lower step and laid his head in my lap. It was the first time all day that I felt completely warm.

"Dan told me," she said into my hair as she kissed the top of my head.

That was good. At least I didn't have to explain anything to her. I didn't trust myself to say some of the words out loud without crying, and I was afraid if I started crying, I wouldn't be able to stop.

"Do you want to talk about it?" she asked.

I straightened up and stretched. "Not yet." Maybe not ever. Tears pricked at the back of my eyes as I thought about talking about Coco being gone and the hole it would leave in my life.

"I'm here if you change your mind." Haley smiled at me. She is two years older than me and we spent our whole lives being "the girls" until our parents died. We were like a unit. Then Mom and Dad had the bad luck of having a tire blow out on Interstate 80 when they were next to a semi. In an instant, we were no longer "the girls." Haley became the grown-up and I became one of the more rebellious teenagers Grand Lake had ever seen.

Sitting next to each other now, the significance of that two-year age difference had pretty much disappeared. We were both tall and thin like our mom. We had both inherited our father's dirty-blond curly hair. Our chins were a little too sharp. Our shoulders were a little too narrow. Otherwise, we weren't bad. Not movie star material, but not bad, and almost interchangeable except for that whole pregnancy thing.

I wiped my eyes on my sleeve and asked, "When's dinner?"

Haley glanced at her watch. "About seven. I'm going to feed my little superhero there first and see if I can get him to fall asleep while the grown-ups eat."

"I don't mind eating with Evan; you know that." Three-year-olds were not the world's best dining companions, and Evan was no exception. I also happened to know that he hated peas, so there was likely to be a Battle Royale if he was eating what we were eating tonight. Still, he was cute as a bug and while I liked the Friday-night dinner tradition my sister had started when I moved back to town, it would be more than okay with me if it wasn't formal.

"I know you don't mind, but Dan called a few minutes ago and said he was bringing Garrett. I don't think Garrett's recovered from the green bean episode yet." Haley giggled.

Evan hated green beans more than peas and the last time Garrett was over, Evan had tried so hard to spit out the somewhat mushy green bean my sister insisted he try that he managed somehow to suck it up and blow it out through his nose. I think we would all always remember it, but Garrett had turned greener than the bean in question and had to go lie down.

"He's not really used to kids," I observed. Garrett was Dan's best friend from college. He'd moved to Grand Lake a few months before I had. He'd gotten tired of big-city life and wanted a change, according to him. Dan had talked about Grand Lake as if it were Nirvana on Lake Erie when they were both at school. Garrett didn't really have any family of his own, which left him free to live wherever he chose, but also left him without nieces or nephews to spew spit-up down his back or blow snot onto his shirt or any of the other things that Evan had done to toughen me up.

Haley snorted. "Neither are you, but you handled it. I think you handled it better than Dan."

"Well, I didn't think a phone call to the urgent care nurse was necessary, although it did put all our minds to rest. Besides, Evan's my nephew. I'm programmed to think all his bodily fluids are cute."

"Hold on to that thought." She handed me the bowl of

peas and stood up using the banister of the porch to lever herself up. "You can give him a bath."

I glanced at my watch. "I'd love to, but I need to run to the store first. Can I do it after that?"

"Why do you need to go to the store?" she asked a little more sharply than seemed necessary.

"I'm out of half-and-half for my coffee in the morning." There was a possibility that we were living too close to each other if Haley had to know why I was going to the store.

Haley rubbed her lower back. "We have half-and-half. Take ours."

"Then what will you and Dan put in your coffee?" Something was not right here.

"Milk. Or nothing. I don't need the extra calories anyway. I'm huge as it is," Haley said.

Something strange was definitely going on. "You're pregnant, not fat, and I don't want your used half-and-half. I want my own."

She pressed her lips together. "Fine. I'll ask Dan to pick some up for you on the way home."

I leaned back on my hands and looked up at her. "Lee, how come you don't want me to go to the store?"

She sighed and leaned against the post. "They have a new display up."

It took me a second to get what she meant. "Antoine's new line launched today, didn't it?" No wonder he had texted me so many times. He was trying to find out if I'd seen it without actually asking me.

She nodded. "There's a life-size Antoine cardboard cutout at the end of the pasta aisle. In fact, it might be more than life-size. I'm pretty sure Antoine isn't that much taller than me."

If I thought I could escape living in Antoine's shadow when I left Napa, I had been mistaken. His television show,

Cooking the Belanger Way, kept getting more popular, and he'd launched a line of salad dressings three months ago. The pasta sauces launched this week. He was everywhere. There were articles in magazines, ads on TV, and now apparently life-size replicas in supermarkets. There was no way to escape him. Most people didn't really understand why I'd wanted to. Sometimes I didn't understand, but then I remembered all the lonely nights waiting for him to come home from the restaurant or a taping. All the lonely days waiting for him to come home from a trip. All the lonely hours when he was home, but was too busy planning menus for L'Oiseau Gris, creating new dishes and writing scripts for his television show to talk to me or even notice I was still alive.

I met Antoine Belanger when he did a series of guest lectures at the CIA when I was still a student. He liked my béarnaise. He liked it a lot. He liked it so much that he showed up the next week and asked me out.

I went.

We were married six months later.

Whirlwind? You bet. Romantic? Absolutely. Deeply flawed? Oh, baby. More fatally flawed than a fallen soufflé.

"I can't hide from him," I told Haley. "Although I appreciate the effort."

Haley had never exactly approved of my marriage to Antoine. She'd gotten married the way she felt we were supposed to get married: in a white poufy dress with half the town there to see who caught the bouquet. Antoine and I had gone to the justice of the peace in downtown Napa with the maître d' and hostess from L'Oiseau Gris as witnesses. I hadn't even told Haley we were getting married until after the fact. For a while, I thought she'd never forgive me.

Luckily, she's not that kind of sister.

Four

I gave Evan his bath, which seemed like a travesty to me when I picked him up from his booster seat after Haley fed him his dinner, which did not include peas. He smelled like grass and apple juice, pretty much the best cologne I'd ever sniffed. Why wash that away? I put too much bubble bath in the tub and an epic battle between a plastic stegosaurus and a Fisher-Price boat was waged. We were both pretty much equally soaked by the time I got him out to put him in his jammies.

He was also getting sleepy and had molded himself to me as I carried him downstairs on my hip. Dan and Garrett were on the back porch with the grill fired up while Haley finished making a salad in the kitchen. She smiled as I walked in and reached her arms out for Evan.

I shook my head. "It's the last thing your back needs. He's getting bigger every second, I think."

"I know. I'll go get Dan. He'll want to tuck him in." Her

brows furrowed. "The timing's not so great. Maybe Garrett can take over grilling the steaks."

I sighed. "Haley, I have a degree from the Culinary Institute of America. I can handle a grill. I can probably even make the steaks do fancy flips as I turn them."

"Could you just maybe make sure they're cooked through and not charred anywhere?" She waved me on.

"Consider it handled." I opened the back door with my free hand. "Hey, Daddy-o. I think your services are needed."

Dan looked up from the grill. He'd changed out of his uniform into a T-shirt and jeans and he looked like my old high school buddy Dan more than Sheriff Cooper again. I swear his whole body melted a little as he looked at his son. I nodded my head at Evan. "Haley says you want to be on bedtime duty."

"Best duty ever." He held out his spatula to me. "Trade?"

"You bet." I handed over Evan and took the spatula, then went to check the grill. It was a classic kettle running on charcoal. Dan was an old-fashioned guy. Sprocket came up from where he'd been lounging in the yard and settled at my feet, most likely hoping I'd slip up and drop one of the T-bones. With Sprocket around, there was no five-second rule. Whatever got dropped got eaten before it ever had a chance to hit the ground, much less languish there for an entire five seconds.

"How's it going?" Garrett came over to stand next to me as I inspected Dan's handiwork. I nodded. I'd taught Dan well. There was melted butter ready to go.

"I've been better." I liked Garrett. Really, I did. He just somehow also made me nervous. As usual, he looked like he'd come straight from his law office, which he probably had. He was wearing dress pants and a button-down shirt. His tie was gone, the shirt's top two buttons were undone and the sleeves were rolled up, but he still looked pretty corporate.

I never looked corporate. Even when I tried to look corporate I looked like I had emerged from a tornado. My hair never stayed in place. My shirts never stayed tucked in. My skirts always wrinkled. One of the fabulous things about opening POPS was that I didn't have to try to look corporate or even kitchen corporate. No suits. No toque blanche. I was a blue-jeans girl every day of the week now.

Garrett leaned against the railing of the deck, arms crossed with a longneck bottle dangling from between his fingers. He was tall and lanky and loose-limbed and looked like he was born to stand exactly like that. Well, maybe not in the lawyer clothes. "You look like you were caught out in the rain."

I looked down at my damp jeans and peasant shirt. "Hurricane Evan," I confirmed.

He reached into the cooler that sat near the railing, pulled out a beer and offered it to me. "I hear you had a rough day."

I took the beer and nodded. "You heard right."

"I'm really sorry. Dan says you and Coco were close." He retreated back to the railing.

I nodded and gave the steak at the edge of the flame a little touch with my forefinger and then touched my chin. I flipped them over.

"What did you just do?" Garrett stared at me, brows slightly furrowed.

I thought through my last few actions, not sure at first what he was talking about. "Face tested the meat. Why?"

"You what?"

"Face tested it." I explained. "If you touch it and it feels like your cheek, it's rare. If it feels like your chin, it's medium. If it's like your forehead, it's well done. Haley and Dan like their steaks medium. When the steaks feel like my chin, it's time to flip them."

He shook his head. "You're a strange woman, Rebecca."

"Perhaps, but I grill a great steak." I shut the lid and consulted my watch. "Could you tell Haley the steaks will be ready in four minutes?"

"Not three or five?" He laughed and took a long swallow of his beer.

I didn't laugh. Instead I took a long swallow of my own beer and looked at my watch again. "Now it's three minutes, thirty seconds."

"Seriously?" he asked.

"Three minutes and twenty-five seconds," I replied.

He set his beer down and held his hands up. "Fine. I'm going. I'm going."

"Three minutes and twenty seconds," I called after him as he went into the kitchen.

I poured some of the melted butter onto the serving platter and took another swig of beer. At the appointed moment, I took the steaks off the grill, brushed both sides with butter and went into the house, Sprocket at my heels, hoping against hope that those steaks would slide off the platter.

Haley had everything on the table ready to go. I set down the platter and everyone helped themselves.

Garrett took a bite of his steak and made a moaning noise. "So this is what they teach you at that fancy California cooking school? To make steak taste like this?"

"Among other things." Like how to care for my knives and how to season food and the right way to julienne a carrot and how to keep a soufflé from falling. I would have learned none of them if Coco hadn't encouraged me to go, hadn't insisted I go, hadn't held my hand and led me out of Grand Lake, then held my hand again and led me back. I held up my wineglass. "To Coco."

Dan, Haley and Garrett all lifted their glasses and echoed, "To Coco."

And then they all gave me the best compliment a person can give any chef: They stopped talking and ate.

Our plates were empty, but no one was leaving the table. It was one more reason it was so weird to be back in Grand Lake. My parents' dinner parties had always been like this. Everyone leaning back in the upholstered chairs, finishing the last of their wine from the Dublin Crystal goblets, laughing and arguing about all the things you're not supposed to bring up in polite company like politics and religion and money. I remembered it all with a golden glow on it. Maybe I romanticized it. I didn't care.

Tonight with the specter of Coco floating over us, there wasn't so much laughter. Other than that, it was pretty much the same. Same two-story house. Same dining room with the same bay window and floral drapes. Same dining room table with its extending leaves. Same floral-patterned china. I twirled my glass, watching the legs the wine made on the side. I thought it might be the same damn Dublin goblet.

The one thing that was definitely not the same: me. I'd left here a wild child full of anger and returned a chastened woman. Humbled by the big bad world. Down, but not out, thanks in large part to Coco.

I went to the kitchen and got my popcorn balls. I brought them out to the table on a platter with another smaller platter of special ones for Haley. "Everyone ready to be my guinea pigs? Except you, Sis. I made you nonalcoholic ones."

I got pretty much the same reaction from Dan and Garrett as I had from Annie. This time I allowed myself the sense of satisfaction I generally got when my food was well-received.

"How many of these would I have to eat to get a decent buzz on?" Garrett asked, leaning back in his chair.

"Probably a lot," I admitted. "It's more the spirit of the thing, you know? That and the flavor."

"I'll keep that in mind." He grinned, then turned to Haley. "And how is your dessert?"

Haley licked the last of the unadulterated chocolate sauce off her fingers and then said, "Fabulous."

"I was working on these with Coco," I said, brushing off my own fingers. "I wish she'd had a chance to try this batch. I think she would have approved."

"So what have you found out, Dan?" Garrett asked.

Dan leaned forward onto his elbows. "Not a whole hell of a lot, to be honest. Jessica left the shop at around four thirty, so Coco was alive then."

"Why did Jessica leave so early?" Jessica usually stayed until at least close to closing time. She taught preschool at the church in the mornings and then helped Coco in the shop in the afternoons and then walked around with butter not melting in her mouth the rest of the time. She also ran the church youth group and helped out with the historic preservation committee. She was everywhere. I was finding it harder to get away from her than it was to get away from Antoine.

"Something about doing some shopping for the Thursday night teen social at the church. Honestly, it got a little garbled, but I guess she'd promised the kids a make-your-own-sundae night and she had to get everything ready." Dan shook his head. "She feels terrible that she might have been able to stop whoever broke in if she'd stayed later."

"Seriously?" Jessica is about five foot nothing. She might have been able to stop an attack by a big bunny rabbit or a rambunctious grade-schooler, but anybody else could have probably steamrolled right over her.

Dan shrugged. "She feels guilty. She feels like she should have been there."

I had a momentary twinge of sympathy for Jessica. I felt like I should have been there, too.

"Any idea what's going to happen to the store?" Garrett finished the last of his wine.

I polished mine off, too. "It'll go to Jessica. That was always the plan. Leave the store to Jessica." I stopped there. I doubted that any of the other plans would be relevant anymore.

Dan's eyes narrowed a bit. "Only the store? Not the recipe?"

Figured that I couldn't slide that past him. "Well, that was the plan." For the past ten years, Jessica had been trying to get Coco to sell her chocolate recipe to one of the big chocolate companies. There would have been licensing money and all kinds of residuals, but then the recipe would no longer be Coco's and Coco's alone, and Coco was a big believer in God blessing the child who had her own. She knew once she was gone that Jessica would be able to do whatever she wanted with the recipe. Unless, of course, she didn't leave the recipe to Jessica.

Dan sat up a little straighter. "Do you know where Coco kept the recipe?"

"In the safe in the office." It wasn't like Coco needed to consult it. She probably knew it better than her social security number, and she'd had that for a seriously long time. "Did anyone mess with the safe?"

"No. It looks a little like Coco might have heard the glass breaking in the back and instead of calling 911, went to see what was going on." Dan shook his head. If he had his way, we'd all be calling 911 for every branch scraping on a window and every neighborhood cat knocking over a garbage can. Better safe than sorry seemed to be his motto these days. I wished I could tell his high school self about this. High School Dan would have squirted milk out his nose he'd be laughing so hard. Or possibly beer. Yeah. More likely beer. He'd changed, too, I guessed. We all had. Except possibly Jessica.

"How do you know?" Haley asked, starting to stack some plates.

"There was glass on the feet of her quad cane. She must have walked through some of it and tracked it back to the office. As if maybe whoever it was backed her into the office and she dropped the cane by the door in her hurry. She might have been going for the phone when the perpetrator confronted her." He turned and looked at me. "Of course, it's not like our crime scene is pristine."

So we were back to this again, were we? "What was I supposed to do? Leave Jessica screaming in there and not go see what was wrong?" I glared at him.

He thought for a second. "No, but you should have left everything alone after that. You definitely shouldn't have messed with the quad cane."

I rolled my eyes. "I didn't touch the quad cane except to keep from tripping on it, and no self-respecting woman would have left Coco with her dress up around her waist like that."

"Amen, sister," Haley said, and we bumped fists. I handed her my plate and Dan's.

"You sure about the quad cane? You didn't clean it off or something?" Dan's eyebrows creased.

"I only touched it to move it out of the way. Why?" I picked up a few wineglasses to carry into the kitchen.

"Just, yours were the only prints on them. Everything else had been wiped." He drummed his fingers on the table.

"I only touched what anyone would have touched." I carried the glasses into the kitchen and then came back out.

"Jessica didn't touch anything," Dan pointed out. "Absolutely nothing. She stepped over the quad cane."

"Jessica this. Jessica that," I said in a singsongy voice. Sprocket raised his head up and cocked it to one side. "Jessica stood around and screamed and didn't do anything and still is somehow right and I'm wrong when I'm the one who actually called the police."

Haley laughed. "Oh. My. God. You still have it in for Jessica?"

I threw my hands in the air. "I do not and did not have it in for Jessica. Jessica had it in for me. She was just so sneaky she always made it look like my fault."

Haley and Dan started to laugh. Garrett leaned forward. "Let me in on the joke, guys. It sounds like a good one."

I sat back down in my chair, crossed my arms over my chest and scowled. "It's not funny."

"Oh, come on, Bec. It's been so long. Can't it be a little bit funny?" Dan reached his hand out to me.

I didn't take it.

"Besides," Haley said. "You never did have any proof that Jessica did it."

Garrett thumped the table. "What did Jessica do? Or not do?"

I rolled my eyes. I couldn't believe I had to tell this story again. "I was making chocolate mousse for the French club in the home ec kitchen. Jessica was making a Gâteau Breton at the same time."

"And you threw down over who got to use the electric mixer?" Garrett leaned forward. "Girl fight over gâteau?"

"No. Someone put salt in the sugar container so my mousse came out like something only a deer would like. You've never seen so many kids spit chocolate out that fast." I cringed, remembering the horrified looks on everyone's faces and how everyone raved over Jessica's gâteau.

"Why do you think Jessica did it?" Garrett's eyes had narrowed a bit.

"Because somehow she magically put sugar in her cake despite the fact that the container was mislabeled." I sat back, arms crossed over my chest. "And who got detention?"

"You wouldn't have gotten detention if you hadn't slapped her, although that was totally epic." Dan gave up on me taking his hand and leaned back in his chair. "The yearbook committee was going to put it in as the most mismatched girl fight in Grand Lake High history, but Mr. Danforth took it out."

Jessica is five foot nothing. I am five foot ten. I'd had to stoop to slap her. "She bit my knee," I pointed out. "I could have gotten blood poisoning from her dirty little mouth. Or rabies."

Garrett's eyes went wide. "She bit you?"

"Yeah. And, like always, didn't get into trouble for it. Principal Pittman said she was just defending herself from a larger attacker."

"She bit you and she couldn't get any higher than your knee?" Garrett was clearly fighting the urge to laugh and wasn't winning the fight.

"Everyone was like, 'Oh, poor Jessica. Mean Rebecca slapped her in front of the whole school.' It was as if nobody could even see how she manipulated the situation." I was not going to laugh. It still pissed me off. You could call me names and make me write bad checks, but mess with my mousse and you will be in for a world of hurt.

"Why? Why would she do that?" Garrett asked.

"Well, first and foremost, I suspect she's a sociopath and that's how she gets her jollies. Secondly, Luke Reed was supposedly going to ask me to Homecoming and Jessica wanted him to ask her." Luke had had a Mustang convertible. I had really wanted to go to the dance in that pony.

"Did he ask her?" Garrett leaned forward.

"He did. Rumor had it that he wasn't interested in going

on a date with an Amazon who picked on Munchkins." I nodded. "I went to Homecoming with Dan."

"You don't have to sound so disgusted. We had a good time." Dan stretched in his chair.

We had. We'd gotten drunk before we even walked in the door and danced like crazy people, but it wasn't a date. Pity dates don't count.

"I think Jessica was more jealous of your relationship with Coco than she was of your relationship with Luke." Haley stood and stretched. "That's part of why she wanted to sabotage you in the kitchen."

I got up and took the stack of plates from her. "I know."

Coco had offered me a job at Coco's Cocoas as charity. She'd seen it as a way to try to tame me a bit. It was there that I discovered how much I liked to cook and Coco discovered how much I understood about food on an intuitive level.

Jessica was fine in a kitchen, but she wasn't great. She could follow a recipe, but she couldn't make it her own. To Jessica, ingredients were things you mixed together to make something. To Coco and me, ingredients had personalities that needed to be managed, and you didn't just throw them together any more than you'd dump a bunch of strangers into a room with booze and call it a cocktail party. Jessica didn't understand that she wasn't great in a kitchen, either. That made it about a bazillion times worse. She truly didn't understand what Coco and I were talking about half the time.

As Coco's heir, Jessica felt she should be the one who Coco talked to about plans for new chocolates, truffles and fudge. She wasn't. Coco talked to me. Even after I left, Coco would still talk to me. She'd call or e-mail. We'd talk for hours. Now that I was back home, we had been talking even more. I knew Jessica didn't like it, and frankly I didn't care. Everyone else always thought Jessica was such a sweet thing.

It must have been the clouds of blond hair and the big blue eyes and teensy tiny petite frame. I knew better, though. I knew what kind of a selfish brat she was even if no one else seemed to recognize it.

When we were waiting in the principal's office the day of the Mousse Mess, she'd turned to me and said, "If you'd tasted your mousse while you were making it like Aunt Coco always says we should, you would have known before you served it. You're not as great in the kitchen as you think you are or as Aunt Coco thinks you are."

That's when I knew she had definitely pulled the switch-eroo on me. Somehow the principal didn't feel that was defin-itive proof. All he saw was the red outline of my hand on Jessica's porcelain-skinned cheek. He'd barely looked at the teeth marks on my knee. I spent the next two weeks serving time after school under the vice principal's watchful eye.

Garrett and I did the dishes together. I washed. He dried. Dan put stuff away, and Haley, after a lot of argument from all of us, sat down and put her feet up. Someone, I'm still not sure who, slipped Sprocket an awful lot of table scraps.

Haley's eyes looked heavy and she was doing that slow blink that people do when they're trying not to fall asleep. Apparently building entire human beings in your own body was tiring. Go figure. I announced that it was time for me to go home.

Garrett diplomatically said he'd be on his way, too. Haley made sure I got the half-and-half that Dan had picked up for me on his way home and then Garrett and I were on the front porch. The wind had whipped up, making the trees toss their branches around like wild dancers at a rave. The slightest scent of fall—moist soil and crisp leaves—edged the air.

"Can I walk you home?" Garrett offered as the front door

closed behind us. "It's probably not safe to walk around alone at night until Dan catches whoever did that to Coco."

"I live over the garage, Garrett. I can see my door from here. I think I can make it there in one piece, especially with Sprocket next to me." It was hard to feel in danger on my own front porch. It was hard to feel in danger of anything more than being a topic of gossip in Grand Lake even after having seen Coco's body this morning.

Garrett looked down at Sprocket. "You know that's a poodle, right?"

I looked at my beautiful dog and he looked back up at me with something that seemed an awful lot like a grin. It was the look that had melted my heart at the shelter when I'd first seen him. Like he'd seen who I really was and liked it. "I'm aware."

Garrett leaned against the post that Haley had leaned on earlier and jammed his hands in his pockets. "You know the original Sprocket was a sheepdog, right?"

I knew what was coming. "So?"

"Well, it's kind of like naming a Chihuahua Lassie, don't you think?" He smiled and scratched Sprocket between the ears.

"I didn't name him after Sprocket because of his breed, I named him after Sprocket because he embodies the spirit of Sprocket. I think if you found a Chihuahua as noble and self-sacrificing as Lassie, you should name it Lassie. Good luck with that, by the way." I might have been the slightest bit touchy about my dog's name. I found myself defending my choice on a fairly routine basis.

He crouched down to scratch Sprocket under the chin. "The spirit of Sprocket?" Sprocket licked his cheek.

"Yes. The spirit of Sprocket. You got a problem with that?"

He stood back up, wiping his cheek with his shirtsleeve. "It's hard to have a problem with something I don't understand."

"I don't understand how you can know Sprocket from *Fraggle Rock* and not understand that." I stepped down off the porch and walked toward the garage. He stayed next to me. "You're seriously walking me to my door?"

He nodded, then followed me up the stairs to the granny flat. I unlocked the door and turned to say good night. He was standing way closer than I expected, his face suddenly serious.

"Will you be okay?" He was close enough that I could smell the starched linen scent of his shirt.

I thought about it for a second. "Yes. I will. I'll miss Coco terribly, but I'll be okay."

He leaned even closer to me. "Glad to hear it. She was my client, you know? Or she was going to be."

"Really?" I hadn't known.

"Yeah. She called the office a couple of days ago and set an appointment up for next week."

"Did she say why?"

He shook his head. "No. I was a little surprised. She's been Phillip Meyer's client for time immemorial."

That was no news. Most of the town had been Phillip Meyer's client. He'd been the only lawyer here that I could remember until Garrett hung out his shingle a few months before.

The wind swirled the leaves in the yard and a wisp of a cloud scuddered over the moon. Then suddenly Garrett lurched forward, pinning me against the door with his body, his hands on either side of my head while making a sound that was awfully close to a squeak.

I put hands on his chest and pushed him back. "What the hell are you doing?"

He held his hands up in front of himself, backing away. "It wasn't me! It was Sprocket. He . . . uh . . . he . . ."

I glared. "He what?"

"He kind of goosed me." It was a little hard to tell in the porch light, but I was pretty sure that Garrett was blushing.

I looked around Garrett. Sprocket sat behind him, his nose pretty much level with Garrett's tush. I swear that dog winked at me. "Sprocket! Bad dog!" Seriously?

Sprocket lay down and put his paws over his eyes, but he wasn't fooling me. He wasn't the least bit sorry. I could see his doggy grin. I shook my head, turned around and finished opening the door.

Garrett stared at Sprocket for a second and then turned back to me. "The spirit of Sprocket. I think I get it."

Great. It took a nose up his butt to get him to understand me. "Thanks for the escort, Garrett. I'll take it from here."

"Do you want me to check inside?" He looked suddenly serious again.

"I'm fine," I said firmly. I gave Sprocket's leash a tug. "Come on, nosey."

I went inside with Sprocket on my heels and shut the door.

Five

Sprocket and I got to POPS at about seven thirty Saturday morning. Saturdays can be busy, especially if the weather is good, and I don't like to still be in the kitchen when it's time to open the store. Susanna would be in by noon, after her game, and I'd be able to take a break. Right now I needed to get cracking.

I don't have a big breakfast bar crowd on weekends. My biggest sellers on Saturday are my caramel cashew popcorn and my chili cheese popcorn, so I started with those. Here's the thing about corn poppers. They're noisy. Not so noisy that I have to wear earplugs, but noisy enough that I can miss stuff. It was a lucky break that I was dumping my first batch into bowls for mixing when I heard the thump behind the store.

My heart pulsed a skittering rhythm like the first few kernels popping in the pan. I froze. Maybe it had been my imagination. Then I heard it again. It sounded like a door being shut.

Was whoever killed Coco back in our alley again? Wasn't

returning to the scene of the crime a thing? I swallowed back the fear that was rising in my throat and slunk to the back door, trying to peer out its glass panes without being seen. Back against the wall, I peered around the door. As soon as I was sure it wasn't a raccoon, I'd call 911.

Then I swore. Allen freaking Thompson. Make that Mayor Allen freaking Thompson. He was prowling around in my back alley. He'd parked his car in the spot behind Coco's and was sneaking around the back of our shops.

Her corpse wasn't even cold yet and here he was. I didn't have to ask what he was after. I knew. He already owned most of the block—my shop included—and he'd been after Coco's for years. Years! She'd always refused to sell. She felt strongly about owning property. She was forever trotting out Virginia Woolf's quote about a woman needing money and a room of her own to work independently and without interruption. Coco's Cocoas was most definitely Coco's room of her own, a room that Thompson had coveted for years.

I threw open the door of POPS. "What the hell are you doing here?" I marched out onto the back porch into the early morning chill with Sprocket beside me. Sprocket growled. I put my hand on his head and said, "Steady, Sprocket."

As if Sprocket would ever attack anyone or anything. I'm pretty sure he's more likely to lick a burglar to death than bite him, but I liked that he had made an attempt to sound menacing. I made a mental note to give him a treat when we got back inside.

"Whoa!" Thompson raised his hands in front of himself. "I'm a friendly."

I crossed my arms over my chest. Friendly, my ass. "Why are you poking around behind Coco's shop?"

"Just checking things out." He took a few steps toward me and put one foot up on the steps leading to my back porch.

I planted my feet right in the middle of the top step. I wasn't budging. Thompson had been mayor of Grand Lake since before I left town at eighteen. At the time, I thought he was ancient. I realize now that he'd taken office in his early thirties. He wasn't even fifty yet and he was a town institution. An institution who was also a property owner. And a member of the preservation committee. And perpetual president of the Grand Lake Downtown Business Association.

"Coco's not even in the ground yet, Allen. Don't you think you should at least wait until after the funeral to start picking over her corpse?" My voice broke a little at the end and I felt tears build up in my eyes. Damn it. I wanted to be strong. I wanted to be the line that would not be crossed, the immovable object, not a sniveling little girl.

He smiled up at me with his ridiculously white teeth. It pained me to say it, but Thompson was a handsome man if you went for that silver fox kind of thing, which I did not. At least, not anymore. I was so over my Daddy issues. I had Antoine to thank for that. Thompson was tan from sailing all summer, which made his white teeth and graying hair look that much more distinguished, along with the crinkles next to his star- tlingly blue eyes. He had that athlete's build, too. The square broad shoulders and narrow hips. The long legs and arms. The loose-limbed easy grace. He looked like he was born to wear the suit he had on, even if it was a little bit rumpled.

I didn't care. There was only one reason for him to be nosing around in the alley behind our shops. It had to be some- thing to do with Coco's shop. He probably was trying to find something wrong with Coco's so he could get Jessica to knock some money off the price so he could gobble it up like he'd gobbled up most of the rest of downtown Grand Lake.

"Rebecca, why do you always think the worst of me?" Thompson said, his hands spread in a gesture of supplication.

"Because you've never given her any reason to think otherwise." And then there was Annie, striding down from Blooms toward us. Gray hair streaming behind her. Peasant skirt like a sail in the breeze. Annie hated Thompson as much as I did. Maybe even a little more since she'd been running a business in this town for longer than I had and had had to deal with him that much more. She brushed past him and walked up the steps to stand beside me. I made room for her on the top step.

"Well, I can see I'm outnumbered here," Thompson said, starting to back away.

Neither of us said a word. Annie crossed her arms over her chest, too.

"I guess I'll be on my way," he said, still smiling as he turned and headed back to his car.

"Don't let the door hit you in the ass on your way out," Annie muttered under her breath.

I fist-bumped her. "The nerve. Can you imagine? Sneaking around back here like some kind of vulture?"

Annie shook her head. "Some people have no sense of propriety."

I looked over at her, trying to figure out what was different. "Are you wearing lipstick?" I looked closer. "And mascara?"

"A little," she admitted, sounding sheepish. She tilted her head. "What do you think?"

"Nice," I said. "Enhancing without looking like clown makeup. Why, though?" I didn't think I'd ever seen Annie wearing makeup before.

She shrugged. "Thought I'd try making an effort for a change."

It seemed reasonable. She was a beautiful woman without anything on her face at all. The makeup made her eyes even more vivid and her lips look plumper. She even had a little blush on her cheeks. "Coffee?" I offered.

"Yes, yes, a thousand times yes." She followed me into the kitchen off the porch. It's not that Annie's shop—which, like Coco's and mine, is in what used to be a house—doesn't have a kitchen in which she could make her own coffee. It does. She uses it for things like starting cuttings, soaking greenery and other nonfood-related activities. Plus, she's a terrible cook. I mean, really terrible. Like "never accept a dinner invitation from her unless it's accompanied by a restaurant reservation" terrible.

"Do you think Thompson could have been here for another reason?" It was possible I'd misjudged the man. Maybe Annie would have a different take.

"No, I heard Jessica has already reached out to him about buying Coco's Cocoas. She's not wasting any time. It's probably a matter of days before she puts everything inside up for sale, too. Any news from Dan about Coco's case?" Annie asked, taking up her usual spot at the table.

I poured two mugs of coffee, then pulled the cream from the refrigerator. "No. He has some theories, but as of last night, theories were all he had." I poured the cream into a pitcher and set it on the table with the sugar bowl and then put one cup of coffee in front of Annie and one at my place.

"You didn't have to make a fuss," she said, pointing at the pitcher. "I can pour milk from the carton."

"It tastes better if it's served well." I shrugged. My phone chirped. I glanced at it. Antoine. Again. I shook my head. "He has paid more attention to me in the last six months than he did in the last six years of our marriage."

"He wants you back." Annie smiled at me. "As any intelligent man would."

I sipped my coffee. "No. He doesn't like to have failed at something. It irks him." It didn't happen often to Antoine. Pretty much everything he touched turned to gold. Except me. I turned into something else all together, something I hadn't particularly liked.

The phone buzzed again. "Is he going to keep texting until you answer?" Annie asked.

"Possibly." I picked up the phone, ready to tell him to leave me alone—as if that had worked at all the last twenty times I'd done it. But the second message wasn't from Antoine. It was from Dan.

It read:

Heads up. We made an arrest in Coco's case. Jasper in custody.

Dan came by the shop at about noon. "Want to have lunch?"

I looked over at Susanna, her long dark hair pulled back into a ponytail and still damp from her postgame shower. She smiled at me. "I've got it. It's kind of slow anyway."

She was right. It had been a quiet day, which was a good thing. I'd been all thumbs in the kitchen the entire day. I'd pushed a wooden spoon down too far in the food processor and ended up with splinters in my sauce. I'd dropped a glass measuring cup and shattered it into about a bazillion pieces. I'd burned my thumb by trying to pick up a saucepan without a pot holder. I seriously was a menace to myself and others. "Let's go."

In another month we'd start to need jackets. It wouldn't get seriously cold until January, though. I wasn't looking forward to that. California living hadn't exactly kept me weatherproof for winter in the Midwest, one of the lessons I'd learned accompanying Antoine to an appearance in

Minneapolis in January. Today, however, was perfect. The sun was shining. In the distance, I could see the lighthouse, stark white against blue sky.

And Coco's murderer was in jail.

Dan and I didn't talk until we'd gotten a booth at Bob's Diner. We slid into the orange vinyl bench seats and then all I had to say was, "Tell me."

He watched while apple-cheeked Megan Templeton poured us each a cup of coffee, gave her a smile and a nod and then said, "I wanted to ask him a few questions, see if he'd seen anything when he picked up the popcorn you'd left him."

"Makes sense." I'd wondered the same thing. "So what happened?"

Dan pressed his lips together and shook his head. "He acted strange from the second we got there. Too friendly at first. Inviting us in. Asking us if we wanted anything. As if either Huerta or I would be willing to get even a glass of water in that dump he calls a house."

"Dan, you don't arrest people—even crazy people like Jasper—for being too friendly." I sipped my coffee and sighed. It was weak and tasted a little like it had been boiled. I set it down and pushed it away.

"No. I don't arrest people for being too friendly. I do arrest them for having a large wad of cash that appears to be about the same amount that would have been taken from Coco's register and several trays of truffles hidden in their home." He placed both hands palms down on the table and took a deep breath.

I sat back. That was a lot of reasons to arrest Jasper. I'd always thought of Jasper as addled, but harmless. Sure, he was a big guy, but I'd never felt threatened by him. I shivered thinking of how I'd encouraged him to come by my shop after hours to pick up the leftover popcorn. "Did he say why he did it? Why he hurt Coco?"

"Nope. In fact, he says he didn't do it." Dan took a sip of his coffee and didn't grimace at all. Did the man have no taste buds?

"Did he say why he had all that stuff, then?" I asked.

"Of course he did. He said that someone had left the money and candy on his doorstep during the night. He said Coco's place was fine when he went into the alley. He walked up onto her porch because sometimes she leaves treats for him, too."

We all did. Jasper was sort of a town responsibility we all shared, like snow removal and lighthouse upkeep. "What time did he come through?"

"He said it was around nine thirty. We're checking to see if anybody saw him." Dan drank some more coffee as if it were a totally acceptable beverage.

I thought about it for a second. "Could he be telling the truth?"

Dan ran his hands back through his hair. "If he was telling the truth, I'm not sure why he felt compelled to smack Huerta in the back of the head with a frying pan and make a run for it."

"He did WHAT?" I squawked.

Megan picked that moment to come back over and take our orders. I somehow doubted it was coincidental. I ordered the grilled cheese and curly fries. Dan got a burger. Megan lingered long enough that I realized she wanted to hear about Jasper's arrest as much as I did. News travels fast in a small town. When she finally left, I whispered, "He hit Huerta in the head with a frying pan? Is Huerta okay?"

Dan snorted. "Huerta's head must be made out of granite. He did one of those cartoon *doing-doing-doing* faces for about three seconds, shook his head and took off after Jasper like he was still playing nose tackle for the Grand Lake Otters. Jasper did not stand a chance."

Jasper wouldn't. Jasper shambled. He did not run or even walk with purpose and determination. He stooped over with his long matted gray hair around his face like he was hiding inside his tent of dirty, baggy clothes. I didn't think I'd ever seen him in anything that wasn't mud colored. "And what was Jasper doing in the kitchen while you were questioning him?"

Dan looked confused for a second. "Oh. You think we were in the kitchen because he had a frying pan. Nope. He pulled that sucker out from underneath the couch. I'm telling you, we should have gotten shots before we went into that shack."

Our food came and I stared at it. Why had I thought I'd be able to eat? Dan was already tearing into his burger. I picked at a fry. "Why would he have let you and Huerta into his house with the money and the chocolate lying around?"

Dan shrugged and took another bite of burger. "He acted like he didn't even know anything bad had happened to Coco. It was after we told him there'd been a break-in and that Coco was dead that he pulled out the frying pan. I'm just glad that we can put this to bed. I wasn't crazy about the idea of a murderer roaming the streets of Grand Lake on my watch."

"Me, neither." Apparently someone capable of murdering Coco had been wandering the streets of Grand Lake for pretty much as long as I could remember. I shuddered. I'd been alone in the alley countless times when Jasper had come along to pick up the leftover popcorn from me and dig through the trash behind the diner. I shuddered harder when I thought about the times he'd come by when Susanna was alone at the shop. And that was only since I'd moved back! It was crazy to think about how long we'd all discounted

Jasper as crazy, but not dangerous. It was devastating to think about how wrong we'd all been.

Dan waved a hand in front of my face to get my attention. Apparently, I'd been staring into space a little too long. "So be happy it's over. I know it won't bring Coco back, but at least no one else will get hurt." Dan took another bite of hamburger.

"Wait a second." I ate another French fry while I figured out what was bugging me. "Do you think Jasper was telling the truth about what time he was in the alley?"

"We're going to be double-checking to see who saw him that evening, but it sounds about right." He pulled my plate toward him and started eating my grilled cheese sandwich.

"What was Coco still doing there that late? That's not like her." Coco was pretty much an "early to bed, early to rise" kind of gal. I couldn't think of anything that would keep her at her shop that late.

Dan shrugged. "Working on her books? Planning new truffle recipes? I have no idea."

I didn't, either. And now we'd probably never know.

Sunday morning is my morning to sleep in. POPS is a seven-day-a-week prospect at this point, but all work and no play makes Rebecca nearly as homicidal as Jack Nicholson in *The Shining*. So I don't open POPS until two o'clock on Sunday afternoons and I don't get up until I wake up. Unless, of course, my cell phone rings at eight thirty in the morning. Then I roll over and fumble for the phone as it vibrates its way across my bedside table.

"Hello," I mumbled into it, not looking to check the caller ID.

"Darling, are you all right?" Antoine asked with that hint of a French guttural *R* in *right* that used to drive me wild in a good way as opposed to the way it was getting on my last nerve at the moment.

"I was all right. I was sleeping." I checked the time again. If it was eight thirty here, it was five thirty in California. Of course Antoine was up already. He'd probably already been to the farmers' market and the fish market to pick out whatever he would use in tonight's menu at L'Oiseau Gris.

"I have just heard about poor Coco. *Quelle tragedie!*"

I pushed myself up into a sitting position in the bed, careful to keep from knocking my head on the sloping ceiling. There are some downsides to an over-the-garage apartment and I'd learned that one the hard way the first week I'd moved in. Luckily, my head is almost as hard as Huerta's. "How do you know about Coco?"

"It is right here on the front page of the *Grand Lake Sentinel*! How could I miss it?"

"Why are you reading the *Grand Lake Sentinel*? What could possibly interest you in that paper?" Seriously, they didn't even have a Food section unless you counted the recipes they ran in Penelope's Corner once a month, and most of those were for casseroles that involved crumbled up potato chips as a topping. Delicious, I grant you. Haute cuisine? Not so much.

There was a pause. "You interest me, so I am interested in what happens in the town you live in."

I leaned forward and rested my forehead against my knees and let that sink in for a moment. "Like you were interested in me in Minneapolis, Antoine?"

"Oh, *chérie*, will you ever find it in your heart to forgive me for that?" He sounded sad, but I knew better.

"Probably not." Once you've been abandoned in Minneapolis in January, you pretty much carry it forever. Antoine had been taping a segment on winter comfort food. As the taping finished, he'd gotten a call from his agent telling him that he had a gig in Miami the next day. Antoine sent an assistant to get his stuff from the hotel and check out.

I'd left the hotel to go to the Guthrie for the day. I came back to find out I had no hotel room and no clothes but the ones on my back and that my husband had already flown from the frozen wasteland of the upper Midwest in January to go to sunny Florida. He'd forgotten I was even there.

"You have no idea how sincerely I regret that lapse in memory, *mon coeur*, but now we have more important things to discuss. It is not safe for you in this Grand Lake. Your friend, your mentor, your neighbor has been murdered! You must come back to California where I can keep you safe."

I felt a twinge. Life with Antoine had definitely been easier. I hadn't had to work unless I wanted to. Doors opened for me magically, if for no other reason than someone behind the door wanted to get to Antoine. I hadn't had to worry about paying bills or calculating sales tax or how to take a day off. I also hadn't been very happy.

I considered all the various responses possible to me. I settled on, "No," and hung up the phone.

Six

Coco's Cocoas stayed dark Sunday afternoon. There was no sandwich board on the sidewalk advertising whatever Coco had picked to feature that day. There were no lights on in the window. No fudge set out on doily-covered crystal platters in the window. It would have been disrespectful for Jessica to open the shop so soon, but my heart twisted uncomfortably in my chest anyway when I saw the dark windows. Jessica had already made an overture to Allen about selling the shop. She might never open the shop again. I wasn't sure she should. She'd never be able to do Coco's recipe honor. She didn't have the kitchen sense.

Kitchen sense, however, was pretty much the only decent sense I had. I certainly didn't have good sense in picking men. Or life paths. Sense and cooking muscle memory led me through my prep in POPS's kitchen. Well, sense and Sprocket occasionally nosing me to break me out of staring into space.

Grief sucked.

Everything was almost ready. I flipped the sign on the door from Closed to Open and flicked the switch that lit up my window display. I was still putting popcorn balls on display trays when Janet Barry came in, pushing her double stroller.

"I wasn't sure you'd be open," she said as I held open the door for her. It wasn't easy getting one of those land cruiser strollers through a door on your own. Her two-year-old, Lucas, was asleep in the back of the stroller, one chubby arm flung up over his head, the other dangling a woolly stuffed sheep over the side. The one-year-old, however, was wide-awake and banging his *Yo Gabba Gabba!* teether on the front rail of the stroller like he was auditioning as a drummer for Yo La Tengo.

"I wasn't sure I would be, either," I admitted. "Was there something in particular you wanted?"

"A tiny bag of the caramel cashew?" She said it as if she were asking for a little bag of crack, all whispery and furtive.

"If you give me a second. The fresh batch is almost ready. It's best when it's warm." I patted little Jack on the head and turned to go into the kitchen.

He pointed the teether at Sprocket and said, "Bow wow wow!"

Sprocket replied with something along the lines of "Aroo roo."

Jack laughed with such an open mouth that I could see all four of his teeth. Then he pounded even harder on the stroller. Sprocket crept closer and sniffed his tiny sneaker. The baby giggled.

"I'll be right back." I'd barely made it into the kitchen when Sprocket dashed past me to his bed in the corner of the kitchen and wailing started in the shop.

Poodles have notoriously soft mouths. It comes from back

when they were hunting dogs. Sprocket apparently likes to show this off by stealing toys from babies or items out of purses or, really, whatever he thinks he can get away with. It's not nearly as useful as carrying a duck without leaving any teeth marks, but he was still darned proud of it. Right now he was carrying the woolly sheep toy that I'd just seen in the hands of the sleeping Lucas.

I stood in front of Sprocket, hands on hips, and looked directly into his eyes. He sat.

"Drop it," I said.

He did.

Lucas was wide-awake and screaming. Janet was trying to console him.

"I'm so sorry," I said as I handed the toy back to Janet after rubbing the dog slobber off on my jeans.

She took it from me between her thumb and index finger like it had been dipped in Ebola rather than a little dog spit.

"The popcorn's on me." I turned to go back to the kitchen.

"Never mind," Janet said. "I'll come back later." She trundled her way out of the shop, Lucas still screaming and Jack still banging with his teether and yelling, "Bow wow wow wow wow."

I turned to give Sprocket a dirty look. "You keep losing me customers and I'm going to start buying the generic dog food for you."

He lay down and put one paw over his eyes.

The door jingled and Susanna came in. "What'd the beast do this time?" she asked, going to get her apron.

"Stole a toy from a baby." I shook my head in disgust.

"Again?" She shook her head at Sprocket. He sunk lower and put his other paw over his eyes as well. "Well, at least he feels bad."

"He's faking it. Don't be taken in by those big brown

eyes." I headed into the kitchen to finish getting the caramel cashew popcorn ready in case Janet Barry actually did come back.

When I came back out, Sam Vander sat with his ridiculously long legs stretched out and propped on the chair opposite him. "Sam, get your shoes off the furniture."

"Yes, Ms. Rebecca." There was something about Sam's tone of voice. I was never sure if he was being sincere or being so incredibly sarcastic that it sounded sincere. He gave me his full smile now and I decided it didn't matter as long as he got his feet off the chair, which he did.

"And you have to get up if we get real customers," I added.

"I'm not a real customer?" Sam scratched Sprocket under the chin. Sprocket's back leg thumped the floor in appreciation.

"No. You're not." What Sam was was Susanna's boyfriend. Maybe. They certainly spent a lot of time together for two kids who didn't have a lot of spare time. Susanna had lacrosse and youth group at the church and, of course, her job at POPS. Sam, who had a wingspan that could almost rival Michael Phelps's, could stand in the goal and block soccer balls all day while barely moving his feet. Plus he went to the church youth group meetings, too, and, come to think of it, spent an awful lot of time at POPS as well.

I went back into the kitchen and got two popcorn balls that had come out more like popcorn amoebas and gave them to Sam. He ate the first one in two bites. Honestly, it was like watching a snake unhinge its jaw to swallow a goat. "I think you might be the shop garbage disposal."

He laughed. "That's what my mom says about me, too. And coach. And Miss Jessica sometimes."

"Poor Miss Jessica," Susanna said. "She's not doing so hot."

"Grief is hard." I knew that all too well. "What's going on with Miss Jessica? Something in particular?"

"She feels so guilty about not checking on Ms. Coco. She kind of collapsed at church this morning. Mr. Meyer had to drive her home," Susanna said.

I did not roll my eyes and I did bite back the twenty-seven sarcastic remarks that were on the tip of my tongue even if swallowing them down was harder than swallowing a dry scone. It was like Jessica was going all over town making sure people saw how much she was grieving. "We all feel guilty about not checking on Ms. Coco. Annie feels terrible. She was on the back porch to drop off sachets and didn't go in. I feel awful, too." I wasn't collapsing publicly and making it all about watching me have appropriate emotions, though, was I?

"Yeah, but Miss Jessica was out. It wouldn't have taken her more than a minute or two to check on Miss Coco," Sam said.

I smiled. Ah, the egocentrism of teenagers. "I'm not sure I'd call running the ice cream social for the youth group being out. What time did you finish up?"

"I helped Miss Jessica carry the last few things to her car at about nine fifteen. She was going to the store to buy some bandages for the burns on her fingers and then going home." Sam ate the second popcorn ball and then let Sprocket lick his fingers clean.

I made a face. "Wash your hands, Sam. That's pretty precise recollecting."

He grinned. "I didn't have to be home until ten and neither did Susanna."

Nine fifteen. Just a few minutes before Jasper would be looking in Coco's back window, breaking it and then killing Coco for a few hundred dollars and some truffles. No wonder Jessica felt guilty. If she'd driven by, she'd have caught Jasper in the act. I felt another twinge of sympathy for her.

I'd never forget her red eyes and pale face at the shock and horror of finding her aunt dead. I shook myself. She didn't check on her aunt. She hadn't seen Jasper and Coco was dead. No wonder she was falling apart all over town.

I told Sam to stop tilting his chair back before he broke it and went back to the kitchen to make more popcorn.

Sprocket and I were getting ready for bed when I heard Dan tear out of the driveway on Sunday night. I texted Haley: **What's going on?**

A few seconds later, my phone chirped with Haley's return text: **Another break-in.**

Me: **Where?**

Haley: **Granny's Nooks and Crannies**

Crap. That was only a block from POPS. It was run by Barbara Werner, one of Coco's closest friends and another fiercely independent little old lady. I texted again: **Is Barbara okay?**

Haley: **Still breathing.**

I pulled on my Ugg boots, threw on a fleece jacket, snapped on Sprocket's leash and we flew down the stairs and into the night. The streets were empty. No one was out. A little fingernail slice of moon hung over the lake. As I hustled along, streetlights made the trees cast shadows that felt as if they were reaching out to grab me with gnarled fingers. I kept a tight grip on Sprocket's leash and pulled my jacket tighter around me. The fleece didn't keep out enough of the cold. I'd need a real winter coat this year, something with down or wool or both. The only other moving thing I saw was an SUV gliding down Marina Road as Sprocket and I sped by on foot. Whoever was driving didn't stop. By the time we actually made it to Granny's, I'd started to calm down only to have my heart rate ratchet back up again when I saw the ambulance with its flashing lights parked in front of the store.

Huerta shepherded the EMTs out of the store. Sprocket barked twice and Huerta looked up. "Rebecca, what are you doing here?"

"I heard there was a break-in. Is Barbara okay?" My breath made puffs of steam on the cold night air.

Huerta looked down at the gurney being pushed by the two EMTs. I looked, too. Barbara's face was as white as bleached flour, but the side of her head was dark with matted blood. "I'm fine, Rebecca," she said in a voice that sounded anything but.

"What happened?" I walked over and took her hand. It was even colder than mine.

"I don't really know. Whoever it was came up from behind and clonked me but good." She grimaced.

"I can see that. Why?" It seemed so unnecessary.

"Cash register's cleaned out," Huerta said, by way of explanation.

"Like Coco's?" I asked.

He nodded. "Just like Coco's. Right down to the back window being smashed in."

"I don't know why I didn't hear it." Barbara shook her head and then winced. "Didn't even have to do it, for that matter. I hadn't even locked the door yet."

"Ma'am?" one of the paramedics said.

I looked around and then realized he was talking to me. "Yes?"

"We'd really like to get Ms. Werner here to the hospital to get more thoroughly checked out, if you don't mind." He gave me a look that said his tone might be polite, but it wouldn't stay that way if I didn't get out of the way.

"Sorry. I'll stop by tomorrow, Barbara," I called as I stepped back and they loaded her into the back of the ambulance.

Her hand fluttered at me, and then she was gone.

"Jasper's still locked up, right?" I asked Huerta.

He nodded. "I still gotta ask, though, Rebecca. Why are you here?"

I opened my mouth to answer and then realized I didn't have a good response. "I'm not sure. Haley told me there'd been another break-in and I guess I wanted to see for myself. Barbara was good friends with Coco. I suppose I was feeling a little protective."

Huerta muttered something into the walkie-talkie thing on his shoulder and in a few seconds Dan was out on the sidewalk, too. "Go home, Rebecca," he said without preamble greeting or anything. He didn't look even remotely happy to see me.

"What?"

"I said go home. There's no reason for you to be here. Go home, lock your door and go to bed. This isn't your concern." His face was grim in the flashing lights of the police cruiser and the ambulance.

"Excuse me, but business owners in the neighborhood where I own a business are being clubbed over the head in their stores. I think it might be my concern." Maybe I would be next.

He shook his head. "Don't start with me. This isn't a joke. Coco is dead and Barbara is lucky that she's still alive. Go home and let me do my job." And the person he'd arrested for Coco's murder had an airtight alibi for the attack on Barbara. He didn't say that part, but it couldn't have been far from his mind.

Sprocket was already tugging at his leash back in the direction we'd come from. He was such a traitor sometimes. "Fine. I'll go."

I did. But that didn't mean I didn't stop by on my way to work the next morning.

Huerta was right. Barbara's back porch looked exactly like Coco's had. Like, too exactly, especially since Barbara had said the back door wasn't even locked. Of course, part of the resemblance was that a lot of the little bungalows in this area had all been built at about the same time by the same builders and had pretty much the same floor plans. Even given that, though, the similarities were startling. The burglar had broken in the lower left-hand pane of the back window in both places, I guessed to reach in and open the door from the inside.

That's when I froze. It was kind of a long reach from that windowpane to the doorknob. I walked up onto Barbara's porch. Someone had taped cardboard over the broken pane, for what good that would do. It was a matter of a couple of seconds' work to peel that back. I reached my arm through and reached for the knob.

I couldn't reach it. It was on the opposite side of the door. I pulled my arm back out, snagging my favorite blue sweater as I did it. "Damn it," I muttered. I tried to inspect my elbow, not exactly the easiest thing on the planet to do. It would have to wait until I got to the shop and could take it off to see how much damage I'd really done. I glanced at my watch and realized how late I was running. I put a little more hustle in my step and Sprocket and I got to the shop by six forty-five. It would be enough time to have everything made, fresh and ready, when I opened the doors at seven thirty, but only barely. As I unlocked the front door, I heard the sound of a car in the alleyway. Annie didn't usually get in this early unless she had a big order. I went through to the kitchen to see if it was her and got there in time to see Mayor Thompson's Lexus pull out.

Seven

It was another busy day at POPS. The *Sentinel* had led that morning with the news of the attack on Barbara with a little bit of speculation on whether or not it was linked to Coco's murder. I wasn't sure whether business was picking up on its own or if people were using a visit to the shop as an excuse to rubberneck at the closed sign on Coco's Cocoas. Annie said she was experiencing the same thing over at Blooms.

"The number of people who suddenly need fresh flowers for their front hallways or someone's desk has pretty much tripled," she reported as she settled down at my kitchen table.

It was two o'clock and we were having an afternoon coffee break. "It's kind of gross." I set out some of the popcorn breakfast bars that hadn't sold that morning. Apparently no one wants raisins in their popcorn. It had been worth a try.

Annie took one bite and set hers down. "Not one of your better efforts, Rebecca."

"I realize that now. I'm a little off, I think." I took a bite. On second thought, raisins in popcorn were not worth a try. I wondered what I'd been thinking when I'd decided to do that this morning. The answer was I hadn't been thinking about cooking. I'd been thinking about two older business-women in the community having both been hit on the head while working at night in their shops.

Annie patted my hand. "We all are. It's so weird to think that Coco won't be here. She's been such a fixture in all our lives."

"More like a rudder for me. I can't count the times she's righted my course when I've veered off." This kitchen, for instance, wouldn't have been possible without Coco. She'd lent me the money to remodel it into the kitchen I needed. I'd kept the old wooden cabinets, but the stove and the refrig-erator were brand-new, state of the art.

Annie made a face. "Seriously? Sailing metaphors?"

I laughed. "You're right. I'm starting to sound like the honorable Mayor." Which reminded me of something. "Have you seen him hanging around here again? He keeps popping up in the back alley like he can maybe swoop up Coco's shop before anyone notices."

"Allen? Hanging around here?" Annie stood up to take the remains of her raisin popcorn bar over to the trash. "I hadn't really noticed."

"Maybe it's just me, then." Two sweet little old ladies get beat up and a person was bound to get paranoid.

She shrugged and brushed the crumbs off her hands. "Maybe. Well, time for me to get back to Blooms. I've got centerpieces for the Elks Lodge to start on." She gave me a quick hug and slipped out the back door, little bells on her skirt jingling as she went.

* * *

After Susanna showed up, I packaged up some breakfast bars (the ones with chocolate chips, not the ones with raisins), left Sprocket with Susanna and went over to the hospital to check on Barbara.

She sat propped up in the hospital bed, the threadbare gown hanging off her skinny shoulder. The gauze dressing had slipped to a somewhat jaunty angle on her head. "Hey, Barbara. How are you doing?"

She waved a hand taped with various tubes at me. "Fine. All this fuss is ridiculous. I'd be better off at home."

"When are they going to let you out?" I pulled up a chair to sit down next to the bed. I was about to offer her the box of breakfast bars when I saw there was already a box of cookies on her bedside table.

"They say tomorrow or the day after. Some social worker has been around making noises about how I don't have anyone to stay with me at home. It's nonsense. I've been living alone since Gerald died and I've been fine. I can take care of myself."

"Popcorn bars," I offered.

She took a small piece, but didn't bite into it right away. "Jessica was already by with those." She gestured at the cookies. "Some sort of gooey thing. Have one."

I picked one up. A Nutella-stuffed cookie. I gave her props for difficulty. Then I took a bite and promptly took back my props. I'd be willing to bet she hadn't frozen the dough before she started scooping it out based on how flattened they were. I wrapped the remains of the cookie in a tissue and slipped it into the wastebasket.

Barbara snorted. "Not my sort of thing, either. I usually

like anything with hazelnut, but there was something about those that put me off. Maybe . . ." Her words trailed off.

"Maybe what?" I asked.

"It's strange, but I could have sworn I smelled hazelnut right before I was hit. It's like drinking too much and getting sick. You never want to drink that kind of booze again." She laughed. "But it was nice of her to come by."

I nodded, wishing I had something to wash down the cookie remnants. "That's Jessica. Always nice." At least on the surface.

Barbara eyed me as if she could read my thoughts. "I've never trusted that one completely. She's way too interested in what other people think and way too good at manipulating those impressions."

I almost hugged her, but then realized it would probably hurt her. "I think you and I are the only ones who think that."

"I'm a bit of a maverick." She grinned, but then the grin faded. "I think my maverick days may be done, though. I tell you, Rebecca. I'm thinking maybe it's a sign. Maybe it's time to close up shop."

I sat back in the chair. "But you're a downtown fixture, Barbara. It wouldn't be the same without you."

She rolled her eyes. "For a day. Maybe two. In a month, people would have already adjusted and in a year no one would even remember I ever had a shop there. Folks are fickle." She narrowed her watery blue eyes at me. "You should know that, girl. Your shop might be your life's blood, but to everyone else it's just a shop."

"Fine. But then your shop is your life's blood, too. What would you do if you closed it?" Barbara still walked a mile along Lake Erie every day. No way she was ready to sit in a rocking chair and knit.

She snorted. "I'd retire. I'd take the money Allen Thompson

has been offering me for the house and property and hightail it out to Arizona. I love that dry heat."

Mayor Thompson again. It was like he was everywhere. At least, everywhere that little old ladies were getting clunked on the head. "Allen's been trying to buy your shop?"

"Allen's been trying to buy every shop he can get his hands on since he was out of diapers." Barbara took a bite of popcorn bar.

I knew he'd been trying to get Coco's shop, but I hadn't realized he'd been after Barbara's as well. The similarities between the break-in at Barbara's and the one at Coco's started to sicken me. It had to be more than a coincidence. Two older women shop owners at their stores late at night. Both hit on the head. Both back windows broken. "What were you doing there so late, Barbara?"

She smiled. "I started an online store. There's only so many antiques a person can sell to tourists who come through Grand Lake. I've been listing smaller items online and doing quite well with it. Amazing how much more demand there is if you open it up to the whole world."

Another parallel with Coco. Barbara still had plans to expand her business. I wanted to ask her more about the online store, but realized I'd better get back to my own shop if I still wanted to have a business, too. "Is there anything I can bring you? Toothbrush? Nightgown? Slippers?" I asked as I started to gather up my things.

"I wouldn't mind some clothes to go home in. Do you think you could stop by my place and pick up some clean stuff? They made a mess of the dress I was wearing when I came in." Barbara plucked at the hospital gown. "I don't exactly want to go home in this haute couture."

"Of course. I'll bring them by tonight." Sprocket and I could stop by after we closed POPS.

"Thank you. There's a spare key under the second flower-pot on the right from the front door. Grab my velour tracksuit from the second drawer of my dresser and my sneakers from the closet. Oh, and give me another piece of that popcorn bar. Good stuff, kiddo." She winked at me. "Good on you."

When I opened the back door to take the garbage out to the Dumpster, I saw a figure hovering in the shadows. I froze. "Who's there?" I called, feeling a little stupid for laughing at Dan asking about mysterious strangers lurking in the area.

The figure stepped out of the lengthening shadows. Tom Moffat. One of Jasper's buddies from the park. "Hi, Rebecca," he said, his voice gruff.

He was cleaner than Jasper generally was, but he had that same stoop-shouldered shuffle that Jasper had. "Hi, Tom. What are you doing back here?"

"I, uh, well, was hoping that maybe you might still put out the popcorn you didn't sell. Jasper said you used to do that for him and that it was pretty good." I could see him looking up at me out of the corner of his eye, like he wanted to see my reaction but didn't want to meet my eyes.

I didn't particularly like Tom Moffat, but it wasn't like I was all that fond of Jasper, either, and it always seemed like a waste to throw out food if someone could use it. "Sure," I said. I held out the bag that contained the leftover popcorn.

He scurried up to the porch and took the bag from me, backing away quickly. "Thanks." Then he shuffled off down the alleyway. I watched him go, slightly uneasy that there was another person who might have a reason to come in and out of the alley.

I took off in the opposite direction. I'd made a list of the items Barbara wanted and wanted to stop off at her place on my way home to gather things up. It was a little later than I wanted it to be and it was already starting to get dark when I got to her house on Magnolia Street. Barbara may have specialized in overstuffed Victorian doily-covered furniture at her shop, but her own house was as sleek and modern as a spread from a Danish design catalog. A black leather couch faced a flat-screen television wider than my bed. A bowl of green apples sat on a glass and chrome coffee table.

Her bedroom was more of the same. A queen-sized platform bed with black-and-white bedding dominated the center of the room. A stark abstract print with swirls of red and orange topped it. I went to the dresser and found the track-suit exactly in the drawer where she'd said it would be. I grabbed some underthings and was getting the sneakers from the closet floor when I heard the *whoop whoop* of a siren out on the driveway.

I looked at Sprocket and he looked back at me, his doggy eyebrows all askew. I went to the bedroom window and looked out in time to see Huerta get out of his squad car and run toward the house in a low crouch. I heard the front door bang open—I hadn't locked it after I walked in—and then Huerta yelled, "Police! Come out with your hands up!"

I crossed my arms over my chest and glared at Dan from across his desk. "Hand to God, Dan! Barbara asked me to pick up some stuff for her! You can ask her yourself!"

"Huerta's asking her right now." He squared his desk blotter with the edge of the desk and leaned back in his chair.

"Dan, be serious." This was ridiculous. He knew what I'd been doing there. He'd even had Huerta take the bag of clothing and toiletries I'd gathered up for Barbara with him to the hospital. "Who even called you guys?"

He eyed me for a second. "Jessica James. She said she was cruising by Barbara's to make sure everything looked okay there and saw the lights on in the house. She thought maybe whoever broke into Barbara's place would know she wasn't there and might take advantage of that."

Jessica. Of course it was Jessica. "What a busybody."

"What happened to the elbow of your sweater, Rebecca?" Dan leaned forward and pointed to my arm.

"My what?" Then I remembered. I'd snagged my sweater on the broken glass in Barbara's back window. Speaking of busybodies . . . "I, uh, must have caught it on something."

Dan pulled a plastic bag with a few threads in a color that looked suspiciously like my sweater out of his desk and set it down between us. "Like maybe the back window of Barbara's shop? The broken one?"

I sank down in my chair. "Maybe."

"Want to tell me how that happened?" he asked.

I sat back up. "Don't you think it's kind of strange that the scene behind Barbara's shop looked exactly like the scene at Coco's?"

Dan stared hard at me. "Not if we're looking for one person who might have broken into both stores."

"Exactly. I was looking at it and realizing that the setup at Barbara's is a little different. There's no way to reach the door-knob from that broken windowpane. I tried. You know how long my arms are." Seriously, I'm like a gorilla. "Someone broke that window to make it look like the break-in at Coco's. There was no other reason to do it. What self-respecting serial burglar makes it that clear that he's on a crime spree? Someone went to a lot of effort to make sure you linked both crime scenes. And that someone couldn't possibly be Jasper."

Dan pinched the bridge of his nose. "I know. I can't figure

out why. It's almost as if someone wants to make sure we know Jasper is innocent."

"But really this only proves that someone else knew what the back of Coco's shop looked like and that Jasper didn't bonk Barbara on the head," I said. Sprocket stood up, turned around three times and then lay back down again as if to settle in for a long night. I was afraid he might be right.

Dan leaned forward on his elbows. "Who else knew exactly what Coco's back porch looked like?"

"I don't know. Whoever did it and me, I guess." I shrugged.

Dan looked at me meaningfully.

What he wasn't saying finally dawned on me. "You have got to be kidding."

"Rebecca, it's not funny and I'm definitely not kidding about it. You do remember that Jasper is still in jail, right? There's no way he was at Barbara's. You knew what happened at Coco's better than anyone else around here except the police. Now I find fibers from your sweater in Barbara's broken window? What am I supposed to do with that?" He threw his hands in the air.

I had an easy answer for that one. "You're supposed to believe me when I tell you what happened."

He tapped his pen against the desk blotter. "I do, but there's going to come a point when someone else might not. Haley is going to pitch a fit if I have to arrest you for real. Please don't make me."

"Did you realize that Allen Thompson was trying to buy Barbara's shop?" I blurted out.

Dan put away the bag with the threads from my sweater in it. "So?"

"Well, he was trying to buy Coco's, too. Had been for years." Now it was my turn to give Dan a meaningful look.

Dan shrugged. "That's Allen's thing. He likes to buy property. It's a little greedy, but not prosecutable."

"You don't think that's a little convenient? That two properties he was after owned by two little old ladies are suddenly coming available after the two aforementioned little old ladies were attacked?" There. I'd put it on the table.

Dan froze. "Let me get this straight. Are you implying that Allen Thompson—our mayor—is beating up old ladies to try to get their property? And alternately framing and clearing suspects?"

When he put it like that, it sounded ridiculous. "Maybe. Or maybe he wants it to look like there's a madman on the loose in Grand Lake so we'll all close our shops and sell them to him. You got Jasper too quick."

"Rebecca, you have lost your mind." He said it like it was a verifiable fact and not just his educated opinion. He minored in psychology at Oberlin. Somehow he thinks that makes him an expert.

I leaned forward. "Dan, I've seen him lurking behind my store. I thought he was there to check out Coco's property, but maybe he's making sure he picks up whatever evidence he left when he killed Coco, and he's casing my place and Annie's place, too. If he did kill Coco, he'd know what it looked like and be able to replicate it at Barbara's."

"Rebecca, listen to yourself. First of all, Allen already owns your building. He doesn't need to bonk you over the head, as tempting as that may be." He took my hand from across the desk. "I get it, Bec. Everyone's on edge. This is scary. But you're not doing yourself any favors by indulging in paranoid fantasies."

I bit my lip. I wanted to argue. I wanted to fight. I wasn't paranoid. "I hate this, Dan."

"Me, too, Bec. Especially since it's my job to make sure

this kind of stuff doesn't happen. Will you please stay out of this? Do not get into trouble I cannot get you out of." He didn't sound angry. He sounded tired.

Dan had been working for years at keeping me out of trouble. I'd been the kid to jump on the tree swing before checking that it could hold me and to sled down the hill before checking for trees. Then there were my wild days in high school. Dan was always the one who was there to pick me up when I'd run out of gas, or hold me up when I'd had too much to drink, or hold me back when I was ready to coldcock someone. If I was trying to prove I was a responsible member of society, I might want to hold off on doing things that the sheriff had to get me out of.

"Sorry, Dan. I'll try."

"Do more than try, Rebecca. Do a lot more."

Eight

Pretty much the entire town turned out for Coco's funeral. The front page of the *Sentinel* was devoted to a profile of Coco and all she'd done for Grand Lake. Unfortunately, the below-the-fold article covered my arrest for breaking into Barbara's house. I closed the shop for the day, as did most of the shop owners on Main Street. We all wanted to pay our respects. Coco had truly been the Grand Dame of Grand Lake business. She'd started her shop when Main Street was a run-down couple of blocks close to the lake. She'd been the anchor for a lot of what came after. Pretty much anyone with a business in town owed Coco a debt of gratitude for that if not for something more concrete. Based on the turnout at the funeral, everyone knew it, too. We were all there in our Sunday best—or in my case, my best black cocktail dress. It wasn't one hundred percent appropriate for a funeral, but it was the closest thing I had to widow's weeds.

Haley had looked at me as I'd slipped in beside her and said, "A little flashy for a funeral, don't you think?"

"It's what I had." I smoothed the chiffon down as much as I could.

"People will talk," she said, staring straight ahead.

"There's nothing I can do about that. Besides, they'd talk no matter what I wore." I looked around and saw most of Grand Lake's business owners. Annie. Bob. Camille. Jacqueline. Allen Thompson was there. Appropriate, although seeing him made me grit my teeth. I felt Annie stiffen as he walked down the aisle of the church past us. I patted her knee and she relaxed.

Then Jessica came down the aisle like a reverse negative bride, blond hair gleaming under black netting and against her plain black dress, being supported on the arm of Russ Meyer, son of Phillip Meyer. "How long have those two been an item?" I whispered to Haley, who sat on my other side.

She shrugged. "Couple of weeks. Not much longer than that."

"I thought she and Jordan Peterson were practically engaged." I was pretty sure it had been Brendan Hansen before that and maybe Kyle Cooper before Brendan.

Haley shook her head. "No. They broke up before you came back."

"Why?"

Dan leaned forward to look at me around Haley, which was getting tricky considering how much space her tummy took up. "Quiet. You two can gossip later."

I opened my mouth to protest and then snapped it shut. He was right. What did it matter anyway? It was Jessica's business and I did not want to be any part of anything that was Jessica's business. With Coco gone, I wouldn't be, either. I sighed and sat back in the pew.

Reverend Lee stood and walked up to the pulpit. He cleared his throat and the low thrum of whispers in the sanctuary quieted. "It is not often that I am so sad to see such a full church. We gather today to honor Cordelia Bittles, known fondly as Coco to all of us here in Grand Lake."

There was a little murmur through the congregation and a choked sob from up in the front row. He smiled down at where Jessica must have been sitting. Then he went on. He talked about Coco's life, about how she started her business and how she helped other people start theirs. He talked about her kindness and her wit. Then he said, "And now Coco's niece, Jessica James, would like to say a few words."

I looked over at Annie, who shrugged back at me. I supposed that Jessica was as good a person as any to do Coco's eulogy. She made her way up to the pulpit, looking even tinier than usual dwarfed by the soaring ceiling of the church. There was a nervous giggle that ran through the crowd as Reverend Lee fetched a little step stool over for her to stand on so she could be seen over the microphone.

"Thank you, everyone, for coming today to help me say good-bye to my aunt Coco," she began, then had to take a second to compose herself. "I'm sure she would be tremendously pleased to see how many people came out to honor her today."

Jessica dabbed her pink nose with a tissue. "Everyone knows what a wizard Aunt Coco was with chocolate. I doubt there's anyone in Grand Lake who hasn't had one of her truffles or one of her signature chocolate lighthouses or a mug of her amazing cocoa. Some of us have had all three at once." She paused to let everyone laugh. "She touched so many lives and not just with her sweets. She gave generously of her money and time to charity. She helped businesspeople start new ventures." And now Jessica made eye contact with me.

I nodded at her and tried to smile, but my face crumpled up as tears filled my eyes. I looked down to get a tissue out of my bag.

Jessica cleared her throat. "She seemed tireless to me as a child. Even though as an adult I could see her slowing down as she made plans to retire, her energy amazed me."

I sat bolt upright as if I'd been singed on the behind with a kitchen torch, bumping my knee against the pew in front of me and knocking loose a hymnal. The sun must have slipped out from behind a cloud because suddenly the lamb in the stained glass window behind Jessica's head glowed. The black netting of her hat became a reverse halo and I could see worn spots in the industrial carpet that covered the pulpit. Annie and Haley both looked at me. I looked up at the pulpit, but Jessica was no longer making eye contact with me. "What?" Annie whispered to me.

"Coco wasn't planning on retiring," I whispered back. "She was planning on starting a new business venture. With me."

I barely heard anything else anyone said for the rest of the service. Haley nudged me every time I was supposed to stand or sit or change position in some way. She gave up on getting me to read the responses.

I was too busy seething.

When the final prayer was said, the crowd started moving in that horrible stop-start motion toward the church basement. I paused at the end of the pew we'd been sitting in and turned to Haley. "I can't. I can't go down there."

Haley's shoulders sagged. "Rebecca, you have to go down there. You know what will happen if you don't. There will be talk. Endless talk."

"I don't care." I heard a note of my teenaged self in my voice.

"Well, I do," Annie said from behind me. Her voice had a surprising amount of steel in it. "This isn't about you, Rebecca. It isn't about Jessica, either. It's about Coco, and if you can't suck it up and act like a person for Coco then you are not the woman I thought you were."

I drew back as if I'd burned myself on a hot pan. In fact, it felt a little bit like I'd been burned. "Jessica is lying," I hissed. "Coco and I were making plans. Big plans. Not retirement plans."

"So?" Annie snorted.

"So? So it makes me too damn mad." I managed to stop myself from stamping my foot.

"So do people who leave their carts in parking spots at the grocery store and people who don't use their turn signals. Are you going to stop going to the store or driving?" Annie crossed her arms over her middle. "Rise above, Rebecca. Rise above. You know that's what Coco would have told you to do."

"Fine," I huffed. "I'll go, but I'm not speaking to Jessica."

Haley mouthed "thank you" at Annie as if I couldn't see her and then we rejoined the zombie stumble of the crowd heading downstairs.

I damn near bolted again when we got into the basement and I saw what Jessica had set up for food at the reception. Amid the cakes and cookies and punch were popcorn bars and balls. They just weren't my popcorn bars or balls. She would have had to have driven at least thirty miles to get to another gourmet popcorn shop, but she'd done it. She'd done it to snub me.

"Keep walking," Annie commanded. The grip she had on my elbow didn't brook much discussion anyway. "You'll notice the flowers didn't come from my shop, either, so stop whining and keep walking."

I hadn't noticed that the flowers weren't from Blooms. I'd been too busy focusing on my own outrage. "I'm sorry," I whispered.

"Whatever. It doesn't matter." But I could hear in her voice that it did, like it mattered to me that my life's work had been deemed not good enough to honor Coco today.

I extricated my elbow from her pincerlike fingers. "You can stop frog marching me. I'm not bolting."

She nodded. "Now let's go see what your competition is up to."

Annie had a point. Jessica had done me what had to be a very unwitting favor. I could sample what were probably the best offerings of my nearest competitor without putting on a funny nose and glasses and sneaking through his shop. Not that I'd ever felt that Pete's Popcorn Emporium was much competition. Pete was two towns away and frankly wasn't worth the sea salt in my caramel.

I sidled over to the food table and grabbed two mini–popcorn balls and one bar. I will admit the bar irked me a bit. POPS's breakfast bars had been my own invention and had been crazy popular since I started offering them. I'm pretty sure the quality of my coffee was a factor, too. Bob's was a cute diner but that coffee tasted like lake water that had sat in the bottom of a boat for a while. Regardless, Pete had clearly been scouting me, and while imitation might be the sincerest form of flattery, it also pissed me off. As I scuttled toward the corner to really taste the bars thoughtfully to see if I needed to step up my game or if I could learn anything from his attempt, I ended up scooting between where Jessica was holding forth to a group of people and a knot of Jasper's friends who hung out at the park talking conspiracy theories and panhandling. The latter group were talking and filling up their pockets with as much of the food they thought they could smuggle out without anyone noticing.

"I only hope that Jasper will finally get the help he clearly needs." Jessica held a tissue to her lips and sniffled. "Even if he's not responsible for what happened to Aunt Coco, he's clearly more dangerous than any of us ever suspected. I mean, hitting Deputy Huerta over the head with a frying pan! He could have really hurt him! I know I will be doing my Christian best to forgive Jasper for whatever his involvement was."

For a second, I thought I was going to gag.

Then, in the knot of Jasper's buddies, Tom Moffat said, "Well, if Coco had gotten married, settled down and had some kids none of this would have happened. It's what you get when women go out in the workplace and think they're in charge of everything. Tragedy. A goddamn tragedy, and it could have been avoided."

I inhaled so sharply that I got a kernel of popcorn stuck in the back of my throat. Instead of scuttling safely to my corner to thoroughly examine my competitor's cheap imitation of my brilliant idea I suddenly could not get air into my lungs and the room started to go dim around the corners.

I glanced around, desperate for a glass of water to dislodge the wad that was stuck (was that caramel making it adhere to my soft tissue like glue?) and instead saw a ring of faces around me starting to blur into funhouse mirror shapes.

Then strong arms were grabbing me from behind. A fist was placed in my solar plexus and with a sharp upward thrust the popcorn clump flew from my mouth into a slimy saliva-covered wad on the industrial-grade carpet of the church basement floor.

I turned to face my rescuer.

"Garrett Mills, as I live and breathe," I said, my voice hoarse. "Where did you learn to do that?"

He shrugged. "I made it through undergrad waiting tables at an upscale fish restaurant. Being able to Heimlich a fish bone out of the throat of a hungry diner was basic training."

"Lucky me." Although now that I looked around and realized that the entire room had gone still and silent to take a really good opportunity to stare at me, I wasn't feeling super-duper lucky anymore. I bent down and picked up the offending popcorn clod with my napkin. "I think I better get out of here."

"I'll walk you." He took my elbow and guided me toward the stairs. As we passed by Jessica, I heard her say, "Leave it to Rebecca to make a scene. Coco would be so embarrassed. And what is she wearing?"

I started to turn, but Garrett's grip on my elbow was surprisingly strong. Between him and Annie I was going to have bruises.

"Keep walking," he whispered in my ear. "You don't want her biting your knee again."

He had a point. I held my head high and walked.

Once we made it outside, he asked, "So what exactly led you to aspirate a giant hunk of popcorn ball?"

I shook my head and sat down on the church steps. "Stupid Tom Moffat spouting his misogynistic claptrap on the heels of Jessica mouthing platitudes about forgiveness and Jasper getting help made me want to scream. I accidentally breathed in the popcorn with the air I needed to tell them both exactly what I thought about them."

Garrett sat down next to me. He slipped his suit jacket off and draped it around my shoulders. I hadn't even noticed how cold I was until I felt its warmth envelop me. It smelled good, too. Like laundry soap and sunshine. "I'm not sure it's totally hypocrisy on Jessica's part," he said. "She's visited Jasper every day since the arrest. Most days she brings him cookies."

"Cookies?"

Garrett nodded. "Homemade ones at that."

"How do you know that?" I demanded.

"Because even a philistine like me can taste the difference between a homemade cookie and a store-bought one." He smiled, which made the corners of his eyes crinkle in a nice way.

"Not about whether or not the cookies are homemade, about the fact that Jessica is bringing Jasper cookies at all." Dan hadn't said a word to me about it. I couldn't believe he'd tell Garrett.

"Yeah, well, I'm sort of representing him." He ducked his head.

I jerked away from him. "You're what?"

"Representing him. It's a thing we lawyers do." He leaned back on his elbows. "It's super fun if you like arguing with people."

"But I thought you were the kind of lawyer who did wills and trusts and stuff. Not the kind who went to court and argued." I twisted a little on the step to look him in the eye.

He shot me a look with one eyebrow raised. "All lawyers are the kind who go to court and argue. Don't ever let one of them tell you different."

"And how did Jasper become your client?" The sky had gone gray and the wind was coming in from over the lake. I pulled his suit jacket a little tighter around me.

He shrugged. "Dan asked me."

"Why would Dan do that? And why you?"

Garrett sat back up and turned the collar of the jacket up around my neck. "Because Dan believes in the judicial system and part of that is making sure everyone gets a decent defense and because I used to be the kind of lawyer who went to court and argued about criminal cases before I became the kind of lawyer who does wills and trusts and stuff."

My eyes narrowed. "You were a criminal defense lawyer?"

"Yup. And a fairly decent one at that." He stopped, a pained look passing briefly over his face. "Sometimes a little too good."

I bent forward and rested my head on my knees. "I can't believe this."

Garrett put his hand on my back. "I know. These kinds of cases are always surreal. And to spice it up a little more, Jasper's been asking to talk to you."

"Why?" To say that I didn't want to talk to Jasper would have been an understatement along the lines of saying that I didn't want to use imitation caramel sauce in my popcorn balls.

Garrett shrugged. "He won't tell me. He's pretty insistent, though. Would you be willing to talk to him?"

I thought about it for a minute. "If he tells me one thing that is incriminating, I'm taking it directly to the prosecuting attorney."

"That's fair." Garrett nodded.

"And I'm not baking him anything."

"Also fair."

I sat up to look Garrett in the eye. "If he had anything to do with Coco's death, I'm not forgiving him. Whoever killed Coco took one of my favorite people in the world away from me. I will never forgive that person for that. Never." My voice choked up and I could feel my face going all squishy the way it always does when I cry.

Garrett reached around me into the pocket of his jacket, pulled out a handkerchief and handed it to me. "Just don't forget about that whole 'innocent until proven guilty' thing with Jasper, okay?"

"But why did he have the money and the candy? Was it a Robin Hood kind of thing by the person who did it? And why did he bang Huerta over the head with a frying pan? For fun?" My indignation had the benefit of warming me up a little.

"I'm not telling you anything. I'm asking you to keep an open mind." Garrett reached over a tucked a piece of my hair that had escaped my bun behind my ear.

There was a stillness to him, a quietude that was nice. "I'll keep my mind as open as I possibly can," I promised. Then I leaned my head against his shoulder.

"For the record," he said softly into my hair. "I really like the dress."

Nine

After I got home from the funeral, I changed into yoga pants, a hoodie and sneakers and took Sprocket for a walk. It was like he could read my mood and even though he'd been cooped up in the apartment all afternoon, he didn't bolt down the sidewalk or jump on me. We took our usual route, out to the lighthouse at the end of the pier and back.

The air had turned crisp, but the sun was still warm. We wandered up the river toward the lake where the lighthouse rose up from the end of the pier. About three-quarters of the men of Grand Lake had proposed to their sweethearts in the shadow of the lighthouse. I'd participated in a make-out session or two by it. It's that romantic.

No one was making out there now, though. A black SUV and a blue station wagon sat in the parking lot, but I didn't see any people. When we got closer, I saw that the door to the lighthouse was open. I stopped to peek in. "Hi, there."

Gina Paoletti came out from behind the circular staircase that dominated the middle of the lighthouse with a broom in her hand. She was a plump woman in her fifties with dark hair and a bit of flash in her brown eyes. "Hello, Rebecca. What are you doing here?"

"Just taking a walk. Trying to clear my head a little." I pointed toward her broom with my chin. "You're on lighthouse-keeping duty?"

She nodded. "It's my turn this week." The Grand Lake Historical Society had a regular roster of people who took turns keeping the lighthouse tidy. "Terrible thing about Coco."

I nodded. "Terrible."

"You okay now that you got that popcorn lump out of your throat?" she asked, looking down at the floor and I suspected trying not to laugh.

I sighed. "Just fine. Thanks. See you." Terrific. My near-death experience at my dear friend's funeral was going to be the town's go-to joke for a while.

"I thought the dress was fine, by the way," she called after me.

Terrific again. Sprocket and I walked the rest of the way down the pier. The lake was calm so I sat down and kicked my legs against its rough wooden edges while the ebbing sun shone on my face and my doofus of a dog leaned against me. A little bit of calm seeped back into my soul.

I'd missed living by water when I was in Napa. Which wasn't to say wine country in Northern California wasn't gorgeous. It was. But it doesn't have a lake so big you can't see to the other side. It doesn't have the sounds of water lapping against pylons or the romance of a lighthouse built from melted-down Civil War cannons still flashing its Fresnel light to keep sailors safe on dark and stormy nights. The sunlight doesn't dance along waves there, sparkling like diamonds on a fall afternoon.

It wasn't home.

Grand Lake was home, but one of the main reasons it was had died. I stopped fighting them and went ahead and let the tears spill for my Coco. I put my arm around Sprocket and cried into his doggie neck until there weren't any more tears to cry. Then I pulled Garrett's handkerchief out of my sweatshirt pocket, dried my face and stood up. It was time to soldier on. Like Coco would have wanted.

My cell phone chirped. I glanced at the screen.

Antoine: **R u ok? Do you need legal representation?**

Me: **?**

Antoine: **Heard about your arrest.**

It took me a second to figure out what he was talking about. It must have been my little adventure with Huerta at Barbara's house. The funeral had put it completely out of my head.

Me: **All taken care of. Nothing to worry about.**

I was going to have to see if I could get Ned Twirby to cancel Antoine's subscription to the *Sentinel*. He was getting far too much information about me for my comfort.

Sprocket and I headed home. Dan was sitting on the front porch drinking a beer as we walked up. I sat down next to him, took the bottle and took a long hard swig.

"You want one of your own?" he asked with the polite tone of a man who really wanted to drink his beer himself, but knew better than to say that out loud.

I nodded.

"In the fridge, but be quiet. Haley and Evan are both napping," he said with a nod toward the house.

I left Sprocket with Dan and tiptoed into the house, avoiding the board in the hardwood floor in the entryway that creaked. I made it back out with a longneck in one hand and a Milk-Bone in the other as silently as a sous-chef trying not to disturb a soufflé. I lowered myself back down on the step below Dan's and Sprocket settled onto my feet. Dan pulled one of my corkscrew curls and let it bounce back. "You okay?"

"I've been better."

He tugged the curl again.

"Hey," I protested. "Stop pulling my hair, okay?"

He dropped his hand back to his leg. "You got it, Bec."

We drank in silence for a second or two before I asked. "How come you didn't tell me that Garrett was representing Jasper?"

He didn't answer for a minute, which meant he was thinking. Dan rarely said anything without thinking about it. "It's not really your business, Bec. Plus, I didn't want you to get mad at Garrett."

"Not my business? Of course it's my business. It's the whole town's business. And who cares if I'm mad at Garrett?" None of what he'd said made sense to me.

"That's my point. It can't be the whole town's business. It has to be done right. That's why I asked Garrett to step in. And I don't want you to be mad because it makes my life easier when all my friends get along." He rubbed his chin.

I settled back down and gave Sprocket a scratch behind the ears. I knew he had a point about the town and about the friends. "You should be more worried about Garrett being mad at me once he sees what I did to his handkerchief." My mascara had run when I'd started crying by the lighthouse. It was going to take some serious stain remover to turn that thing white again.

"So why did you think Jasper needed a fancy lawyer anyway? Why isn't the public defender good enough?" I picked at the label on my beer with my fingernail.

It took Dan a really long time to answer. "Because I'm not convinced Jasper's guilty. Even before the attack on Barbara something didn't seem right."

"He had the money and the truffles," I pointed out.

"And he bonked Huerta on the head. There are other factors, though." Dan held up one finger. "Number one: the break-in at Barbara's. Whoever did it had to, at the very least, know what the back of Coco's shop looked like after the break-in there, and Jasper was locked up when it happened."

He held up a second finger. "Two: no glass on his shoes. Any of his shoes. Crime scene folks tested every pair from Jasper's house—not that there were many."

"He could have thrown them out somewhere between Coco's and his place," I pointed out.

"Yeah. I thought about that. But why throw out the shoes and keep the money and the truffles in plain sight?" Dan's eyes narrowed a bit as he looked out over his yard. "Doesn't make sense."

He had a point. "Is there more?"

"Honestly, motive. He doesn't really have any."

"Uh, money. Chocolate." There were totally times in my life when I would have killed for a truffle.

"Jasper's done a lot of things, mainly centered on being a public nuisance. You know what he doesn't have anywhere in his record? Any kind of theft. No shoplifting. No purse snatching. No pickpocketing. Nothing like that." Dan sighed. "Also nothing violent. He occasionally gets het up and yells at people in the park about how the Scottish independence referendum was fixed and that Eisenhower had secret meetings with aliens, but he's never hit anyone, never laid hands on anyone, never even threatened to do anyone physical harm."

"People snap. Or get desperate," I pointed out.

"They do. But there's usually a reason." He sat up again. "Listen, Jasper really wants to talk to you."

"Garrett told me."

"Will you?" Dan put his hand on my back. "Maybe he'll tell you something that can push this one way or the other."

"I don't know, Dan. Why me?"

"Jasper won't say. I think the only way to find out is for you to talk to him. Will you do it for me?"

I rested my head against him. As if he even had to ask. "For you, I'd lasso the moon, Dan."

"Bec, can you remember if you turned on or off the lights when you came into Coco's office?" He patted my head. It was nice. No wonder Sprocket liked it.

"Why would I walk into a room and turn off the lights?" I knew I'd been a little unpredictable recently, but I wasn't crazy.

He shrugged. "I don't know. Maybe you were so upset about seeing Coco . . . the way she was . . . that you turned out the lights?"

I raised my head to look at him. "No. I did not turn off the lights. That would be ridiculous."

"Do you think Jessica might have?" he asked.

Jessica hadn't seemed capable of much of anything at that point. I didn't think I would ever be able to forget her eyes huge and red in the stark whiteness of her face. I wasn't sure I'd ever seen such a picture of woe. "I think she was too busy standing in the middle of the room screaming like a teakettle about to boil over to turn anything off or on. Why?"

"I'm just trying to make sense of the fact that the lights weren't on in Coco's office." Dan let his beer bottle swing and tap against the step.

"None of them were? Not even the one over her desk?" Coco would have had her desk light on by late afternoon.

Her eyes had been getting worse and worse and she snapped on the light to do just about anything. She couldn't even read the labels on her measuring spoons without her glasses and extra light—not that she needed to read them. She could tell a teaspoon from a tablespoon in her sleep.

"None of them. Not her desk light. Not the office overhead light. Not the porch light. Nothing." He kept tapping.

"Dan, that's weird. If she was in there, she would have had the light on." I thought for a second. "Were there any fingerprints on the light switch?"

"About a dozen. Coco's, Jessica's, yours, Annie's, plus some that we haven't identified yet," he said.

I sat up straighter. "But, Dan, if someone turned those lights out after Coco was dead, then that person's fingerprints are probably on that light switch."

"Wow, Sherlock, do you really think so?"

I stuck my tongue out at him. "No need for sarcasm."

"Oh, there's every need for sarcasm. There's too much at that crime scene that doesn't make sense, Bec." Dan took a deep breath and blew it out.

I'd been focused on how senseless the crime was. It hadn't occurred to me that it hadn't made sense, either. "What else?"

"There's glass on the feet of Coco's quad cane. There's glass on the bottom of your shoes and Jessica's shoes," Dan said.

"That makes perfect sense." Jessica and I had both walked through the broken glass in the kitchen. I'd walked through it twice, once on the way in and again on the way out. I'd taken Jessica out the back door of Coco's Cocoas to go to POPS to wait for the police. The glass on Coco's quad cane must have gotten there when she walked through the glass to see what had made the noise.

"There's no glass on Coco's shoes," Dan said.

That brought me up short. "None?"

"Not a single shard, according to the lab."

"But there is glass on the cane? The cane that was way over on the other side of the room from Coco?" He was right. I was having trouble coming up with a scenario that would make that all make sense.

Dan took a long pull from his beer. "Yup. Time of death according to the coroner doesn't match up, either."

I turned it all over in my head. "What does that all mean?"

"I think the break-in part of Coco's death was staged. Someone came back and did that all later." His tone was flat, but he was clenching and unclenching his jaw. "Maybe it was an accident. Maybe Coco stumbled, fell, and hit her head and whoever was there panicked. They used the cane to break the back window, took the money and the truffles, and left Coco there for Jessica to find her the next morning."

"Then what's the deal with Barbara? Is it some kind of copycat? And, if so, why?" My mind raced. "You've got Jasper in custody. Whoever broke into Barbara's would have to know that would make Jasper look innocent. What would be the point?"

"I'm not sure." He started to pick at the corner of the beer bottle label.

I gazed up at the clouds puffing along in the sky. "Could Barbara's break-in be a way to throw you off the trail?"

"The trail of what?" He looked down at me.

"Of whoever killed Coco. Maybe the break-in at Barbara's was a way to make us think that there was a serial burglar of little old ladies' stores to cover up something about Coco's murder." I wasn't sure what there was to cover up, but maybe there was something.

Dan snorted. "You mean because I'm so hot on the trail of whoever it was who shoved Coco into that desk? I got nothing, Bec. Nothing. No one has to try to throw me off the trail because I'm not on one."

"That you know of." I leaned down to give Sprocket another pet.

"That anyone knows of," he countered.

"Except whoever did it," I pointed out. "Whoever did it knows exactly what you are and aren't on the trail of."

Ten

The next day after Susanna got to the shop in the afternoon, I walked up the steps of the Grand Lake Sheriff and Fire Department as promised. It was a great building, at least from the outside. All arches and stone and carved lintels. It had been built in the 1930s and had that serious weathered look that old buildings got after they had some decades under their wainscoting. Dan bitched about it nearly nonstop. They had had no clue about the kind of wiring needed for sophisticated 911 call systems and Internet connections in 1934 or the kind of staffing it would require to run even a small town sheriff's department.

I slowed my steps at the top of the stairs. I didn't want to go in. I didn't want to see Jasper, but I'd promised Dan and Garrett. I pushed open the heavy doors and walked up to the reception area. Deputy Huerta sat at the main desk.

"Hi, Glenn," I said, leaning my elbows on the high marble surface. "I'm here to see Jasper."

He shook his head. "If I'd known I could get all the single

ladies of Grand Lake to come visit me, I'd have gotten myself arrested years ago."

"What do you mean?" I asked as I scribbled my name in the visitor register. He didn't need to answer. I saw the name on the line above mine. Jessica.

The whole town would miss Coco, but I doubt anyone grieved for her the way Jessica and I did. I felt a connection to Jessica because of that, and it made me want to hug her. At the same time, I couldn't forget the intentional way she'd snubbed Annie and me—Coco's closest friends—at the funeral, using other vendors for the flowers and popcorn snacks. That made me want to pull her hair. I was glad I'd missed her. If I'd had to talk to her, my head might have exploded.

"What did Jessica want?" I set the pen back down.

Huerta shrugged. "Same as yesterday, I guess. Wanna cookie?" He pushed the box toward me.

I looked inside. Snickerdoodles. A solid choice. "Doesn't Jasper want them?"

"She brings a dozen by every day. He can't keep up." Huerta took one and took a bite.

Well, they weren't poisoned. That was for sure. I took one. The flavor wasn't bad, but the texture was all wrong. Either she hadn't let the butter soften and the eggs come up to room temperature before she started or she'd overmixed or both. I wrapped the rest of the cookie up in a napkin. I wasn't going to waste the calories on a substandard Snickerdoodle. "Garrett said Jasper wanted to talk to me."

Huerta pointed at Sprocket and said, "He has to stay with me. He can't go into the interrogation room with you."

"Fine, but don't feed him any cookies." I handed over the leash.

Huerta nodded and motioned for me to follow him. "Jasper's made it real clear he wants to talk to you. You going to be okay talking to him alone? He's said that he doesn't want anyone listening in on your conversation."

Was I? I supposed so. "It's . . . safe, right?"

Huerta rubbed the back of his head. "Well, he doesn't have access to any frying pans in there. It should be okay." He opened the door to a small room with a table that was bolted to the floor and two chairs. "I'll bring him in in a second."

I settled myself on one of the hard plastic-and-chrome chairs and waited. Huerta was back with Jasper nearly as fast as he'd promised. Jasper was wearing handcuffs and an orange jumpsuit with legs that were too short and arms that were too long. It was a slight improvement over his usual clothes in that the jumpsuit was clean. Huerta cuffed him to a metal ring in the table. He pointed to a button on the wall. "Hit that if you need help."

Then he was gone.

Jasper leaned across the table and whispered, "I didn't do it, Rebecca."

Even with the jumpsuit and the cuffs, he somehow looked more together than any other time I remembered seeing him. There was something about his eyes. They weren't circling wildly. Also his hair was brushed. That always helped people look a little more together. Maybe finally having done something unforgivably crazy had shaken him sane.

"Why are you whispering?" I asked. "I'd think your innocence would be something that you'd pretty much want to let everyone know. Maybe even take an ad out in the *Sentinel*. They get pretty good circulation on Tuesdays."

"I'm not joking." He threw himself back in the chair.

"Fine. You're not joking. Why should I believe you?" There was something weird going on. Jasper was looking me in the eye and not muttering to himself.

He cocked his head to one side. "Because you're probably

one of the few people in this town who would understand what I've been doing all these years. I figured I could explain it to you and maybe you'd explain it to your boy, Sheriff Dan. Then he'd see these charges are bogus and let me out."

"Dan is not my boy. He's my brother-in-law." Why I thought that was the part of that statement to pounce on, I'm not sure.

"Fine. Brother-in-law. BFF. Bestie. Brother from another mother. Whatever you want to call him. You two have been tighter than twins for years." Jasper sat up straight and folded his hands on the table. "I want you to explain to Dan why I'm not crazy."

"But I do think you're crazy, Jasper." Everyone thought Jasper was crazy. Jasper talked crazy and acted crazy and looked crazy. I was pretty sure that all added up to crazy.

"Yeah. But I'm not. Hear me out, okay?" This was not how Jasper generally spoke. There were no weird half-quotations or references to conspiracies or biblical quotations thrown in for good measure.

I'd told Dan and Garrett I'd listen to Jasper. I liked to be true to my word. "Fine. Lay it on me."

"I was a graduate student at the university in the seventies," he said.

Fine. We were going way back, then. I could totally buy Jasper as a graduate student. Didn't sound crazy yet. "Go on."

"I got involved with some of the antiwar demonstrations." Jasper folded his hands on the table. "Really involved."

I still had no idea where this was going that might possibly have anything to do with Coco's death, but I nodded.

"I got arrested." Jasper looked down at his folded hands. "More than once."

I couldn't help myself. "Jasper, what does this have to do with anything?"

"Hear me out." He took a deep breath and let it out. "It's hard to keep up with your studies when you're in and out of lockup. Plus there were all those meetings . . ."

"And?"

He shrugged. "I flunked out." His voice broke on the last word and tears stood in his eyes. "Me. A failure."

It was clear how much it cost him to tell me that. "I'm sorry, Jasper. That must have been hard."

He used his shoulder to wipe away the tears that had begun to spill onto his cheeks. "You have no idea. Hard and humiliating. I was the first person in my family to go to college and then I flunked out. It was crazy." He stopped again. "So I went crazy. For a while."

Now we were getting somewhere. "What kind of crazy?"

"The kind where maybe you drink a lot and take some pills and then they lock you up for a few days to keep you from hurting yourself. The kind that makes you realize that crazy isn't really worth it. When I got out, I went to the bus station and took the first bus. It was coming here. The last thing I wanted when I got off was to tell people what a failure I was. So instead I told them I'd just been released from Western Ohio Psychiatric, which was the truth. Just not the whole truth. Everyone left me alone. A few people who felt sorry for me left food out or gave me odd jobs now and then. I did a little panhandling. I inherited a little money when my folks passed on. Not a lot, but enough to keep me going. It hasn't been a bad life."

I stared at Jasper, attempting to grasp what he was trying to tell me. Everything I knew about him had been an act to get sympathy, money, and food. I'd certainly fallen for it. So had Coco. Had it cost Coco her life?

"So, you see, I'm not crazy. It was just easier to pretend that I was crazy so I didn't have to deal with everyone looking at me like I was a failure." He smiled as if this explained everything.

This was enlightening, but I still wasn't sure why I was there. "And you felt you had to tell me this why? I mean, why not explain it to Dan or Huerta or your lawyer?"

"Because you, of all people, would understand." He lifted his cuffed hands as far as they would go and pointed at me. "You could help me explain it to them."

I still didn't get it. "Why?"

"Because, you know, you're, uh, well, the same." Jasper's smile started to fade.

"You think I'm acting like a lunatic?" I knew some of my habits were a little too "California" for some people in Grand Lake, but I wasn't preaching about conspiracy theories in the park, and I bathed on a daily basis.

"No. I think you're a failure who had to come back to your hometown. You know how hard it is. You know how humiliating it can be with everyone whispering about you behind your back and pointing. So you'd get why it'd be easier to pretend to be crazy. That is, until someone tries to frame you for murder." Jasper leaned forward onto the table.

I sat back. "Dude, that's seriously how you want to ask me for a favor? By telling me that you think I'm a failure?"

He blushed. "I get that it doesn't sound good when you put it that way."

"Why didn't you ask Jessica for help? I heard she's in here every day anyway." With substandard cookies, but still here.

"Jessica has never left here. She's never had to come back." Jasper sucked in the ends of his mustache and chewed on them for a second. "Besides, Jessica is a lot more interested in you than she is in me."

"Excuse me?"

He shrugged. "She keeps asking about what I saw out in the alley that night, if maybe I saw you coming or going or if there were lights on in your store."

Now I sat back in my chair. "Did she say why?"

"No. She didn't. Then again, I didn't ask her." Jasper drummed his fingers on the table. "You'll talk to Dan, then?"

"I don't think me telling him you're not crazy is going to change anything, Jasper." After being called a failure, I didn't really feel like I had to put Jasper's mind at rest by telling him that Dan already thought he was innocent. Besides, wasn't acting crazy for all those years kind of crazy all by itself? Like maybe even crazier than actually being crazy?

Jasper got a wily look in his eye. "But you will talk to him?"

I shook my head. "Jasper, tell Garrett and Dan yourself. Leave me out of this." Besides, he'd taken advantage of me and everyone else in town with his little act. Why should I do him any more favors?

Jasper tried to cross his arms over his chest, but couldn't because of the cuffs. "You are kind of mean, Rebecca."

I stared at him. I supposed I was being a little mean. "Fine. I'll tell him, but Dan's still not going to let you out, you know," I said. "At least not right away."

He rolled his eyes. "I know. I should never have hit Glenn with that frying pan. I admit it. I panicked when they told me about Coco. It hadn't occurred to me that the money and the truffles were anything but a gift until then. That doesn't mean I should go down for murder, though."

He was right. If I came home and found money and truffles on my doorstep, I'd think I'd hit the jackpot, not that someone was trying to set me up for murder. "I'll talk to him." I stood up and knocked on the door.

"Rebecca," Jasper said.

"Yeah?"

"Be careful. Remember. I didn't do it. That means who-ever did is still out there."

We were running low on butter and sugar at POPS. Normally I would have headed out to the warehouse store in Amherst, but I didn't have the energy or the time for it. Sprocket and I got into the Jeep. I even rolled the passenger side window down for him so he could loll his head out of the window and let his tongue wave like a freak flag in the breeze.

I hustled into the local grocery store and grabbed a cart. Susanna had lacrosse at five and I'd promised I'd be back in time so she wouldn't be late. If I kept moving, I'd just make it. I made it to the baking aisle, put two bags of white sugar and three of brown sugar into my cart and then half-jogged to the dairy section. I rounded the corner and walked smack-dab into my ex-husband.

Well, not my actual ex-husband. A life-size cardboard cutout of my ex-husband. Well, not actually life-size. Haley was right. Antoine wasn't that tall. Two-dimensional Antoine towered over me. Real Antoine was only about three inches taller than me.

Two-dimensional Antoine looked down at me, a twinkle in his eye, a half smile quirking up one side of his mouth and his hand stretched out toward me in invitation. I knew the look. He wanted me to try something. Something a little bit naughty. In this case, it was apparently the brand-new Belanger line of pasta sauces. Probably better than the time he'd wanted me to try that thing with the ice cube. Well, maybe not. The ice cube thing had been kind of fun.

I stared up into those blazingly blue eyes, caught in their beam like a deer in the headlights even if the beam was at least half in my own mind. Haley had warned me. She'd tried to protect me from it. I'd forgotten, too wrapped up in Coco's death. Now I was standing in Kroger, unable to move, almost unable to breathe.

Antoine. I was never going to be able to get away from him. I was never going to be able to get away from any of my past. Everyone knew everything about me here. From my wild child days in high school to my marriage to a cele-buchef to my divorce. What's more is everyone had an opinion. I was a loser, a failure, a bomb, a fiasco, a flop, a zilch, a zero, a big giant goose egg.

"You okay, miss?"

I turned. A pimple-faced boy wearing a dorky red hat and apron stood there. "Fine. I'm fine," I said.

He laughed. "Lots of ladies stopping to stare at that guy." He pointed to two-dimensional Antoine. "He sure is popular. Want me to show you where we shelve his sauces?"

"Th-that's okay," I stammered out and practically ran to get my butter and leave. At least that kid didn't know who I was.

Eleven

I squealed into the alley behind POPS, nearly colliding with a black SUV on my way in. I ran into the store through the back door with Sprocket on my heels. "I'm here," I called out.

"I'm outta here," Susanna called back. I heard the bells on the front door jingle behind her before I even managed to set down the sugar and butter on the kitchen table. I'd made it just under the wire for her to leave and still get to practice on time.

I put the butter in the refrigerator, the sugar in the cupboard, washed my hands and was tying on my apron when I heard the bells jingle again. Sprocket growled low in his throat. I walked into the front room saying, "Can I help you?" Then I saw who it was.

Jessica. She had on a skirt and a sweater set and heels. I looked down at my jeans and tunic top and scarf and felt somehow diminished before Jessica even opened her mouth.

"Can I get you something?" I leaned one denim-covered hip against the counter.

She sniffed and gave the tiniest shake of her head. "No. Thank you. I wanted to stop by and talk to you. Alone."

"Seriously, Jessica? Not even my coffee is good enough for you?" I was still stung by the funeral snub.

She rolled her eyes. "Fine. A cup of coffee, then."

I gestured to the table and chairs. "Make yourself at home."

She hung her purse off the back of one of the ice cream parlor chairs, then sat with her tiny little feet barely brushing the ground.

I went into the kitchen to get the coffee. I'd just finished warming the cups when I heard a shriek, then Sprocket shot by, leapt into the dog bed I kept in the corner of the kitchen and hid his head. "What did you do?" I whispered to him. He kept his paws over his nose, so I went into the shop to find out what crime he'd committed now.

"Keep your filthy dog's nose out of my purse!" Jessica screamed at me, clutching her Coach knockoff to her chest.

"He's not in your purse and he's not filthy. He's quite clean." The nerve of some people!

"Well, he was in my purse and I don't care if he's sterile. I don't want his slimy nose in my purse. Seriously, Rebecca, can't you even control your dog? You are so irresponsible." She put the purse on the table, wiping it down with a napkin like it had been soiled. "And don't you know that Sprocket was a sheepdog? Who names a poodle Sprocket?"

I did not dignify her question with an answer. If there was someone who would never understand the spirit of Sprocket, it was Jessica James. Instead I shook my head and went back into the kitchen to get the coffee. I put a couple of popcorn balls on a plate and brought them, too, for good measure. Right before I left the kitchen, I whispered to Sprocket, "You are not helping."

He harrumphed and kept his back turned to me.

I set the plate and cups down on the table and sat down across from Jessica. "What did you want to talk about?" I asked.

"I've been going through Auntie Coco's papers. I didn't know she'd lent you money, Rebecca." Jessica took a tiny sip of coffee. She didn't say anything, but I saw the look on her face. I made a nice cup of joe.

My face flushed. I hadn't wanted to take any money from Antoine, but I hadn't had enough to start POPS the way I thought it should be started. Coco felt strongly that it was the right thing to do and had offered to make up the difference. "Then you'll have also seen that I've been paying her every month." I only had a few more months to go before the whole loan was paid off.

"Yes. I saw that, too. When do you think you can have the balance paid off?" She pulled a tissue out of her bag with her bandaged fingers and brushed at her nose.

What I hadn't considered until that moment was that I no longer owed Coco the money. Now I owed it to Jessica. The idea of being beholden to Jessica was enough to make me want to run around in circles screaming while banging the top of my head with a wire whisk. "I can have the money to you by the end of the month." It wouldn't be pretty. I'd be running lean here, but with some artful shifting of resources and perhaps eating a few more—or maybe all—of my dinners with Haley and Dan, I should be able to pull it off.

"Excellent. That's all I wanted to talk about." She stood up and wobbled for a second.

I grabbed her elbow to steady her. "Are you okay?"

"I'm fine, Rebecca. You don't have to be so dramatic." She pulled her arm away from me and swayed again.

I took a harder look at her. Her eyes were red-rimmed and sported bags too big to carry on a commercial flight. That wasn't why she was swaying on her feet, though. Now that I was close, I could smell it. Someone had been putting a little something extra in her morning coffee and it wasn't me. Jessica smelled of booze. Even though it might not have been the right time, I couldn't stop myself. I had to ask her. "Why are you telling everyone that Coco wanted to retire?"

Jessica sighed. "Rebecca, Coco was seventy-two years old. How much longer did you think she was going to keep working?"

"At least a few years longer. She wasn't planning on retiring any time soon. She wasn't planning on winding things up. She was planning on starting new things. With me." I couldn't keep the heat out of my voice. I fought to turn down the flame since I wanted a favor. "We were making some plans for a business we were going to start. Would you let me look in her office for the notes? I'd really like to have them."

Jessica walked right up to me, so close I could smell the strawberry scent of her shampoo over the perfume of bourbon. "No. I won't let you rifle through her papers. And I won't have you spreading lies about some business she was starting with you."

"They're not lies, Jessica. We had plans." They had been big plans to me, too.

"Can you prove that, Rebecca?"

Her voice was so cold it made me shiver. "I could if you'd let me look for the plans we were making in her papers."

She shrugged. "Then I guess it would be your word against mine about that. And who would care anyway?" Now she looked up at me, a sly smile on her face. Suddenly her face twisted. She sniffled. Her big blue eyes welled up with tears. One spilled over her bottom lashes and ran down her cheek. "Someone out there made sure that Coco wasn't going to do anything more, ever. Whatever she was planning is never going to happen now anyway."

I felt terrible. Whatever else I thought about Jessica, I knew she was genuinely distraught over Coco's death. Those puffy eyes. The day drinking. I could at least be sympathetic. "I'm sorry, Jessica. You're right."

Her face returned to normal as fast as if she had some kind of hidden switch. "I am right, Rebecca. And don't you forget it. Have you considered this? If you hadn't been pushing Coco to stay in business, maybe she wouldn't have been there so late that night. Maybe she'd still be alive!" Then she stomped out of the shop.

My heart raced as I watched her walk out the door. I turned to Sprocket, who had come back into the shop, and said, "Did you see that?" The way her face had changed as if she'd flicked a switch chilled me. How much of what she showed to the world was an act?

He licked my hand, which I took to be a yes.

"No one will believe us, you know." I patted his head. "No one ever." The whole town believed the face she showed them. Somehow they never saw her when her mask slipped.

But damn it, I was going to make my point. I flipped the shop sign to Closed and barreled down the sidewalk after Jessica. I caught sight of her as she turned into Bob's Diner. By the time I got there, Jessica was already seated in a booth.

"You know that's not true about Coco. Whether I was here or not, she wasn't planning on retiring. If anyone was pushing anyone, it was Coco pushing me to do something more with her." I slid in across from her.

"What I have to ask—what everyone is asking—is why on earth would Coco go into business with you?" Jessica leaned back and tilted her head to one side.

"She wanted to start something new." I thought about what else Coco had said when she'd first approached me about it. "She wanted to do something new and she didn't want to do it alone."

"You're still not answering my question, Rebecca. Why you?" She smiled. "I mean, we all know you're okay in the kitchen."

"Okay?" I started to rise up.

Jessica held her hand up. "Hear me out, Rebecca. You're okay in the kitchen, but clearly not good enough to have made it outside Grand Lake. I mean, you had Antoine Belanger vouching for you and you still couldn't make it in California."

My mouth dropped open and I started to sputter. "Antoine didn't back me. I was on my own."

"And didn't cut it. The only thing you did was marry someone famous and you didn't even manage to do that well." Jessica set her coffee down. "Coco was kind. I'm sure when you came to her with this crazy idea of yours she didn't want to hurt your feelings."

"I didn't come to her. She came to me," I protested.

Jessica snorted. "Sure she did, Rebecca. Because that's what all businesswomen in their seventies do. They go to younger broke people who owe them money and ask if they want to go into business with them. That's totally how the world works. You know, if you hadn't been hounding her maybe she would have already retired. Maybe she would have already handed the shop over to me and she wouldn't have even been there that day and she'd still be alive."

"Jessica, I'm telling you. Coco came to me with an idea to combine our businesses. She wasn't going to retire. I don't know why you're telling people that, but you're wrong."

"Rebecca, you're going to have to keep your voice down."

I whirled around. Megan stood behind me, wringing her hands.

"I have to keep my voice down? What about her?" I pointed at Jessica.

Megan winced. "Her voice isn't raised. You're the one who's yelling."

"Yelling?" Now I actually was. "You call this yelling?"

"Rebecca, please," Jessica broke in, her voice sickly sweet.

I turned back to Megan. "You're actually still buying this act? All these years and you still think she's all sugar and spice and everything nice?"

Megan pursed her lips. "You mean because she stayed here in town and helps teach preschool and run the youth group at the church while taking care of her aunt? That act?"

I threw my hands up in the air. "Yes. That act. Because that's what it is. An act."

"Well, it's a pretty convincing one." Megan shrugged.

I was about to explain why it wasn't a convincing act when I felt a tap on my shoulder. I turned around. It was Dan. My shoulders slumped. He gestured toward the door with his head. I followed. At the door, though, I turned and pointed my finger at Jessica. "This isn't over, and you know it."

"Are you threatening me, Rebecca Anderson?" Jessica asked.

"Yes. I mean no. I mean, stop telling people Coco was planning on retiring when you know it's not true."

Jessica shook her head. As we went out the door, I saw people already starting to cluster around her.

* * *

I strode down the sidewalk toward POPS, the fire of indignation fueling the fire of my pace.

"What the hell was that, Rebecca?" Dan took a couple of long strides to catch up with me.

"That was me telling Jessica to stop telling everyone that Coco was planning on retiring when she wasn't." I pulled the keys out of my pocket and opened the door. Sprocket sprang up from where he'd been sitting beside it. I gave him a quick pat on the head. "Good boy."

"No. I'm pretty sure that was you publicly threatening a fellow business owner." Dan flipped one of the chairs around and straddled it. "What's gotten into you?"

As my anger ebbed away, something else took its place. I brushed at the tears that were forming in my eyes. "Did you hear what she said about me, Dan?"

He nodded. "I did. It wasn't nice. It wasn't true. You've got people lining up here in the morning for your popcorn bars. It wasn't anything you should let get to you. You know that."

"No. I don't think I do know that anymore. Let me tell you what Jasper wanted to talk to me about." I filled Dan in on that fun conversation. "So basically the whole town thinks I'm a loser. The whole town thinks I'm a failure. Jessica is probably right. The whole town probably thinks I'm making up a story about Coco wanting to start a new business with me."

Dan dropped his head.

I sat back in my chair. "You, too, Dan? *Et tu?*"

"Oh, come on. Don't start with the Brutus stuff. I'm not stabbing and it's a long way from March. You have to admit, it does seem kind of farfetched that Coco would want to start something new at her age." He looked at Jessica's mug on the table. "What does a hardworking cop have to do to get a cup of coffee around here?"

"He has to follow me to the kitchen." I went into the kitchen, dumped out the old stuff and started a new pot.

"Hey! That would have been fine if you microwaved it for a second." He leaned against the counter.

"No. It wouldn't have. It would have been bitter and boiled and nasty. We deserve better. Or at least you do. You're not a loser." I rinsed the grounds out of the French press, rinsed the whole thing again with hot water and ground fresh beans.

As soon as the noise stopped, Dan said, "You know this is part of the problem."

"Decent coffee is never part of the problem. It is always part of the solution. Always." There were few things in life I was certain of, but that was one of them.

"That's not what I mean. You always have to make things harder. Let things be simple. Let the stuff about Coco go." He was almost pleading.

I poured the boiling water in and set the timer for four minutes. "That's easy for you to say, Dan. The whole town isn't calling you a loser."

"No. They're not. They call me *Sheriff* and one of the reasons they call me that is that I encourage our citizens not to go around threatening one another, especially when one of the townspeople has been killed and another has been attacked." He looked at his watch. "You know Megan would have already poured me a second cup of coffee by now."

"And it would have tasted like swill." I heated mugs for us and put out the cream and sugar. "I wasn't threatening her person."

"Good. Don't." The timer went off. "Now can I have a cup of coffee?"

I poured the coffee and he took a sip. "Worth the wait?" I asked.

"You know it is. Stop showing off and explain to me about Jasper again. I always wondered how crazy he actually was." He sat down at the table. "I caught him looking normal way too many times."

I sat down and took a sip of my own coffee. I hadn't been showing off. I'd been doing what I'd been taught, doing things the right way. Which is when it occurred to me that showing people I wasn't a loser was a much better plan than stamping my feet and telling them that I wasn't one.

Now I just had to figure out how to do that.

After Dan left, I had another surge of business with people picking up popcorn balls for desserts. I took another hour to close after that. I slogged through emptying the display cases.

No one else was around when I took everything out to the Dumpster. Being out there alone in the alley gave me another little frisson of fear. Someone had been out here looking at the backs of our stores, and it hadn't been Jasper. I wasn't sure if it was more frightening to think about a total stranger being back here or it being someone I'd known for years who had suddenly become violent. I wasn't crazy about either scenario.

I must have been more deeply lost in thought than I knew because when Allen Thompson turned down the alley in his utterly ridiculous Lexus I almost jumped out of my skin. He slowed down as he pulled abreast of me. "You okay, Rebecca?"

"I'm fine, Allen. What are you doing here?" I rubbed my arms.

"Oh, just cruising by."

"In the alley? Because that's so scenic and all?" I mean, who wouldn't want to take a tour of the Dumpsters of Grand Lake?

He smiled that white-toothed politician's grin at me. "I'm the mayor of the whole town, sweetheart. Not just the storefronts."

He was also the owner of most of the storefronts, including mine, but still not Coco's. "Are you sure there isn't a particular reason you're interested in this alley, Allen?"

"I—I don't know what you mean," he stammered.

That was interesting. He looked guilty. The question was of what. Everybody knew he wanted to buy Coco's shop. He'd wanted to buy Barbara's, too. Now Coco was conveniently out of his way and possibly Barbara as well. "I was just thinking about Coco. The last time I saw her was Thursday around noon. We were going to have coffee the next morning. When was the last time you saw her, Allen?"

His brows furrowed. "I'm not sure. Probably Tuesday night at the chamber of commerce meeting. She almost never missed one of those."

"Oh. So you didn't see her on Thursday at all?" I tried to make the question sound casual. "Didn't stop by to chat about business? About maybe her selling her shop?"

"Not that I recall." He stopped. "What exactly are you implying, Rebecca?"

"I'm not implying anything. I'm just curious about why you've been hanging out around this alley so much lately and why you look so guilty when I ask you about it." My hands balled into fists at my side.

"Rebecca, stick to making popcorn. Let Dan worry about what's happening in the alleys of Grand Lake." He didn't wait for my response, just gunned his engine and drove away.

I watched him drive off to the other end of the alley and out onto Second Street and then went back inside. "I don't like that man, Sprocket. I don't trust him."

I packaged up the leftover popcorn to leave for Tom—not that the misogynistic asshat deserved even my stale leftovers. Really, who spouted that kind of nonsense about women staying in their places anymore? Sadly, I knew the answer was more people than I cared to count. I was most decidedly not in California anymore.

My hand froze on the door handle for a second as I went to put the package on the back porch for him anyway. How much exactly did Tom dislike women who ran their own businesses? It didn't help that his shaggy face popped up into the glass frame of the door at just that second.

I leaped back with a gasp.

He scowled.

I looked down at the bags in my hand. It probably wouldn't do to piss him off any further if he was the person attacking women business owners. I opened the door and handed it to him. He grabbed the bag from me without a thank-you and left.

"You're welcome," I called after his retreating back. He didn't turn around. He had a total lack of charm in common with Jasper. No wonder they were friends.

I locked up and we took our evening walk out to the lighthouse. I could feel the weather starting to turn and it seemed like it was getting darker faster. Or maybe that was my mood. It was too cold to sit and dangle our feet, so Sprocket and I contented ourselves with standing at the end of the pier and watching the sun slowly sink toward the water. I wrapped my sweater tighter around myself and turned to go back toward town.

And nearly ran headfirst into Garrett Mills. Or, more

accurately, he nearly ran headfirst into me, since he was the one who was actually running.

"Rebecca! Sorry!" He stopped, panting, and wiped the sweat off his forehead with the back of his hand.

"You're wearing shorts." I'm an amazing observer. Almost nothing gets past me.

"Yeah. Dress for the second mile, right?" Garrett bent over slightly to rest his hands on his thighs, which were shockingly muscular. Again, I was only observing.

"Sure. Whatever you say." Second mile? He was running more than one? I began to question his sanity, but it seemed rude to mention it. I resumed walking. Garrett fell into step beside me. "Are you stalking me, Counselor?" I asked.

"Maybe it's the other way around. Maybe you're stalking me. I run here every day," he said. "There's something about the water . . ."

"You don't run here every day. I walk here every day and this is the first time I've seen you." I was pretty sure I'd remember seeing him in his running gear, what with the muscles and all.

"I usually go in the morning, but it's getting a little dark and cold for my tastes. I thought I'd try after work instead, but I'm glad I ran into you. I heard about the, uh, thing between you and Jessica this afternoon." His breathing was returning to something that sounded vaguely normal.

Fantastic. Of course he had. My conversation with Jessica must have run through the town gossip line like a hot knife through butter. "What? Did she take out an ad or something?"

He shook his head. "No, but word gets around. Did you really threaten her?"

"Is that what they're saying?" It figured. Jessica had timed it perfectly again. Everything she'd said to get under my skin had been said without an audience or in that sweet reasonable tone of hers. I was the idiot who said whatever I was thinking no matter where I was or who I was with and tended to say it at a greater decibel level than was perhaps strictly necessary.

"Yeah. Along with something about you owing Coco money, and a few other choice tidbits." He glanced over at me as we walked.

I tightened my jaw. "Whatever."

He reached out to take my arm. "I know we haven't known each other very long and it's none of my business, but you might want to be careful."

"Of what?" I stopped.

"Let's call it the court of public opinion. It can be pretty damaging. I've seen it." Garrett dropped my arm and bounced lightly on his toes. It must have been getting cold for him with barely any clothes on.

"Yeah. I've been tried and convicted by this town before. It's nothing new." I shrugged.

Garrett shook his head. "It is new, Rebecca. This isn't about the behavior of a distraught high school kid. Some-one's dead."

I turned away from him. "And there's no one with less reason than me to want it that way!"

"So you say."

Great. Garrett didn't even know me and he thought I was making up the whole story about Coco and me going into business, too. I turned away from the lake and sped up my pace as I walked away, but Garrett easily matched it so I slowed down instead. "Thanks for the advice," I said hoping that my voice showed exactly how very much it was not welcome.

"Call me if you want to talk," he said, and then he was gone, jogging off into the sunset.

I watched him for a second. Do all joggers bound like that? He looked like he was actually having fun. "Haters gonna hate, Sprocket, but we're gonna show 'em, right?" I was starting to think of a way that I could. I'd show them all.

Only suckers waited for permission.

Twelve

One of the first things Coco gave me when I came back to Grand Lake was a set of keys that included the keys to her house and to her shop. She had a set with my house keys and shop keys on them, too. Sprocket and I walked past POPS and Coco's Cocoas and directly to Coco's house a few blocks farther on.

The sun was starting to set and no one was out as we walked up the driveway and around to the back door. Most of Grand Lake was inside cleaning up after supper and getting ready to settle down to a nice night of television or reading or needlepoint. I waited as an SUV went past on the street and then we let ourselves into Coco's. I reached out to turn on the light and then thought better of it when I remembered the whole Barbara debacle. It would be better if no one knew we'd been here. I turned on the flashlight app on my phone instead.

I shone the light around the kitchen. A coffee mug and a bowl sat in the drying rack. I ran my fingers over them. Of course Coco hadn't left dirty dishes in the sink. That wasn't her way. She liked things neat and tidy. She said it was part of why she'd never wanted to get married. She didn't want to deal with anyone else's mess.

I made my way to Coco's office and stood looking around for a minute or two. Where would she have kept the notes for the business plan she was writing for us? Where would I have kept them? That was easy. I would have kept them in some messy pile that was sliding off the edge of my desk. What would be the opposite of that?

There was a wire rack with folders slotted into it. I halfway remembered Coco putting whatever she'd been working on in that for easy access. I pulled out the first folder. It was a lot of stuff about insurance. The next folder had her will. My heart sank a little. Maybe Jessica was right. Maybe Coco had been tired and wanting to retire if she was reviewing her will. Maybe I had been pushing her too hard to start our new venture. Maybe the coffee we were supposed to have together on Friday had been for her to let me down easy. A whole "it's not your popcorn, it's my chocolate" kind of breakup talk.

I sat down in the chair behind Coco's desk. Then I saw Coco's to-do-list pad. I'd definitely know what she was planning if I could see what she'd put on that list, but the top page was blank. I held it up at an angle. There were some depressions on the top page. It would be easy enough to run a pencil over it gently to get at least a glimpse into what Coco was up to that last day.

I was rummaging through the desk for a pencil when I heard the sirens. They were probably heading over to one of the taverns a few blocks away. At least, that's what I tried to tell myself. Then the flashing lights strobed through the window to stripe Coco's study walls in red and blue. Okay. Maybe there was something happening on the block. Please let there be something else happening on the block. I heard a car door slam.

I looked at Sprocket and said, "Not again."

I could swear he laughed.

Then Coco's front door was slamming open and Huerta yelled, "Police! Coming in! Freeze with your hands up!"

I slipped the notepad into my purse and raised my hands.

At least this time Huerta put the window of the squad car down so Sprocket could hang his head out on our way to the station.

I glared at Dan from across his desk. He glared back. "Bec, just tell me what you were doing in Coco's house. I'm sure we can clear this thing up and then we can all go home."

"I'm not talking until my lawyer gets here." I pressed my lips together and mimed locking them and throwing away the keys.

"Can't you charge her with being uncooperative or something?" Jessica asked from her seat over on the side of the office.

Jessica. Of course she was the one who called the cops on me. Again. Of course she had happened to be passing by her aunt's house and saw my flashlight beam inside. Sprocket growled a little deep down in his throat.

"And can't you make that animal wait someplace else?" Jessica pushed back in her chair away from my dog.

"Sprocket won't hurt anything and Rebecca does have the right to counsel, Jessica." Dan rubbed his hand over his face. He looked tired. Good. I couldn't believe it when he told Huerta over the radio to arrest me. For the second time in the space of a week. Me. His best friend. The person who created a diversion when he stole his first candy bar. The person who helped him glue down everything on Ms. Vigler's desk in sixth grade.

Come to think of it, Dan was kind of a juvenile delinquent back in the day. He probably didn't want to be reminded of it this minute, though.

"I suppose next you're going to tell me she has the right to break into my aunt's home and rifle through Coco's belongings at will." Jessica sniffed.

"There was no breaking. There was only entering," I protested. "I have a key."

Dan's eyebrows went up and I remembered that whole "not talking until my lawyer got there" thing. Luckily, he showed up about then.

Garrett looked like we'd interrupted an evening of watching basketball on the couch. In fact, I was pretty sure we had. He had on jeans and a Case Western sweatshirt. His hair was still wet from a shower, but he had a five-o'clock shadow going. He looked decidedly un-corporate and not even a teensiest bit lawyerly. I was relieved, however, that he wasn't still wearing those shorts. They were distracting, and I needed to stay focused.

"Rebecca," he said, sneakers squeaking on the tile floor. "If you'd wanted to see me again, you could have called. You didn't have to get arrested first."

"Calling you wasn't my idea." It actually hadn't been. Huerta had stressed the "you have a right to an attorney" thing pretty hard and Dan had actually slipped me Garrett's card.

"So I'm missing the end of the Cavaliers' game for no good reason?" He leaned against the doorframe of the office.

I didn't feel like explaining everything in front of Jessica. "Don't you want to consult with me in private?" Then blushed at exactly how that sounded. Based on Dan's smirk, he'd heard it, too.

Garrett grinned. "Yeah. Right. Dan? You have a spot where I could speak to Ms. Anderson? Privately?"

Dan nodded his head. "Of course. Follow me." He stood up and led us down the hall to a small conference room. He opened the door and stood aside. "Be my guest."

Once we got inside and sat down, Garrett said, "Rebecca, what the hell? Did you not hear what I said to you about the court of public opinion? How do you think rummaging around in Coco's private papers is going to look to people?"

"I was trying to find some notes that Coco and I had made about our business plan. Then I'd be able to show everyone that we were going to start a new business together and she didn't have any plans to retire and that Jessica is making stuff up to make me look bad. Again. That's all. Well, those and some recipe ideas we'd been working on. I could re-create those on my own, but it'd be easier if I had the notes we'd already made." I ran the edge of my thumbnail up and down my jeans. "I don't know why everyone has to make a federal case out of it."

Garrett pushed back in his chair and crossed his legs, ankle to knee. "It's not a federal case, Rebecca. It's a criminal one." He jiggled his foot. He didn't sound amused now.

"I am not a crook," I said. "I didn't find the notes. Besides, if I had found them and took them, it wouldn't be stealing. They were half mine."

"So you removed nothing from Coco's home?" The foot kept jiggling, but nothing else on him was moving.

I slid my hands under my thighs and crossed my fingers while thinking about that notepad. "No. Of course not."

He sighed and stood up. "Let's go talk to Dan. Given the circumstances, there's a chance I can make it home before the end of the fourth quarter. But first, give me your phone."

I handed it over. He hit a few buttons and then handed it

back. "I put my contact information in there in your favorites list. Call me whenever."

"My favorites? Don't you think that's kind of presumptuous?" I asked as I stood up.

He shrugged. "I've got good self-esteem. If I'm not one of your favorites now, I will be soon enough." He held the door open for me.

Sprocket and I trooped after him down the hall back to Dan's office. Garrett motioned for me to sit down. "I think what we have here is an unfortunate misunderstanding."

I stifled a giggle. I'd been sure he was going to say "failure to communicate." Dan, Jessica and Garrett all turned and stared at me. I held my hands up in front of me. "Sorry."

Garrett rubbed at his forehead with his thumb. "Ms. Anderson was simply trying to locate some business plans she had been working on with Ms. Bittles before Ms. Bittles's untimely death. Ms. Bittles had given Ms. Anderson the keys to her home many months ago. Ms. Anderson did not think she was doing anything wrong by letting herself in and looking for the plans." I noticed he didn't mention the recipes.

"She did, too! I already told her no," Jessica burst out. "That's why she was snooping around with a flashlight. She's sneaky."

Garrett turned to me.

I shrugged. "It wasn't a flashlight. It was my cell phone. I didn't know if the electricity still worked. I only wanted what was mine. Nothing else."

Jessica threw her tiny hands up in the air. "You really expect me to believe that, Rebecca? After I already told you I wouldn't let you into her office to look for those papers?"

I leaned back in my chair. "I don't expect anything of you, Jessica."

"What's that supposed to mean?" Now she was on full alert.

"I mean, that if you had been willing to let me in to look for the business plan, I wouldn't have had to let myself in."

She jumped to her feet. "So you admit you were snooping!"

"I admit I was looking for the plans that Coco and I were working on. I might still want to go forward with them," I said in what I hoped was a reasonable tone.

"None of them better have anything to do with her fudge recipe, Rebecca." She jabbed her finger toward me.

I didn't budge. "Of course not. Our plans were based on new recipes, collaborations between Coco and me."

"Jessica, do you still want to press charges against Rebecca?" Dan broke in.

"I suppose not." Jessica put her hands on her hips. "Just remember, Rebecca, whatever belonged to Coco now belongs to me. Me. Not you. Not ever." Jessica shook her head and muttered something under her breath.

Now I was on full alert. "Did you just call me a vulture?" The very same thing I had called Allen Thompson. She couldn't have hurt me worse if she'd used a knife.

"If the feathers fit, Rebecca. If the feathers fit." Jessica looked at me, a little smile on her insipid face.

I was on my feet so fast I didn't even know how I'd gotten that way.

Then Garrett was in front of me. "Get out of my way, runner boy." I tried to feint around him.

He blocked me easily and shook his head. "Nope. Take a second. Think about the optics, Rebecca."

"The what?"

"How this would look. Think about it. Think about your knee." He glanced down at my leg.

It took me a second to put it together. He was talking

about my high school showdown with Jessica. He was right. The optics were bad. Seriously bad. I dropped my hand. "Want to take a walk?"

"Very much," he said, taking my hand and leading me out of the police station with Sprocket guarding my back.

Thirteen

I didn't see the black SUV on my way into POPS the next morning. I'd started watching for it. It gave me an itchy uncomfortable feeling. I did get a few knowing comments about my troubles with the law from some of the breakfast regulars. The *Sentinel* had run the story of my second arrest. I didn't know how they'd heard about it so fast, but I suspected it was Jessica. She'd want everyone to know anything that made me look bad. She always had.

By noon I'd received another set of texts from Antoine. He was certain I needed some kind of legal assistance and he would be happy to pay for it. He suggested that perhaps also I would like to return to California to avoid getting three strikes and being put in prison in Ohio for life.

I didn't respond to any of them.

That evening, Haley and Dan were taking Evan to a Trout Fishing in America concert. I'd been invited to attend but had passed. Having been treated to "I Think I'll Need a Bandaid" on a loop in the minivan on a trip to Cleveland the previous month, I was pretty sure that I'd stick something in my eye if I had to listen to them again. It had actually been a really funny cute song the first fifteen times I heard it. It had started to sour on repeat number sixteen. By repeat number twenty, I'd been done, but Evan had only been getting started. Ah, to be three.

But then when I closed the shop, there didn't seem to be any reason to head back to the apartment, either. No Haley. No Evan. No Dan. Just Sprocket and me. It seemed like a better idea to hang out at the shop and get a little paperwork done.

Paperwork is my downfall. I'd never really had to do it before I opened POPS. When I was a teenager, it was Haley's problem. When I was in school, it was the Institute's problem. When I was cooking, it was the chef's problem. When I got married it was Antoine's problem.

Now it was my problem and no one else's. Coco and Annie had helped me set up a system, but the problem with systems is that a person had to actually then use the system to make it work. Somehow making the system work in the office was low on my priority list, so there was a stack of filing to be done teetering on my desk like an unstable chocolate fountain.

I made myself a toasted cheese sandwich and then I made a second one to share with Sprocket, who had looked at the dry food I kept for him at the store and then at me and sighed heavily enough to rattle the blinds. I settled down at my desk and started working from the left side to the right side, filing whatever I came across that needed to be kept, throwing out the junk and making a significantly smaller pile of stuff that needed me to do something.

I'd gotten a good rhythm going when I heard the sound of a car door shutting in the back alley. Not slamming.

Shutting. Gently. Like whoever was shutting it didn't want to make a lot of noise.

The hair on my arms stood up. Jasper's words came back to me. If he didn't do it, Coco's murderer was still on the loose in Grand Lake. Criminals liked to return to the scene of the crime. We still didn't know why anyone would have broken into Coco's Cocoas when she was there alone working at night and now I was here working alone in POPS. Then I thought about that black SUV that always seemed to be cruising around wherever I was, looking dark and mysterious and dangerous.

I hit the switch and turned off the lamp on my desk. All the rest of the lights were already off. I slid out of the room I used as my office, keeping close to the walls. Sprocket looked up at me, head tilted to one side in as plain a doggie question as I had ever seen. I held my finger up to my lips. He settled back to the floor.

I slipped along the hallway to the kitchen. Annie's back porch light was on, casting its glow into the shadows of the alley. It didn't light up much, but it lit up enough for me to see Allen Thompson walking down the alley. His walk was like his door slam. Quiet. Clandestine. He stayed close to the shadows and kept looking over his shoulder.

I craned my neck a little. The jerk. He'd parked in Coco's spot. It galled me. The flowers hadn't even wilted yet on her grave and he was parking in her spot and scoping out the properties around her business.

That thought stopped me. Why would he be scoping out the other businesses? He owned everything on the block except for Coco's. Her place was the only thing he should be sniffing around.

I waited until he had shadow-walked past POPS and slipped out the back door, not shutting it behind me. I stayed in the shadows of the porch and watched while Allen stopped by Annie's Dumpsters. I held my breath as he looked up and down. Good thing I was wearing black.

After he'd satisfied himself that no one was around, he walked briskly across the alley, up the steps to Annie's back door and directly into her shop. I bit my lip to keep from shouting out. Just because he owned the building didn't mean he could march in and out at his pleasure.

Then another thought occurred to me. A darker thought. Annie could be in there alone. A whole scenario played out in my head. Allen coming to talk to Coco about selling her shop. Her dismissing him. Words being exchanged. Then him shoving her and her falling backward and hitting her head. An accident, like Dan had said.

Then what if Allen had discovered that he liked it? He enjoyed watching the light go out in Coco's eyes. I'd always felt the man had no moral compass whatsoever. Maybe he was a real sociopath and Coco was the first of what would be a string of murdered single women shop owners. Maybe Allen had been shamed by a woman shop owner as a child and now he was going to exact his revenge on the business-women of Grand Lake.

I ran down the steps of the porch and over to Annie's. I tried the door. Locked. Damn it. Allen must have let himself in with his own key. Good thing I had my own set with the spare Annie had given me in my jeans pocket. As I dug the keys from my pocket I heard a noise. Not a noise, a voice. A woman's voice. Inarticulate. Moaning.

My hands shook so hard it took me three tries to get the key in the lock. I charged into the little house, heading toward the noise. Allen had Annie backed up against her potting counter and she was making a noise unlike any I'd ever heard her make before. Without pausing, without thinking, without considering, I picked up one of the clay pots from the back wall and bashed Allen on the head with it, yelling, "Get off her, you monster!"

It was about then that I stopped to wonder why Annie had had her legs wrapped around his waist.

"What. Are. You. Doing?" Annie panted as she scrambled to rearrange her clothes.

I looked down at the cracked pot in my hand. Allen had a heck of a hard head. He and Huerta ought to have some kind of competition. "I thought I was saving you from being murdered."

Annie crouched down next to where Allen lay on the floor. "Allen, honey, are you all right?"

He moaned. "What happened?"

"Rebecca happened." Annie stood up. "Let me get you some ice."

I followed her into the kitchen. "Do you want to explain what was happening back there?"

She shoved a couple of handfuls of ice from the freezer into a bag. "Rebecca, if you don't know what that was after eleven years of marriage, I don't really want to be the one to explain it to you."

My face got hot. "I know what you were doing. I want to know why."

Annie started to laugh as she wrapped the bag with a towel. "Do you really need me to answer that, either?"

No. I didn't. I got that part, too. "Okay. I guess what I mean is, why him? I thought we hated him."

Now it was Annie's turn to blush. Finally. Apparently getting caught with your legs wrapped around the mayor in the corner of your potting room wasn't blush-worthy.

Getting caught with your legs wrapped around a mayor you supposedly hated was another story. "It's complicated."

"I have time." I crossed my arms over my chest and leaned against the counter.

She shook her head and went back to the potting room. Allen was sitting up now, propped up against one of the cabinets. "Give me one reason I shouldn't call the police and press charges against you for assault, Rebecca. Just one reason."

"Just one?" I pretended to think. "Okay. Annie's reputation. How about that?"

Allen pressed his lips together so hard they pretty much disappeared. "Fine."

At least he was a gentleman and at least I wouldn't have to explain to Dan why I'd had the cops called on me for a third time in the space of a week. Although I suspected he might have been happy to have an excuse to leave the Trout Fishing in America concert.

Annie crouched down and pressed the ice against the back of Allen's head. He winced and shrugged away. She made a clucking noise and he settled back down.

"How long has this been going on?" I asked.

They glanced at each other. "Since the chamber of commerce meeting about the snow-plowing contract," Annie mumbled.

"The snow-plowing meeting? The one where you stood up in front of the whole town and accused Allen of using city contracts to line his own pockets? That meeting?" It had been an epic Norma Rae moment. Annie standing in front of the council, her hair a graying halo around her face, laying out exactly how Allen's proposal for snow clearance was going to end up profiting him and costing the town.

"Wasn't she amazing?" Allen looked up at Annie and smiled. She smiled back.

"Yes. But she was exposing your greedy and corrupt ways while she was being amazing. Isn't that a problem for you?" This was all so confusing.

He laughed. "A problem? No. A challenge? Absolutely. Do you have any idea how long it's been since someone has really challenged me? It was . . . exciting. Enervating. Got my blood boiling in ways it hadn't boiled in years." He pulled Annie toward him and kissed her right on the mouth.

I shook my head. "And you? What's your explanation?" I asked Annie.

She arched a brow at me. "Not that I owe you any kind of explanation, but . . . Well, I forgot my umbrella at city hall that night. When I went back to get it, Allen was the only one there. We started arguing again and then, well, we weren't arguing anymore. That line between passion and anger can be very thin sometimes."

Allen reached up, took her hand and brought it to his lips. "You have such fire. I don't know how any man can resist you."

I felt like I'd been dropped down a rabbit hole. "But you two have been mortal enemies for as long as I can remember."

Annie shrugged. "Imagine we're like Rock Hudson and Doris Day in *Pillow Talk* except I don't have those awesome hats."

"And I'm not gay," Allen chimed in.

"So all the times I've seen you prowling around the alley you were coming to meet Annie?" My theory casting Allen as Coco's murderer and Barbara's assailant was rapidly disintegrating.

Allen nodded and then winced again. "We weren't quite ready to go public. You're not the only one who's going to be surprised. My chamber of commerce friends are going to have a hard time getting used to Annie being at our cocktail mixers."

"And imagine what my master gardeners' group is going to think about having Allen for tea!" Annie giggled. "We've been meeting at the store so no one sees us at each other's houses. I didn't think you were going to go all Nancy Drew on us."

I turned back to Allen. "So you weren't looking for evidence you might have left behind when you murdered Coco?"

"When I what?" Allen squawked and started to stand up, then winced and sat back down again. "You thought I did what?"

I looked down at my feet. "I kind of thought you might have murdered Coco."

"Why on earth would I do that?" He looked honestly confused.

"To get her property. I know Jessica is planning on selling it to you. Annie told me." It finally dawned on me how Annie probably knew. Pillow talk, indeed. Ewww. I felt double dirty.

"Of course she is. I'm offering a good price so that I can consolidate my investments here downtown," Allen said.

"And Coco wouldn't sell. I thought maybe you'd killed her because you knew Jessica was an easier mark." A greedier mark, I corrected in my head.

Allen struggled to his feet and over to one of the cane-back chairs Annie had scattered around. "Look. I like business. I like buying and selling. It's like a game to me. Monopoly, but the board is real. I would no more murder someone to get access to a property than I would spit into the wind."

"I also thought maybe it might have been an accident. You argued and pushed her and she fell and then you tried to make it look like someone broke in." I sat down on one of the chairs. I felt tired all of a sudden.

"Please tell me you didn't share your theories with anyone," Allen said plaintively.

"I maybe mentioned them to Dan." I winced. "Sorry."

"And what was his reaction?" Allen asked.

I looked down at my feet. "He told me I was crazy."

"Good man. I'm going to see about getting him a raise."

The next morning on the way to POPS, Sprocket and I were walking up Tulip Lane when we saw the black SUV go through the intersection ahead of us. I hurried down the street to see if maybe I could get a license plate number to give to Dan, but then a green Honda Civic turned onto the street. Well, the driver tried to turn onto the street, but somehow turned too hard and jumped up onto the sidewalk. After bumping up onto the sidewalk, the driver clearly tried to correct, but overdid that as well. The Civic bumped back onto the road and headed directly toward a white PT Cruiser parked on the other side of the street. The driver corrected again, but sideswiped the Cruiser, screeching along the length of the car with that awful metal-on-metal sound that everyone knows heralds no one any good.

Sprocket surged forward, barking at the out-of-control automobile. I pulled back on his leash. Who knew where that crazy-ass car was going next? One place it wasn't going to go, however, was over my dog. Not unless it went over me first.

The driver overcorrected again, jumped the opposite curb and this time, without any cars in its way, plowed directly into the oak tree in the front of George and Cindy Calvin's yard. In the oak-tree-versus-Civic standoff, the oak tree definitely won. Sprocket and I heard the airbag deploy with a giant *pop* and then there was nothing but a hissing noise coming from under the crushed hood of the Civic.

Sprocket and I started to run. We got to the Civic at about the same time Mrs. Calvin came out onto the porch in her bathrobe. "What in the Sam Hill is going on out here?"

"Not sure, Mrs. Calvin. Someone's had an accident." I was pretty sure who was going to be behind the wheel of that car. It wasn't the only green Civic in town, but I thought I knew who drove this one.

"I'll say! Who the h-e-double-toothpicks is that?" She looked reluctant to come off her porch.

Normally I admire the fact that Mrs. Calvin manages to have one of the worst potty mouths in Grand Lake without ever uttering a real swear word. It was from her that I'd learned to call someone a "see you next Tuesday." Today, however, I didn't have time for it. "Call 911."

I grabbed the door handle and tried to pull the door open, but the force of the impact had jammed the door. I knocked on the window and peered in, seeing mainly the pillowy white airbag. "Are you okay in there?"

The blond head turned to look at me. I took a step back. Just as I thought. It was Jessica. Sprocket raised his head and sniffed. I did, too. Gasoline. Visions of the car suddenly bursting into flame exploded in my brain. I pulled again on the door, bracing my feet and putting my full weight into it. It still wouldn't budge. Jessica stared at me through the window. "Jessica, can you push on the door from the inside?"

She still stared at me, her eyes unfocused.

I pounded some more. "Jessica! Unlock the door!" Still nothing. Behind me, Sprocket was barking as if he could open the car door through sound frequency.

I looked around for something, anything I could use and saw the brick edging along Mrs. Calvin's driveway. I ran over, pulled up a brick, went to the passenger side of Jessica's Civic and smashed the window. That got Jessica's attention.

"What the hell, Rebecca?" With her words came a puff of breath that had to be about ninety proof.

I was getting a little tired of people asking me that, so I didn't bother to answer. I reached in and unlocked the passenger door, crawled halfway in and undid Jessica's seat belt. "You have to get out of the car. Can you open your door?"

Comprehension started to dawn in her eyes. She turned to her door and tried to push it open. No dice.

"Climb over this way." I slid back out of the car to give her room, but she got stuck halfway across the console.

"I can't." She collapsed, sprawled across the seat.

"You can, Jessica. You have to." I bent over to look at her. Sprocket shoved his way in and licked her face.

"Oh, yuck! Your dog slobbered on me." She tried to wipe her face, but missed, her hand waving ineffectually in the air.

My heart was thudding in my chest. "Jessica, move. There's gasoline dripping from somewhere. It's not safe for you to stay in the car. You have to get out."

"I'm tired." She laid her head down on the passenger seat. "The leather is nice and cool."

"It won't be for long if your car bursts into flame," I pointed out.

She didn't answer. In fact, I thought I heard a slight snore. Sprocket licked her face again. She waved a hand distractedly in the air like she was brushing away a fly.

Mrs. Calvin came back out onto her stoop. "I called 911. They said they're on their way."

I listened, but didn't hear sirens. The gasoline smell got stronger. I reached into the car and grabbed Jessica under her armpits and pulled. She slid toward the door for a second then stopped. I gave another experimental tug. Nothing. I looked in. Jessica's leg was caught. I clambered over her and moved her leg and then shifted back out again. I tugged again. Still nothing. So I tugged harder.

Big mistake. Jessica came free and I stumbled backward, landing hard on my back on Mrs. Calvin's lawn with Jessica on top of me. Mrs. Calvin screamed an actual expletive. Jessica opened one eye, closed it again and then started to scream. Sprocket licked my face enthusiastically.

As I tried to catch the breath that had been knocked out of me, I heard the sirens.

Fourteen

The paramedics had taken one look at Jessica and whisked her into the ambulance. Dan took a quick statement from me and one from Mrs. Calvin and then headed to the hospital to talk to Jessica after a terse "You and I have to talk" directed at me. Mrs. Calvin offered me a cup of coffee, but I had to get to the shop, and suspected she used instant anyway. As it was, I was late. I barely had the first batch of breakfast bars ready to go before people were lining up at the door.

It didn't help that I was moving slow. My head hurt from where it hit the ground and my rib cage was bruised up enough that it hurt with every breath I took. When the crowd thinned out at nine thirty, I almost wept with relief. I collapsed into a chair at the kitchen table with a fresh cup of coffee with good cold cream and a little sugar. I reached into my purse to pull out the bottle of painkillers I kept there and my hand hit an unfamiliar shape. I pulled it out. Coco's to-do-list notepad. I'd completely forgotten about slipping it into my purse right before Huerta burst in to arrest me. Self-righteous indignation apparently erased my short-term memory.

I set it on the table. Coco always tended to push hard on pens. She said it was a leftover from living in the days of carbon copies. You had to really bear down to make sure the words on the yellow copy were still legible. I thought it was one more sign of her energy and vitality. Even pens had to bend to her will. Whatever the reason, I could see faint depressions on the paper from where her pen had dug in.

I picked out a soft-leaded pencil from the old sugar tin I kept my office supplies in and sharpened it. Then, holding my breath, I started to run the side of the pencil over the depressions with the same gentleness Antoine had taught me to use when making pastry. My streusels will melt on your tongue in a sea of buttery goodness, and Coco's hand-writing appeared on the notepad like cream rising to the top of a stoneware jug.

The date on the top was Thursday, the day she died. My hands started to shake.

The first item was hard to read. I held it at an angle to the light. It looked like it was possibly "Buy sponges." Or maybe something about tongues? Hard to tell.

The next item was easy. Return library books. Coco was a voracious reader and was at the Grand Lake Public Library at least once a week if not more.

Third item: Pick up copies of plan. Could she have meant our business plan? The one we'd been working on together? The one no one else thought existed? But pick it up from where?

Item four, however, took my breath away. Of all of them it was the easiest to read. Coco must have been pressing down pretty hard on that pen when she wrote, "Change will."

* * *

I had known that Coco was planning on changing her will. I hadn't thought it would happen this soon. It was part of the plan that Coco and I had been making to create our personal popcorn-and-fudge wonderland. Coco's will, as it stood now, left everything to Jessica. Her house. Her car. Her shop. Her fudge recipe. The fudge recipe that Jessica had been trying to talk Coco into selling to one of the big national chocolatiers for years.

The new will was going to leave Jessica the house, the car, and the shop, but not the recipe. Coco was going to take that with her to the new shop she was going to open with me. I knew that, but I didn't think anybody else did. With no one believing me about Coco and I going into business together, I figured they'd be even less likely to believe that Coco was going to give the fudge recipe to me.

Dan came in at about noon to have our little chat. He waited until I'd set his coffee down in front of him to say, "I don't know what you were thinking, Rebecca. Why didn't you wait for us? Why did you have to pull Jessica out of that car? You knew Mrs. Calvin had called 911. You knew we were on our way." It didn't escape my notice that I was no longer Bec.

"I could smell the gasoline. I was afraid the car was going to burst into flames. I couldn't stand there and let Jessica burn. She was too drunk to get out of the car on her own." It occurred to me that Jessica might have been happy to let me burn. I hadn't thought that part through at the time. I crouched down next to Sprocket and buried my face in his fur. At least he was on my side.

Dan rolled his head like he was loosening his shoulders. "Cars don't burst into flame in real life. That's a TV thing."

"Well, how am I supposed to know that?" I demanded.

He made a noise in his throat. "Jessica is talking about pressing charges, Rebecca. You dislocated her shoulder."

I had thought I heard a *pop* as we'd gone sailing out of the car. I cringed. That probably really hurt. Good thing she had probably been too drunk to really feel it. "It wasn't on purpose. I was trying to save her from a fiery death." I pulled out my phone, scrolled through to the favorites list and hit Garrett's number.

"Who are you calling?" Dan asked.

I held up the phone to show him. "Garrett. I guess he's my lawyer these days."

"Maybe you should put him on speed dial." Dan got up and left. He didn't even finish his coffee.

Maybe I already had.

I walked into Garrett's office and found Pearl Bartikow-ski behind the reception desk. "Pearl, I didn't know you worked here." Pearl, like her sister Ruby, had been a legal secretary for as long as I could remember. In fact, she'd worked for Mr. Crowner, the attorney who Haley had hired to get me off on the boat joyriding charges that Mr. No Sense of Humor Winthrop had refused to drop.

"I started a month ago." She smoothed her plump hands over her pristine desk. "Mr. Crowner was making noises about retiring and then young Garrett here opened his office. I'm afraid I didn't give him a chance to even advertise the position. I marched right in, sat down, and started answering the phone."

"That's . . . enterprising of you." I wondered how Mr. Big City Attorney had responded to that. Or I guess I didn't have to wonder since Pearl was sitting right here in front of me.

"The commute is so much better and Ruby and I can have lunch together every day." Pearl's sister Ruby worked for Phillip Meyer. Pearl leaned forward to whisper, "It's driving her nuts that I'm working here, especially since so many of Meyer's clients are coming to Mr. Garrett now."

"They are?" That was interesting.

"Oh, yes. I couldn't resist giving her a hard time about Miss Coco making that appointment to redo her will." She wiggled with the pleasure of the memory.

I guess someone else besides me did know. "You knew that Coco was going to redo her will?"

"That's what she said on the telephone when she made her appointment," Pearl said.

"Garrett said he didn't know why she'd made the appointment." At least, that's what I thought he'd said.

Pearl pursed her lips. "Oh, I might have neglected to write that part down, but I'm pretty sure that's what she told me. She wanted to update her will. You should have seen Ruby's face turn red when I told her that!"

"When did that happen?" I asked.

Pearl's face fell a little. "It was the day she died. Such a shame."

"Did Coco say why she didn't want to stay with Meyer?" I asked.

Pearl nodded her head. "She sure did. Said she had concerns about her privacy."

Poor Coco. I couldn't believe she hadn't realized that Pearl would immediately hold that over Ruby's head and thus make sure Coco had no privacy whatsoever.

Garrett came out of his office, shirtsleeves rolled up and tie a little askew. "Rebecca, come on in." He gestured me into his office and then shut the door behind me.

"I hear today we're talking about assault charges. You're

certainly keeping me on my toes." He settled down behind his desk.

I sat down in one of the wingback chairs across from him. "I like to diversify."

"May I suggest that you stop?" he asked. "I'm afraid that one of the charges is going to stick or that Dan is going to have a stroke. Neither seems like a good option."

"I can't promise anything." I couldn't because I knew what I had planned as soon as I left here. If I didn't get caught, it would be great. Since it seemed like I got busted for every little thing—even good deeds like pulling drunk women from potentially fiery balls of vehicular death—I figured there was a good chance of us all ending up at the police station again. "Although I have definitely learned my lesson."

His eyes narrowed and then he held up his hand. "Don't tell me anything. I really need to be able to swear total ignorance of any plans you have to break the law if I'm going to continue to practice."

"Fair enough. I'll treat you like a mushroom. You know how they grow mushrooms, right?"

"Exactly. Keep me in the dark. Then, as for this latest debacle." He shuffled a file folder onto the top of the stack in front of him.

"It wasn't a debacle. I saved Jessica's life when she was too drunk to help herself." Why did everyone keep forgetting that? I was the hero of this story, not the villain.

"Okay. As for your latest lifesaving activities, I'm pretty sure you're protected under the Good Samaritan law." He looked up at me sharply. "Your actions weren't willful or wanton, were they?"

"I wasn't aware I could be wanton while pulling someone out of a vehicle." I hadn't been wanton in a very long time. I wasn't even sure I remembered what wanton felt like.

"I'll take that as a no, then." He marked something down on his legal pad while muttering, "Not wanton."

I leaned back in the chair, feeling a little relieved. "So I'm okay, then? Jessica can't press assault charges against me?"

"I'll check on a few things and we can talk about them." He looked up at me and smiled. It made his eyes crinkle.

"Great. When?" I asked.

He hesitated, then said, "How about tonight? At dinner?"

I blinked. "Like a date?"

"Not exactly. More like dinner with your sister and brother-in-law. It's Friday." He turned an interesting shade of pink. "Not that a date would be awful or anything . . ."

I held up my hand as I stood. "I'll see you tonight."

I suspected Garrett hadn't been wanton in some time, either.

I had definitely learned my lesson about sneaking around at night. It was way too easy to get caught when people saw lights on where they shouldn't be. It was much smarter to let oneself into one's friend's shop during daylight hours. I went up to the back of Coco's store, took out my keys, and let myself in.

The light was dim, but there was plenty to see by, at least for my purposes. I went through the kitchen to Coco's office and froze.

Everything was the same as it had been the day Coco died. Everything. Right down to the blood smeared on the credenza behind her desk.

I was not a squeamish person. I have skinned rabbits and cut up turkeys into pieces. This was different. The blood was Coco's. It was supposed to be inside the person who had been my beacon for so many years.

Coco had spent all of her seventy-two years doing what needed to be done. I would not let her down now. I marched over to her desk, hoping the thudding of my heart would get a little quieter.

I looked around, not really sure what it was I wanted to find. This had been the last place Coco had sat, though. This had been where she'd done all of her lasts: her last thoughts, her last notes, her last breaths.

I saw a little corner of paper sticking out from under the desk blotter. I wiggled it out. It was a ticket, the kind you hand over to someone behind a desk when you're picking something up. It was for the FedEx Office in Amherst. I was willing to bet all the popcorn in the Buckeye State that it was for our business plan.

The printer's "ready" light blinked on and off. I remembered that Coco had been having trouble with it. Sometimes all it needed was to be turned off and then back on again. I switched it off, sang the alphabet song, then turned it back on. Papers started spitting out.

I picked up the top one and nearly squealed. It was the popcorn fudge recipe Coco and I had been working on. The next one was the salted-caramel popcorn fudge. I held them to my chest. I waited until the printer was done and grabbed the sheaf of papers and the FedEx ticket. Leaving everything else untouched, I returned to the back door of Coco's shop and let myself out.

"What on earth are you doing now?" a voice said from behind me.

I let my head drop. Busted again. I really was not cut out for a life of crime.

Annie shook her head. "What on earth are you doing, Rebecca?" She continued over to the Dumpster with the armful of trimmings she had to throw out.

"It's kind of a long story," I said, trying to figure out how to summarize everything that had happened up until then.

"Never mind. I probably don't want to know." She brushed off her hands. "I do want some coffee and a snack, though."

Relieved she wasn't still mad at me for assaulting her boyfriend, I threaded my arm through hers and started to walk back to POPS. "I have just the place."

"You know, you're lucky it was me who saw you coming out of Coco's," she said as we walked up the back steps to POPS.

I really should have looked around before I opened the door. I was not cut out for espionage, apparently. "You mean, instead of Dan or Huerta?"

"Or Allen. Or Jessica. Or any of the other people around here who think you've gone off your rocker." She sat down at the kitchen table.

It was precisely because they all thought I was off my rocker that I had to do what I was doing. I had to show them I wasn't crazy or a loser. "I found this in Coco's office." I pushed the FedEx receipt across to her.

Annie glanced down and then put her hand to her chest. "Oh, my God. A business owner had copies made. Contact the authorities immediately."

"Sarcasm is not welcome," I said, snatching the ticket back from her.

She pointed at me with a spoon she'd picked up. "Not true. You love my sarcasm. It's one of the reason we're friends."

She had me on that one. I did love her sarcasm. "Fine. Be sarcastic. Just be ready for a surprise."

Annie sighed. "After your last surprise for me, which I believe involved bonking my boyfriend over the head with a clay pot, I feel like I'm ready for anything."

* * *

The shop was especially quiet that afternoon, which was a good thing. I kept looking at the recipes I'd printed out at Coco's. They were good. I felt proud of them. More important, the two of us had had a blast when we'd worked on them. The reality that Coco and I would never get another opportunity to spend time in the kitchen together hit me. No more good-natured teasing about the fact that she thought I liked things too spicy and I thought she liked things too salty. No more tasting back and forth. No more laughing together with spoons in our hands.

Then I started to get mad. Someone had taken that from me. Someone had shoved Coco hard enough to have her stumble backward and hit her head on that credenza. Someone had stolen something truly precious to me.

At six thirty, Sprocket and I stomped home. Not even a trip to the lighthouse managed to calm me, especially since I ran into, of all people, Jessica. She was struggling with the door to the lighthouse with her left hand because her right arm was in a sling.

I jogged up to her, Sprocket on my heels. "Let me help you."

She whirled. "I think you've helped me enough today, don't you think, Rebecca?" She didn't look so hot.

"I'm sorry, Jessica. I really thought the car could catch fire. If you hadn't been so drunk that you couldn't get out of the car on your own, you would have been fine." I backed away. Sprocket growled. I looped his leash a little tighter around my hand. He'd never bitten anyone. It would be my luck if he decided to take a chunk out of Jessica as his first biting offense.

"I wasn't drunk." Her voice sounded thick and a little shaky. "I wasn't. I . . . I had taken some cough medicine. It must have made me sleepy."

The old cough medicine excuse. I'd heard that one before. It was possible I'd even used it before. "Whatever. I thought you were in danger. You could at least let me help with the lighthouse door to make up for it."

"Oh, fine." She handed over the keys.

I unlocked the door and handed them back. "What are you doing out here anyway?"

She breathed in through her nostrils loudly and then out in a sniff. "The historical preservation society meets here every Friday. It's my job to unlock the lighthouse and set up the snacks." She motioned to two grocery bags by her feet.

"I can help with those, too." I carried them in for her and set them on the folding tables along the edge of the room. "Can I put this stuff out for you?"

She nodded.

I pulled out some bakery trays of cookies and some little sandwiches, and then put out the drinks. As I was finishing, Brandy Johnson and Olive Hicks walked in. They both froze when they saw me.

"Hello, Rebecca," Brandy said in a tone that was decidedly chilly. "What are you doing here?"

"I was walking by and saw Jessica trying to set up. I thought I'd help her."

"We would have thought you'd helped her enough today." Olive sniffed.

"That's funny. That's what Jessica . . ." My words trailed off. It had been what Jessica had said. It was probably what everybody was saying.

I said good night and went home.

Fifteen

As Sprocket and I walked up the driveway, Evan raced toward us, arms stretched out like an airplane, with his Batman cape streaming behind him. He stopped a few feet before he reached us, jumped into what I thought was supposed to be a karate pose and yelled, "Hiya!"

"Hiya, yourself," I replied. Sprocket licked his face and he giggled.

"Mama won't let me play on the slide in my Batman cape," Evan informed me, falling into step beside me as I walked toward the house. "She says I'll dangle and hurted myself."

"Your mama's pretty smart." And read a lot of parenting magazines as well.

"But I wanna wear my Batman cape and I wanna go down the slide." His sweet face crumpled.

"Life's full of hard choices, little man." I patted him on the head between his Batman ears.

He looked up at me as if suddenly remembering something. "Why'd you hurt Miss Jessica, Auntie Becca?"

Unbelievable. My three-year-old nephew was in on the Jessica gossip. This town sucked. "I did not hurt Miss Jessica. I saved Miss Jessica. Miss Jessica crashed her car because she was dr—"

"You're here." Haley lumbered down the porch, cutting me off. She looked at me through narrowed eyes and mimed locking her mouth and throwing away the key. Evan took off on another airplane swoop around the yard.

"How does Evan know about Jessica and me? Who gossips with three-year-olds?" I demanded.

"No one gossips with three-year-olds, but they notice when their preschool teacher doesn't show up and a bunch of the moms have to step in." Haley sat down on the porch step. "The moms then gossip. Some three-year-olds listen too closely."

I sat down next to her and looked over to where Evan zoomed around making motor noises. "He doesn't look like the eavesdropping type."

"All kids are the eavesdropping type." She nudged me with her elbow. "You were the worst."

I had been, too. I had been all about knowing what the grown-ups were talking about until I became one of the favorite topics of conversation, as in, "What are we going to do about Rebecca?" Then I'd lost interest.

"Plus, it was a big deal. Everyone was upset. Everyone had an opinion. Everyone had heard something slightly different from someone else they felt was an unassailable source," Haley said.

I put my head down on my knees. "I really thought I was helping. I really thought I might be saving her life. I don't suppose anybody mentioned that."

Haley patted my back. "Not so much. Maybe that'll be part of the conversation next week."

"Do you need help with dinner?" I asked. That was one thing I was pretty sure I could help with that I wouldn't screw up.

"Yes, please." She sighed. "My feet are killing me."

I looked down. She had on slippers instead of shoes and her feet looked swollen. "Sit here and watch Evan. I'll take over."

I made my way to the kitchen and surveyed what I had before me. It looked like roasted chicken with potatoes and green beans. Solid choices except that I didn't want to be the one to get Evan to try green beans again. I rolled up my sleeves and went to work.

I loosened the skin on the chickens and pushed butter mashed with rosemary, sage and thyme between the meat and the skin. I rubbed the inside with kosher salt and the outside with olive oil and kosher salt. I slipped some sliced onion into the chickens then trussed those birds up and got them in the oven.

Next up were the potatoes. I washed them, diced them, tossed them with more olive oil, rosemary and kosher salt and then popped them in the oven as well. Easy peasy.

Now I had to face the green beans. I cleaned them while I considered my options. Then I dug in the refrigerator for bacon. I was fairly certain that the addition of bacon could make almost anything better. I chopped the bacon and tossed it in a sauté pan with onions. Once that was done, I removed the bacon with a slotted spoon and sautéed the green beans in the bacon grease.

As always, at some point, I got lost. The smell of the herbs and the butter and the bacon and the chicken and the potatoes. The rhythm of the dicing and the slicing and the chopping. The dance between the stove and the counters and the sink and the fridge. It soothed me. I vaguely heard Haley coming in with Evan at one point.

Then Dan and Garrett were coming in the front door. "It smells amazing in here," Dan said as he made his way into the kitchen with two grocery bags.

"I hope you have wine and appetizers in there," I said, coming out of my reverie.

"Will chips and beer do?" Garrett asked, pulling items from the bags.

I snagged a beer out of the six-pack and toasted him with it. "Any port in a storm, baby, and it's been raining cats and dogs out there."

Dinner was a slightly quieter affair than it had been the week before, but I decided to bask in the glory of having gotten Evan to eat his green beans with minimal fuss rather than worry about the fact that Dan didn't seem to want to look me in the eye. Garrett walked me home afterward. It was the first time I'd let him past the front door. "This is . . . colorful," Garrett said as he stepped inside.

It was possible I'd gone overboard with the color scheme. If I had, though, I didn't care. I'd moved from my crappy student apartment that I'd shared with three other cooking school students in Yountville to Antoine's house in Calistoga. It had felt like a fairy tale to move into his beautiful home up in the hills with its gorgeous artwork and cushy furniture and eight-hundred-thread-count organic pima cotton sheets. I'd practically burned all my own stuff as I'd danced up the drive-way into what felt like a mansion for me. I mean why bring my dresser with the drawer that stuck or even my half-burnt hot pads into that palace of perfection?

I knew the answer now. Because then some of the stuff in that house would have been mine. I don't know if that would have made our marriage last longer or not, but I know it would have helped if I had felt like Antoine's house was as much mine as his, and maybe I wouldn't have always felt like a guest in what was ostensibly my own house. Maybe I would have felt like my own person and, well, what might have happened then?

Maybe I wouldn't be back in my hometown with everyone thinking I'd tried to maim the local preschool teacher. "Hot chocolate?" I offered.

Garrett nodded. According to him, somehow all anybody in the town was talking about was the fact that I'd dislocated Jessica's shoulder. The fact that she smelled like a brewery on her way to teach preschool at the church? Not so much. The EMTs pumped her full of painkillers so by the time anyone thought to see whether she was drunk, it was too late to test her. There was only my word that she'd been drunk driving and nobody was putting too much stock in that since I was facing assault charges. I'd told Dan at the scene that she was drunk, but according to him that wasn't enough.

"You really thought the car was going to burst into flames?" Garrett asked. He sat at the breakfast bar in my kitchen.

"Why is that so hard to believe?" I handed him a mug of hot chocolate. "And why doesn't anybody care that Jessica was drunk driving to school?"

"Because there's no proof of that and there's plenty of proof you wrenched her arm out of its socket." He took a sip of the hot chocolate, stared at the mug for a second and then took a second sip.

I sat down next to him with my own mug. "It sounds so ugly when you say it like that."

He cocked his head to look at me. "How else would you like me to say it?"

"I would like you to say I was trying to save her life." I sat up straight, as befitted a hero like myself.

"By wrenching her arm out of its socket," he pointed out.

I took the hot chocolate back from him.

"Hey, give that back. It's really good."

I held the cup up and out of his reach. "Not until you say it right."

He sighed. "Fine. Rebecca Anderson saved Jessica James's life by pulling her from a car that could have burst into flames at any moment. She should probably be given a medal."

"Better." I handed the hot chocolate back and gave him a chocolate chip cookie to go with it. Sometimes I bake when I'm angry. Of course, I also bake when I'm sad, when I'm happy, when it's raining, and sometimes just because.

"You're going to make me fat." But he took a bite of the cookie anyway.

"Run an extra mile tomorrow. You'll be fine. I'd like to know why no one cares why Jessica plowed into Mrs. Calvin's oak tree." I slumped over my own chocolate. It wasn't cheering me up.

Garrett swallowed his bite of cookie. "Everyone cares. That's why no one's asking."

I shook my head. "You are not making sense. Perhaps you've had too much chocolate and it's gone to your head."

"I'm making perfect sense." He set the mug down. "Jessica is grieving, Rebecca. People do all kinds of things when they're grieving. I would have thought you of all people would know that."

Heat rose up my face. "That's kind of a low blow."

"I didn't mean it that way. Although I do think you'd be cutting pretty much anyone else more slack than you're cutting Jessica." He gestured at me with the cookie. "This is really good, too."

I chewed on that along with my cookie for a second. "I didn't cut her slack because I didn't believe it at first. I didn't think Jessica cared that much about anybody except Jessica." Except she clearly did. She'd been completely distraught since Coco died.

"Do you think maybe there are other things about Jessica that you don't see clearly?" Garrett asked.

I chewed even longer on that and then said, "Nope."

Monday morning, I got into POPS early, made the breakfast bars, brewed the coffee and opened the doors to find absolutely no one waiting on the sidewalk.

I looked down at Sprocket. "Where'd everyone go?"

He looked up and down the street and then went back inside and lay down on his bed.

"Maybe it's the zombie apocalypse and we don't know about it yet," I suggested. Or maybe it was some kind of holiday. I checked the calendar, but no. No holiday today. I looked down the street. No zombies.

I finally went next door to talk to Annie. I should have known it was going to be bad when she refused to come out from behind the counter.

"There's a rumor going around that you're the one who killed Coco." Annie shrank back like I might explode.

It was a good move. "That I did what?" I shouted. "Who would say such a thing? Who would believe it?"

Annie's face crumpled a little bit. "I think you can guess

who might say such a thing if you thought about it for a second."

I plopped down in one of the chairs Annie had set up for consultations. "Jessica. Jessica is telling people I killed Coco."

Annie came out from behind the counter and sat down next to me. "Not exactly, but she is stacking up evidence against you, Rebecca. You need to be careful."

"What evidence? I had nothing to do with it. What possible evidence can there be?" Surely, if you were innocent there would be no evidence. Then again, there were constant stories on the news about people being released from prison after years and years because DNA testing proved they were innocent. I didn't think DNA was going to help me.

"I guess you would call it circumstantial." Annie tapped a pen on the table. "You were the last one out of here that night. You were the one who left the popcorn for Jasper that would lure him here to be set up. You didn't want Coco to retire and maybe she was going to anyway. You were caught going through her papers at her house like maybe you were looking for the fudge recipe, and you're a suspect in the attack on Barbara because there were fibers from your sweater in the broken window and you showed up at the crime scene like a lunatic. Then there's dislocating Jessica's shoulder."

I laid my head down on my pillowed arms. "When am I going to learn?"

"Learn what?" Annie said, patting my head.

"To not let Jessica get me to make myself look bad all on my own. That woman should have gone into the diplomatic corps. She could have probably manipulated everyone to making peace in the Middle East if she wanted to. But no, instead she has to turn her superpowers on me." I really had no one to blame but myself. And Jessica, of course. I could always blame Jessica. That, at least, was comforting.

"Rebecca, are you listening to yourself?" Annie asked.

I flattened myself even farther down onto the table. "I am."

"You do know that Jessica is mourning Coco just like the rest of us, don't you?" Annie's voice was soft but firm.

That was true. Not only had Jessica manipulated me into making myself into a murder suspect, she was also making me look like a selfish twit. I'd seen Jessica's red-rimmed eyes, her uncharacteristic drinking, her shock at finding Coco's body. Whatever else Jessica felt, she had loved Coco and was grieving. Maybe it was natural for her to try to pin the responsibility for that grief on someone she disliked as much as she disliked me.

Nasty and passive-aggressive and sneaky, but still natural.

"Remember, no one can make you do anything, Rebecca. You choose your own course," Annie said.

My head shot up. "What?"

"I said you choose your own course." She straightened some of the catalogs on the table.

That did not sound like Annie. "Have you been reading self-help books?"

Annie blushed. "Just one that Allen gave me. It's got some good stuff in it."

Annie was reading Allen's self-help books. I felt almost as alone as I felt when Antoine had abandoned me in Minneapolis. I stood up. "Well, I think I better go donate my breakfast bars to the homeless shelter and figure out what to do to make the town realize I didn't kill Coco."

"Just remember, Rebecca. You need to be careful." Annie's forehead creased. "I know you didn't kill Coco.

Jasper didn't kill Coco. Allen didn't kill Coco. Someone, however, did kill Coco and probably doesn't want anyone to know about it."

I went to my shop. I mean, how much trouble could I get in there? Annie was right. I needed to stop sticking my nose into other people's business. What did it matter if everyone thought Coco was planning on retiring? What did it matter if I never found the business plan? What did it matter if I spent the rest of my life in the town where I was born where everyone assumed I'd be the reckless screwup I'd been in high school?

The little bell over the door rang and Barbara came into the shop. She no longer wore her gauze bandage fascinator and was looking much more her usual self. "I brought you a little something," she said, plunking down a package on the counter.

"What for?" I asked. It wasn't my birthday.

"I felt bad that you got into trouble for picking those things up for me. Seriously, it's like that Jessica is following you around, trying to catch you being up to no good." She looked around at my empty shop. "It doesn't seem to have been very good for your business, either."

That was an understatement. "I was glad that Huerta didn't insist on keeping your tracksuit as evidence."

"Yes, and thank you for sending him with the clothes. He's quite the eyeful, isn't he?" She chuckled.

I blushed. "Barbara!"

"Oh, please. I'm old, but I'm not dead. Yet. Unless someone else decides to hit me over the head again." She touched the top of her head gingerly. She pushed the package toward me. "Open it."

I did. It was a beautiful antique set of containers for sugar and flour in a blue-and-white willow pattern that would look perfect in my kitchen. "Oh, Barbara. Thank you so much. You shouldn't have."

She waved a hand at me. "Don't get too excited. They were in the shop."

I motioned her into the kitchen and started water for coffee. "Speaking of the shop, did you make a decision?"

"I did." She sat down at the table and looked around. "I really like what you did with this room. It's so much brighter than before."

I snorted. "That's damning with faint praise. It was like a tomb in here before. So what was the decision?"

"I'm keeping the shop. Sort of." She folded her hands on the table.

"How does one 'sort of' keep a shop?" I asked.

"I have this niece in Illinois. She just got divorced. She's been out of the workforce for a while. She's not quite sure what to do with herself. I suggested that she move here and become my assistant manager with a plan to take over the place when I'm ready to fully retire. This way I can still spend a few months a year down in Arizona. She finds a way to make a living. Her kids live in a nice small town that at least used to have a low crime rate. It's kind of a win-win."

"I should say so." I poured us each a cup of coffee. "Do you remember anything more about the attack?"

"No. I wish I could. I'd love to help Dan catch the bastard who did this." She took a sip and winked at me. "Good and strong. Excellent. I can't stand that weak swill they serve over at the diner."

I clinked my mug against hers and took a sip, then started shaking the leftover popcorn into bags.

"What are you doing with that?"

I sighed. "Putting this stuff out back for Tom Moffat. He's been coming by to pick up the leftovers since Jasper was arrested." I made a face. "He may not like women being in the workforce, but that sure doesn't stop him from taking handouts from them." I froze. "You don't suppose . . ."

"Oh, don't mind Tom. That's just a bad case of sour grapes. He's still mad that I wouldn't marry him." Barbara chuckled.

I sat up straighter. "You dated Tom?"

"I don't know if you could call it dating. We had a few dinners together. Maybe shared a few smooches. He was quite the slobberer." Barbara made a face. "Anyway, I said no when he proposed. I think he's still mad."

"I can't imagine spending a lifetime with a slobbery kisser." A shiver of disgust rippled my shoulders.

"Neither could Coco. He made a play for her, too, back in the day." Barbara sipped her coffee.

"I had no idea that Coco had ever even contemplated getting married," I said.

"I don't think she did. Both of us liked being independent too much. We like everything in its place, and men . . . well, men just mess that up."

After Barbara left, I texted Susanna and told her not to come in and closed POPS early. Coco would have shaken her head at me and told me it was important to be open when people stopped by, but I didn't have it in me today.

Instead I went home. Not my apartment. Real home. The home where I grew up. Haley and Evan were deep in the construction of a fairly complicated Brio train-track configuration.

"So what were these big plans you had with Coco?" Haley snapped together a piece of wooden train track while peering at the diagram on the box.

"Oh, you know." I ran one of Evan's little wooden trains up and down my thigh.

"No, I don't know," she said with what seemed like an exaggerated amount of patience. I wasn't sure if she needed the patience for dealing with me or for dealing with the wooden tracks. "I have no idea. I knew you two got together and talked a lot and cooked a lot, but until the funeral I had no idea the two of you were planning anything business-related."

The reason Haley didn't know is because pretty much nobody knew except Coco and me. We were keeping it on the down low until we were ready to put our plans into action. Maybe it sounds paranoid, but we both felt it was best to hold our recipes and plans pretty close to our chests. "We wanted to combine forces. We thought it would be fun to have a kind of chocolate and popcorn wonderland."

"And what would happen to the shops you have already?" Haley got down on the floor and started laying out the track.

Evan started running his little train along it, making *chug-chug-chug* noises. "Finish, Mama! Finish track!" he yelled when he came to the end of it.

"Doing my best, sweetheart." Haley pulled more track pieces from the plastic crate. "Your shops?"

"Well, I'd probably close POPS as it is now, but Coco was planning on giving her shop to Jessica." I hadn't told Coco that I thought Jessica wanted to run that shop about as much as she wanted to run a marathon, which is to say not at all. I'd figured that was Jessica's business and that Jessica could take care of her own.

Haley sat back on her heels to check the box again. "So Jessica would profit quite a bit from Coco and you going into business."

I squirmed a little. "I guess."

Haley turned to look at me. "What are you not saying?"

"How do you know I'm not saying something?"

"You're talking to the sister you spent a good deal of your adolescence lying to in some form or another. What aren't you saying?" She shook a curved piece of track in my direction.

"Coco was going to give her shop to Jessica, but she wasn't going to give Jessica her recipe, remember?"

Haley set both pieces of track down. "So?"

"That would make the shop worth a lot less."

"Did Jessica know?"

"I don't know. I don't think so." Coco wouldn't have told her. I wouldn't have told her. But Pearl told Ruby that Coco had made an appointment with Garrett to change her will. Ruby would have told Phillip. Phillip might well have told his son, who was currently Jessica's boyfriend. "Maybe. I suppose she could have, but it would have made for a really long game of telephone."

"When was it going to happen?"

"Sooner than I thought it would. Apparently Coco made an appointment to talk to Garrett about it," I said.

"Do you have any proof that that was what she meant to do?" Haley asked.

I shook my head. "It was something we were talking about. Coco didn't want Jessica to sell the fudge recipe. She knew I wouldn't no matter what."

"So it's your word about it, like with the plan to open the new business." Haley sighed and picked up the track pieces again. "It doesn't matter, though, does it? Coco didn't change her will. You guys didn't open your new business. The fudge recipe belongs to Jessica along with the shop. Bad timing, I guess."

"And timing is everything."

Sixteen

Amherst, Ohio, is about fifteen miles from Grand Lake. You pop down to Highway 2 and head east. The road is straight, and on a crisp fall day with the trees starting to turn, it's kind of pretty. That still did not explain why on earth Coco would have chosen to take something to be copied all the way in Amherst when we have a perfectly good copy shop two blocks away from Coco's Cocoas in Grand Lake. Especially since Coco liked driving less and less. She said she didn't trust her reflexes the way she used to.

The next day, I left Susanna in charge of the shop as soon as she'd gotten there after school—not that there was much happening. Garrett showed up to buy a breakfast bar, I think just out of pity. Janet Barry came in for her little bag of caramel cashew popcorn, but she acted even more like she was doing a drug deal than usual. She kept glancing over her shoulder and checking who might be on the sidewalk. She actually asked if she could go out the back. They had been my only customers all day. I wasn't sure how long I'd be able to keep the shop open with that kind of slowdown, especially after depleting my bank accounts to pay Jessica all the money I had owed Coco.

Sprocket and I got in the Jeep at around three thirty and headed off to Amherst to pick up whatever Coco had felt was important enough to take to another town to get copied. Sprocket had given me a look and sat down when I'd opened the car door. I'd dangled a treat in front of him to induce him to jump in. Hoisting fifty-plus pounds of standard poodle into a four-by-four with decent clearance was more of a workout than I'd wanted. He still hadn't budged. Finally, I'd said, "No vet." He'd jumped in, scarfed the Milk-Bone down in one gulp and settled in with a grin.

"Dr. Ambrose is not the devil, you know," I'd told him after I got in, but Sprocket had snorted his disdain. I knew better than to argue with him and instead I started the Jeep and we went off on our adventure.

Twenty minutes later, we pulled into the parking lot of the Kinko's on Cleveland Avenue. I cracked the windows on the Jeep for Sprocket, went into the store and got in line. Now I really wondered why Coco had driven this far. There was never a line at Kendall's Copies in Grand Lake.

When it was my turn, I presented the ticket to the stout woman behind the counter and smiled.

She did not smile back. She pushed the ticket back at me and said, "You're not Ms. Bittles."

Surprised that she even knew, I pushed the ticket back to her. "No. I'm not. I'm picking this up for her."

She slid the ticket back toward me again. "Do you have some kind of note from Ms. Bittles saying she gave you permission? Or should I call her?" She leaned back like she'd won some sort of contest.

Coco was one of those people who won people's admiration

and loyalty all the time, but I was still a little surprised that the FedEx counter girl was this protective. "I'm sorry to have to tell you this, but Coco passed away."

I'd said it as gently as I could, but the counter girl reeled back as if I'd shoved her. "She what? What happened?"

I didn't feel like I could possibly go into the details. "The police aren't sure. They're investigating."

She glanced behind me at the growing line, then she called over her shoulder to one of her coworkers. "Paul, can you take over here for a minute?"

A bright-eyed twentysomething kid with curly hair and a nice smile nodded and walked up next to her. "I can help who's next."

She gestured with her head for me to meet her at the end of the counter. She leaned forward and whispered. "Are you saying Coco was murdered?"

"It looks like it might be a burglary gone wrong, but yes."

She put her hand to her heart for a second and then took a deep breath. "And who exactly are you?"

"I'm Rebecca Anderson. I had the shop next door to hers and . . ."

"The popcorn lady. Got it." She held up her index finger. "I'll be right back."

While she went into the back, I leaned back to get a glimpse of Sprocket in the parking lot. He'd moved into the driver's seat and had put both paws up on the steering wheel. Two little boys were pointing and a girl in jeans so skinny they looked like a second skin took a cell phone photo of him.

The counter girl came back and dropped three three-ring binders down in front of me. "Here's the plan."

I waited, but she didn't elaborate.

"Well, do you want them or not?" she finally asked. "I'm pretty sure Ms. Bittles meant one of the copies for you."

I looked at the front cover. It read: Bittles/Anderson Merger Plan: Coco Pop Fudge Empire.

The Holy Grail. The business plan no one believed me about. The one Coco had been working on. I ran my finger over the lettering. They'd have to believe me now.

"I'll take them." I followed Counter Girl over to the payment area.

"What day did you say Coco died?" she asked.

"Two weeks ago Thursday," I said.

She checked a tag on the top binder. "That was the day after I called her to tell her the order was ready." She shook her head. "She said she'd come by the next afternoon before it got dark." She shivered. "Wow. Creepy."

And another piece of the puzzle fell into place. Coco had closed the shop early to come to Amherst to pick up the business plan copies.

Except she hadn't picked them up. And she hadn't left the shop. And she hadn't turned on the lights. And she didn't have glass on her shoes.

I hugged the binders to my chest as I left the shop. I had a lot more questions, but at least I had proof that I wasn't a liar and that Coco hadn't planned on retiring.

On the way home, I called Garrett and asked him to meet me at Dan and Haley's. They were all there together when I got back from Amherst. I plunked the binders down on the dining room table in front of them and said, "See? I told you so."

"What are we looking at?" Garrett took the top binder and pulled it over to himself.

"The business plan Coco was making for us." I drew myself up taller.

"Where did you get these, Rebecca?" Dan's voice was unexpectedly sharp.

"From the FedEx in Amherst. Coco took them there to be copied and put in the binders." It was so like her to have the plan organized into sections with tabs and dividers and everything. I'd glanced through. There were even charts and graphs. Charts and graphs were serious stuff.

"She told you that?" Dan asked.

"No." I was starting to feel like I'd missed something. There was something in his tone.

"Then how did you know to get them there?" His tone was even sharper than it had been before.

"I found the little ticket thing they give you when you drop something off. You know, like the thingie for the dry cleaner." I realized now what extremely thin ice I was treading on.

"Where did you find it?" Dan's shoulders were tense, and I could see the muscles in his jaw as he clenched his teeth.

I stared at him. The clock in the hallway ticked each second as we sat there, eyes locked. Light glinted on his badge. Finally, I said, "You can't possibly believe that I had anything to do with Coco's death. You just can't."

"You're not giving me a lot of choice, Rebecca." He started ticking items off on his fingers. "You were the last one to leave the shops that night. You've been caught rifling through her papers in her house and in her shop. You have a long-standing feud with her heir. Go ahead and stop me anytime."

"Fine. I will. I have keys—keys that Coco gave me—to both her shop and her house. Why on earth would I have bashed in the back window of her shop when I could just let myself in with the key?" I leaned forward, glaring.

"I don't know." He leaned forward, too. "Maybe to make

it look like someone had broken in, to cover your tracks. That would explain why there was glass on the bottom of Coco's cane, but none on the bottom of her shoes. Whoever staged that scene used the cane to bash in the window. Plus, the only fingerprints on that damn cane were yours. There weren't even any of Coco's prints on it."

"So you're drinking the Jessica Kool-Aid, too? You think I had something to do with Coco's death?" I could not believe this. I could not believe Dan would take Jessica's side over mine. "The cane had my fingerprints because I moved it aside to get to Coco!"

"There is no Kool-Aid, and I'm investigating this case. Everyone is a suspect until I say they're not, and you're not helping by going into people's houses and offices and removing evidence." Dan threw his hands up in the air.

I leaned over the table to look at him eye-to-eye. "Well, somebody has to look at the evidence."

Dan's face flushed and I realized I'd gone too far. If I could have grabbed those words and stuffed them back in my mouth, I would have. Being a chef has taught me to eat just about anything, but rarely my own words. I dropped my head. "I'm sorry, Dan. I didn't mean that."

Dan didn't answer for a second. Finally, he said, "I think you better go, Bec. Try to stay out of trouble, will you?"

I left, but with a backward look over my shoulder at Dan and Haley. Dan gripped the edge of the dining room table so hard his knuckles were turning almost as white as Haley's face had gone. I waved and went out the door.

I trudged up the stairs to the apartment with Sprocket on my heels. We went in and I looked around at my apartment. It didn't feel fun and colorful anymore. It looked stupid. Like a child with a too-big box of Crayolas had gone wild in it.

I'd found the business plan, the one that was supposed to prove that I wasn't a loser, and it hadn't proved anything. Even my sister and my best friend didn't think it proved anything. And now, to make matters worse, I'd insulted them.

Maybe I should give up. I'd tried. I'd tried super hard. I'd worked long hours. I'd made plans. I'd tried new things. Where had it gotten me?

Back where I'd been in high school. Feeling like the whole town was against me. Feeling completely alone. Feeling like a total failure.

Antoine wanted me back. It's not like life with him was so miserable. I'd lived in a beautiful home in one of the most gorgeous areas of the country. I was constantly being given fabulous food and amazing wine. I didn't even have to work if I didn't want to and if I did want to, I would have connections everywhere. People would bend over backward to be nice to me so they could get close to Antoine. So what if I'd been abandoned in Minneapolis in January? It's not like he didn't get me on the next plane to Miami. Everybody forgets his wife in a frozen tundra once in a while, right?

All it would take would be one phone call. One word from me. That life could be mine again. I started to reach for my cell phone, but Sprocket chose that moment to bound up into my lap and lick the tears from my face. Stupid dog. Salt water just makes you more thirsty. I'd barely gotten him back down on the floor when there was a knock at the door.

"Rebecca? You in there?" It was Garrett.

"What do you want?" I asked, not getting up to answer the door.

"You forgot the business plans. I, uh, thought you might want them, so I brought them up."

I should probably have told him to go burn them, but then I remembered all the work Coco had put into them. Maybe I should keep them if only as a memento of her sharp brain. I walked over and opened the door.

"Nice of you to carry my books for me," I said, standing back to let him in.

"I try to be chivalrous to my clients even when they're going out of their way to incriminate themselves. You got that ticket out of Coco's house the night you broke in there, didn't you?" He handed me the binders.

"I didn't break in! I had keys!" Why couldn't anyone understand that? "And I didn't find the ticket there. I found her to-do list there."

"Stop splitting hairs, Rebecca." Garrett sounded almost as weary as Dan had.

"They're not hairs. They're facts. I didn't break in any more than I broke into her office where I found that FedEx ticket." If you can't come clean to your lawyer, who can you come clean to?

Garrett groaned. "Seriously? Her office, too?"

"Yes. Her office, too." Why not let it all hang out?

"Did anyone see you?" he asked.

"Only Annie." She wouldn't rat me out. At least, she wouldn't unless she got on the "I hate Rebecca" bandwagon everyone else was riding.

"Not a good idea, Rebecca." He shook his head.

"Says who?" I flopped down on the couch.

"Grand Lake's preeminent defense attorney." He made a bow before sitting down next to me.

I snorted. "Preeminent defense attorney? How'd you get that title?"

"Well, I am currently representing one hundred percent of the murder suspects in Grand Lake. That is if you still count

Jasper as a murder suspect since the judge let him off with time served for his assault on Huerta with the frying pan." He stretched his long arm out over the back of the couch.

"There are two of us. I think your statistics are spurious. Or maybe they're specious. I can never keep those two straight." Plus, my head hurt. Maybe my heart hurt a little, too.

"The important thing about both of them is that they both mean I'm at least right on the surface." Damn, he looked smug when he smiled.

"And the surface is where it stops. Neither Jasper nor I killed Coco, and you know it. So does Dan." I pulled the afghan over my lap.

"I know it. You know it. Dan knows it. At this rate, though, I'm not one hundred percent sure the district attorney knows it, and I'm really not one hundred percent sure that the people of Grand Lake, at least some of whom would be in your jury pool, know it," he said.

"Jury pool?" I squeaked. "I'm going to be tried?"

He held up his hands to stop me. "Not yet, but you've got to try to lie low, Rebecca. You're not doing yourself any favors."

No. I'd been too busy doing favors for little old ladies in the hospital and drunk women in crashed Honda Civics, and look where that had gotten me. "How am I supposed to lie any lower than I've been lying?"

"You could start by not snooping around in old ladies' houses at night and getting yourself arrested for breaking and entering." He brushed the hair off my forehead. He held up his hands. "I know you had keys. It doesn't make it look any better."

I sighed.

"You could also turn evidence over to Dan instead of running off to snoop into things yourself," Garrett said.

"Like what evidence?"

"Like the FedEx ticket and the to-do list. Actually, give them to me now and I'll take them to Dan. I'm not sure he wants to see you right now." I got up and fished the ticket out of my purse and then went and got Coco's to-do-list notepad from my desk and handed them over.

"Did you seriously do the pencil rubbing thing to see her to-do list?" Garrett looked at the notepad and shook his head.

I blushed. It had seemed totally logical to me. "I had to if I wanted to see what was on it."

Garrett stopped shaking his head. In fact, he sat very still. "But the actual to-do list wasn't in her office?"

"Not that I saw and clearly not that Dan saw." I wasn't sure where he was going with this. Then it dawned on me. "You think the killer took her to-do list?"

He shrugged. "I know it sounds pretty far-fetched. It was just a thought." He stood up and headed for the door.

I followed him, and then suddenly we were there somehow standing too close to each other again.

He leaned forward and his lips touched mine. Time ground to a halt. There was me. There was him. There were our mouths joined together. Then I pushed him away and looked behind him.

"Are you looking for something?"

"Sprocket," I said. "I thought maybe he pushed you again."

He laughed and shook his head. Then he looped his arm around my waist and pulled me against him. "No, Rebecca. This is all me."

After Garrett left, which I made him do before any of our clothing got seriously disarranged despite the fact that the kisses had been darn nice, I pulled Coco's business plan binder onto my lap. It started with an executive summary then moved on to a business concept description. I felt I was following pretty well until I hit the financial features and requirements section. There were a lot of charts and graphs and a lot of numbers. Like piles of numbers.

My relationship with numbers was somewhat troubled. Somehow I was fine with them in the kitchen. Cups and ounces, doubling and halving, converting to metric. No big deal as long as it was in a recipe. Put a dollar sign in front of something? It stopped me in my tracks like a deer preparing to become venison in front of a set of headlights.

Here's the thing about recipes. They don't really mean much. They are, in the end, only as good as the person making the dish. You have to be a little like Kenny Rogers's gambler. You have to know when to hold 'em and know when to fold 'em. You have to know when to follow the directions to the letter and when to let your own creativity shine. You have to be able to feel them in your bones. Your blood has to bubble and froth with your soups. Your heart has to beat with the rhythm of your whisk. Otherwise a recipe is nothing more than a set of words on a piece of paper.

I highly suspected a business plan was much the same. It would only be as good as the person who was following the plan.

I equally highly suspected I was not the person who would know how to make a business plan sing. I knew my way around a kitchen. I could make food that would make people feel. I could make a mac and cheese that would make you think you were being held on your grandmother's lap and a Prosecco sorbet that would make you think you had just fallen in love. I wasn't sure I could make a popcorn and chocolate wonderland that would have people driving from all over northern Ohio to experience it without bankrupting my already-broke self.

I slumped down into the red armchair and cursed its cheeriness. Cheery was about the last thing I was feeling at the moment. In fact, I might never feel cheery again.

I picked up the sheaf of recipes Coco and I had been developing. I caressed the page that held our popcorn fudge ideas. Think rocky road, but with popcorn instead of marshmallows to give it that extra salty schwing. Then I sat bolt upright. I might not be able to make a business plan sing, but I damn sure could make this recipe. I generally didn't do much with chocolate or fudge at POPS since Coco's Cocoas was right next door, but Jessica hadn't opened the doors since Coco's murder. Now I knew she was selling the building to Allen, and most likely the recipe was going off to one of the big confectionary companies.

There actually was no Coco's Cocoas next door to me anymore and no reason to not make that fudge. I didn't have a lot of time, but I really only had to make two of the recipes to accomplish what I had in mind.

I did what Coco would have expected me to do. I got to work.

Seventeen

Apparently, the lure of a free piece of fudge trumps the distaste of taking food from a suspected murderess. I set Susanna—who, let's face it, was a draw all on her own—with a table of the tuxedo popcorn fudge and the Coco Pop Fudge in front of the store and plastered a great big Free Samples Today Only sign on the table.

It was like throwing bread crumbs on a lake. The geese flocked to it. Or in this case, the people of Grand Lake.

It started slow, but word gets around quickly in a small town. For once, that was working to my advantage. By the end of the week, there was a line going out the door of POPS at three in the afternoon when they knew that the Coco Pop Fudge would be hitting the counter.

It was a little like having invented the Cronut. Admittedly on a smaller scale, but the same feeling. If forced to give it a name, I'd call that feeling good. Real good.

If forced to be completely honest, it felt even better when Jessica shoved her way into POPS at four thirty, one arm still in a sling, but plenty able to use her other tiny needlelike elbow to get through the crowd. She then screamed at me in front of everyone. Her face red, she shouted, "Rebecca Anderson, what the hell do you think you're doing?"

Everything went silent. The room had been buzzing before, but now you could hear water boiling in the kitchen. I had a feeling no one had ever heard Jessica come even close to swearing before much less yell out the word Mrs. Calvin spelled as h-e-double-toothpicks. I was willing to bet Jessica was calling me a "see you next Tuesday" in her head, but she wasn't quite mad enough to spit that out. Yet.

I smiled and said, "I'm selling fudge."

"Coco's fudge, you mean. You're selling Coco's Signature Fudge, her secret recipe fudge." She jabbed her finger toward my face. Luckily, with the counter between us and the height difference she wasn't going to get anywhere close to my face. Otherwise I'd be worried she was going to jab my eyes out.

"Not Coco's fudge. You know better than that, Jessica. Or you would if you tasted it. That recipe belongs to you and only you. This was a new recipe that Coco and I were working on together. For the new business. The one you said she would never go into with me." I pulled the business plan out from under the counter and put it out for everyone to see.

I heard a few gasps from the crowd and Jessica's face went pale as she looked at the binder. "Give me a piece of that." She grabbed a square off the display and crammed it into her mouth. She swayed while she ate it. Had she been drinking again?

"That's no way to taste something, Jessica. You know that." It wasn't, either. Shoving a hunk of something into your mouth and chewing it like a wad of Bazooka was not a good way to appreciate the subtleties of anything. Even if she hadn't tasted it the way she should have, Jessica got enough of a sample to know it wasn't Coco's secret recipe, either. Which, for me, was not so secret. I'd spent too many years helping Coco in the kitchen to not know that recipe. I also had too much respect for Coco to do anything with it, even if I was pretty sure she was going to give it to me in her new will. That had not been the way the fudge had crumbled. Or melted. Or set. Whatever. That was okay. I had these new recipes, ones I had more ownership of. No one could take these recipes from me.

Oh, it had some of the qualities. The smoothness. The richness. The way it melted against the tongue. It had a few other things as well. The new fudge was a little lighter, a little more playful. It had a little more zing. I'm not saying exactly—because I like to keep my secrets, too—but I had placed a fairly large order for cayenne with my supplier. Also, sea salt is such a nice addition. Maybe even a touch of caramel. Honestly, there's a lot a person can do with fudge.

"This is disrespectful, Rebecca. Terribly disrespectful." Jessica shook her head, making her blond hair swing and then having to take a step backward to steady herself.

I cut off a piece of fudge from another display and held it out. "Wanna try the tuxedo version?"

I thought steam was going to start coming out of Jessica's ears. She knew that Coco had struggled with making a tuxedo fudge that she thought was worthy. Combining white and dark or white and milk chocolates is a tricky proposition. Some people don't even consider white chocolate to be a true chocolate. Finding the right combination of cocoa butter and sugar and milk to have the same consistency as the dark chocolate took some experimentation on our part.

I still might make some tweaks, but the tuxedo popcorn fudge was pretty good as it stood.

Jessica must have thought so, too. I could see her think about spitting it out to show her disgust with me, but she couldn't get herself to do it. It was that good.

"I will be back, Rebecca. With my lawyer," she said as she marched back out.

"And I'll get you my pretty," Susanna said sort of under her breath, but not entirely. The whole room laughed. I felt a glow in the pit of my stomach that had nothing to do with chocolate.

Let her call her lawyer. Mine was a good kisser and I had him on speed dial.

I closed up the shop at the normal time. Tom was in back of the shop and practically snatched the bag of leftover popcorn—which was decidedly smaller than the ones he'd been getting the week before—and left. I watched him go, uneasy about how much he disliked women business owners and how easily he moved in and out of the shadows of Grand Lake.

We'd run out of fudge long before closing, but I needed the time to place orders for more supplies for what were clearly going to be some winning recipes. I decided to have them delivered so I wouldn't have to run into two-dimensional Antoine over at Kroger again. I swept up and then Sprocket and I were on our way to the lake.

I spotted the black SUV a block over as we crossed Court Street. Instead of continuing on, I doubled back and went around the block. The SUV was still there, like a dark hulk waiting for its prey.

Well, I was tired of being prey. I was tired of being pushed around. This was a new me and a new day and I was taking charge.

I walked up to the black SUV and knocked on the window.

It sunk smoothly down into its groove and I looked into the face of a woman probably around ten years older than me. She had a heart-shaped face, a good haircut, and trendy smart-girl glasses. "Can I help you?"

I admired her calm. "Yeah. You can tell me why you've been lurking around Grand Lake."

"I'm afraid I can't discuss that. Confidentiality issues. You understand." She started to close the window, but I leaned on it with both hands.

"No. I don't understand. Who are you and why do I keep seeing you around my shop?" I would not be brushed off like a nobody again.

"I'm sure I don't understand what you're talking about." She smiled that bland smile at me again.

"You know a woman was murdered here and another one was attacked." I didn't really think this woman had done anything, but maybe she had seen something. "The police are feeling a little bit jumpy about strangers hanging around and following women business owners."

"I'm aware. I was very sorry to hear about Ms. Bittles. Her fudge is famous all over northern Ohio. I was a big admirer. I'm a little bit of a foodie. Would you mind moving away from my window so I can go?" Her smile was getting less bland and more anxious by the second.

"I mind a lot. I want to know who you are and what you're doing here. I want to know why you've been lurking around Coco's shop. Who sent you? One of the big chocolate companies? Maybe some developer who wants to buy it more than our greedy mayor?" I leaned forward a little so our faces were very close.

She laughed now, a throaty raucous guffaw. "Big chocolate? Are you serious?"

"Deadly serious," I said, refusing to be put off by her mocking tone. If she didn't know about Big Chocolate then I wasn't going to educate her. She could drown in their syrup before she knew which way the cocoa was blowing.

"You're not going to go away, are you?" she asked.

"Not a chance," I said.

She shook her head and sighed. "Fine. I'll explain. It was a ridiculous assignment anyway." She stuck out her hand. "My name is Leslie Stephens. I'm a private detective from Toledo. Antoine Belanger hired me to keep an eye on you."

"You know, this is really good," Leslie said as she polished off another popcorn ball. It was her fourth. I wondered where she put it all. She was about as big around as my pinky finger. "I desperately wanted some of that fudge everyone has been lining up for, but I didn't dare come into the shop. I was worried you were onto me and I guess I was right. I don't suppose you have any left?"

We were sitting in the kitchen of POPS. After her bombshell of an announcement, I figured we needed to sit down and talk without an audience. I pulled out some of the fudge batch for the next day. "This should be close to set by now." I cut off some and handed it to her.

She took a bite and made a kind of whooping noise. "Amazing. Can I get some to take back to Toledo? I know someone there who will be really interested in this."

As if there was someone on the planet who wasn't

interested in chocolate. Well, not many someones. "How long has this been going on? This thing with Antoine?"

She narrowed her eyes and thought. "A couple of weeks. It's pretty easy duty. It's not every day, so I'm free to take other jobs here and there. You have a routine and you don't waver from it much."

"Thanks. I think." Having a routine made me sound responsible. Or possibly really dull.

"Well, except when you're breaking into houses." She took another piece of fudge off the plate. "That's more exciting."

"I didn't . . ." I decided to let it go. Maybe Garrett was right. Maybe I was splitting hairs. "So you're Antoine's source? The way he's found out about everything going on here in Grand Lake?"

"Well, everything that has to do with you. He's not interested in much else." She cocked her head. "He seems really devoted, and Lord knows he's hot. And rich. Why are you insisting on living in this little Podunk town where people don't even seem to like you that much? If he wanted me back, I'd be on the next plane, and I don't even like guys."

When she put it like that, it was hard to answer. "Let's just say that the devotion thing is new."

She shrugged. "He's still hot and rich. I think a lot of women would settle for that. Hell, most of them would settle for just rich."

"Then they can have him," I said.

"Hey!" she said.

I looked down. Sprocket had his nose deep in her purse. He immediately pulled it out and trotted over to his bed with a makeup bag in his mouth. "Sprocket!"

I followed him over to his bed. I took the makeup bag, but noticed a lump under the cushion.

"What else have you been hiding?" I asked Sprocket as I moved the cushion. One tennis ball, two squishy toys—one of which I was pretty sure was a Teletubby—and a lavender sachet with CB embroidered on it. "Seriously, Sprocket?"

"A whole family of lawbreakers, eh?" Leslie said with her throaty laugh.

•

We said good night soon after and I figured that would be the last I would ever see of Leslie Stephens, but I was wrong. She was back the next morning, waiting at the door with a bunch of my breakfast bar regulars. Apparently once you accepted fudge from a suspected murderess, you might as well accept breakfast bars as well. Everyone was back. I was going to have to consider hiring more help if I was going to have a morning rush and an afternoon rush.

"Back for more?" I asked Leslie when it was her turn.

"Well, yes, but I got a new assignment last night. I have something for you, too." She handed me an envelope as I handed her two dried-cranberry and white chocolate breakfast bars and a cup of coffee.

"What's this?" I asked.

"A cease and desist order," she said with a smile. "Have a nice day, Rebecca. You've been served."

Then she was gone.

I ripped open the envelope and scanned the contents. Then I took out my phone and hit the speed dial for Garrett. It was a damn good thing he'd put his number in my phone. I felt like he was the only one I was calling these days.

"Hi, Rebecca." Just hearing his voice made me feel a little bit better, but only a little bit.

"I've been served." I kept looking through the papers, hoping that there was some kind of mistake.

"With what? Coffee?"

"I wish. Unless of course it came from the diner." I took another look at the papers. They weren't changing. "A cease and desist from Jessica James about my Coco Pop Fudge."

He laughed. "Come in as soon as Susanna gets there and we'll talk."

Annie came by for coffee before Susanna came in. I showed her the papers. "Jessica is suing you?" She laughed.

"Why does everybody think this is so funny?" I took the papers back from her. They didn't appear remotely humorous to me.

"But Coco Pop Fudge is not Coco's fudge recipe," Annie protested. "Even I can taste that."

Annie was a terrible cook, but she wasn't a bad eater. I wasn't surprised she could taste the difference. "Jessica knows it, too. She tasted my fudge. I could see in her eyes that she knew it wasn't Coco's recipe."

"Can you prove it, though? I don't think the look on Jessica's face when she ate it is going to be admissible." Annie stirred her coffee.

"How do you prove something like that? I have my notes in my handwriting about the recipes Coco and I were working on, but I don't have a copy of Coco's recipe in her handwriting." I chewed on my lower lip, thinking.

"Does anyone?"

"Maybe. I kind of doubt it, though. Even the one Coco kept in her safe was typed, not handwritten. It could come from anyone's computer."

"Which means that Jessica could type up a new one that could say anything and no one would be the wiser," Annie pointed out.

"Except me," I said.

"Why you?" Annie's eyes opened wide.

"Because I know Coco's recipe."

Annie's eyebrows climbed up into her hair. "You know Coco's fudge recipe?"

"Of course I do. I probably know it better than Jessica does." I had known Coco's fudge recipe before I knew how to drive a stick shift.

Annie shook her finger at me. "You shouldn't walk around saying that. The recipe was top secret."

"Not if you worked in the kitchen with her as long as I did." I pushed the plate of breakfast bars toward her. "It wasn't hard to figure out."

Annie narrowed her eyes. "Who else worked for Coco over the years?"

"In the kitchen? Just me and Jessica. She had counter help in the summer, but we were the only ones allowed in the kitchen." We had been the only ones she trusted.

"So it's going to be your word against Jessica's word about what the recipe is," Annie pointed out again.

I hadn't thought of that. Jessica could easily alter the recipe. "I guess that's why I'm paying my lawyer the big bucks. Oh, by the way, here's one of the sachets that you made for Coco. I'm sorry. Sprocket must have stolen it from your purse. He's turning into a total klepto." I grabbed the little soft square out of my junk drawer, where I'd stowed it.

Annie turned the sachet over in her hands. "I wondered where these had gotten to. I figured Dan had them down at the station."

"Why would Dan have them at the station? Did lavender become a controlled substance or something?" I poured myself another cup of coffee.

"No, goofball. Because they would have been part of the crime scene." Annie shook her head.

I froze, French press suspended in the air. "Wait. What?"

"I left them on Coco's back porch. I figured the cops had picked them up," Annie said, bouncing the sachet back and forth between her hands.

I thought back. I'd been pretty panicked when I'd run into Coco's store and pretty shaken up when I'd walked back out, but I was nearly one hundred percent positive that there had been no basket of sachets on that porch. "I don't think they were there, Annie. I don't remember them."

She looked at me, gray eyes wide and serious. "Then where did Sprocket get it?"

I stared back at her. "I have no idea."

"Well, wherever he got it, you can keep it. It's got dog slobber on it now." She handed it back to me.

Eighteen

Pearl buzzed Garrett as soon as I walked in the door. "She's here."

"Send her in," his tinny voice said over the intercom.

"I believe you know the way," she said.

I let myself into his office.

"You're generating a lot of business for me," Garrett said. He got up and offered me a chair.

He smelled nice. I'm used to good smells. With the amount of baking I do, I'm surrounded by the scent of butter and cinnamon and chocolate all the time. This was different, though. This was a starchy smell, and I don't mean like a potato. I handed him the envelope that Leslie Stephens had given me that morning. "What kind of cologne do you wear?"

He read over the papers. "I don't wear cologne and I also don't think you're focusing. This is a cease and desist order from Jessica regarding your popcorn fudge."

"You mean my Coco Pop Fudge," I corrected.

"Yeah, I do, and that's part of the problem. She wants you

to stop using that name. She wants you to stop using anything with the word 'Coco' in it." He leaned back in his chair.

"That's not trademarked," I pointed out.

"Yet," he countered.

"Well, when it is I'll cease and desist." I started to get back up. That had been easier than I'd expected.

"That's not all, Rebecca." He motioned for me to sit back down. "She wants you to prove that you're not using Coco's fudge recipe."

"That's ridiculous, Garrett. Jessica knows I'm not using Coco's recipe. She tasted Coco Pop Fudge and Tuxedo Coco Pop Fudge. I could tell by the look on her face that she knew it was a brand-new direction. Plus, I have all the recipes that Coco and I made together." I flung myself back in the chair. Nothing is ever easy. Nothing.

That got his attention. He leaned forward onto his elbows. "You have documentation?"

"Well, they're my notes that I made while we were working on them, but if you want to call it documentation that's fine with me." I ran my thumbnail along the outside seam of my jeans.

"That's excellent." He nodded and stared out into space for a second. "I might have to actually taste this Coco Pop Fudge to be absolutely sure."

I had anticipated that request. I reached into my bag and plopped a wrapped box onto his desk. "Have at it, Perry Mason."

I watched as he unwrapped the box and took out a square. He took a sip of water first and then bit into the fudge. I could see the moment the sweet and salty main notes hit the front of his tongue and when the spice of it hit the back of his tongue. "Oh, my word, Rebecca. I think I love you," was all he could manage to say.

"Thank you, although I do generally expect at least one date before a guy professes his undying love." Either that or I expected him to have at least tasted my béarnaise.

He brushed his hands off and stood. "We'll see what we can do about that after we deal with this cease and desist nonsense. I'm going to file for a declaratory judgment."

So far, deciding not to be the victim was working out okay for me. I had Coco's business plan for us. My Coco Pop Fudge was a hit with the people of Grand Lake and had elicited a declaration of love. So maybe I had a little court case going. I felt like I was definitely going to put that one in the win column as well. I was feeling less and less like a loser on a minute-by-minute basis. I decided to push it a little farther.

Before heading back to the shop, I went to the park to look for Jasper. He was the only other person who had been on Coco's back porch between when Annie had left the sachets there and when I had gone running in the next morning. At least, the only other person who I knew of for sure. The only other person who wasn't the murderer. Had he seen them? Dan was barely speaking to me. I didn't want to ask him, especially when I wasn't sure if it was significant or not.

Jasper wasn't there. Tom Moffat was holding forth on the biological details of why we should never elect a woman president. He stopped spouting supposed scientific data on women's hormone fluctuations long enough to tell me that he hadn't seen Jasper since Jasper had been released from jail. Then he suggested that my life would be a lot easier if I had stayed with my husband and that most of my troubles could be traced back to the fact that I didn't properly respect the men in my life. When he started to discuss his theories about my losing my father at an early age, I left without saying good-bye.

Next I tried the diner. Megan said she hadn't seen Jasper, either. That is, she did when I could get her to acknowledge my existence. Coco Pop Fudge was apparently not enough to get Megan back on my side. She either still thought I was a potential murderess or she was upset about Jessica's shoulder or maybe both. Either way, she practically ground her teeth while she told me that she hadn't seen Jasper since Dan released him from jail.

The library was the only other place to look. No luck there, either. Or at least, no Jasper. He'd apparently been lying low since his release from the hoosegow.

There didn't seem to be an alternative, so I walked down to the south end of town to Jasper's house. I picked my way around a metal bed frame and two bicycles that looked like they'd been scavenged for parts. Eventually I made it to Jasper's front door with Sprocket right at my heels. Four large garbage bags slumped on the sagging porch. No wonder Dan got the heebie-jeebies talking about going inside this place. It was a walking advertisement for keeping your tetanus shots up to date.

I knocked on the door, almost hoping that Jasper wasn't home. I didn't really relish the idea of being told what a loser I was again, but I needed to talk to him.

I supposed I didn't blame him. I'd certainly felt the weight of shame in my life. I could see not wanting to face the townspeople you'd essentially hoodwinked for years. I knocked on the door.

A man answered. "Rebecca," he said. "What can I do for you?"

I stared at him, trying to fit the familiar voice into the very unfamiliar face I was looking at. "Jasper?"

"One and the same." He pulled the door open wider. "Come in. I'm trying to do a little straightening up, so watch your step."

I stood in the doorway and stared at him. The long gray shaggy hair had been cut close to his scalp, almost a Caesar. The beard that had often appeared to serve as a storage place for snacks was gone. So were the layers of baggy dirt-crusted clothes. He had on a pair of clean Levi's and an untucked dress shirt with the cuffs rolled up over a T-shirt. He looked . . . good. He looked like a regular guy on the street. In fact, he looked a little better than most of the regular guys on the street. He looked a little like Richard Dean Anderson. He looked like someone I'd be tempted to fix up with Annie. Maybe I should. I was seriously doubting her taste in men.

Jasper turned back when he realized I hadn't moved. "I decided to make some changes."

"I should say so." I still didn't move. It wasn't just the clothes and the hygiene. He stood different. Taller. Straighter. Who knew his shoulders were that broad?

Several garbage bags and boxes stood open around the room, partially filled. He gestured to them. "I'm going to clean this place up. Make it a decent place to live. I finally realized that I deserve that in my life." Then he pointed at me. "And I have you to thank for it."

I took a few steps into the room. "Jasper, I'm flattered, but I can't imagine what I did that helped you."

"You looked me in the eye and made it clear that you didn't care what anybody else thought about you. You were going to hold your head high and keep going until you made it all work." He sat down on the couch. "You weren't going to let what anybody else might whisper behind your back stop you in your tracks for decades. You weren't going to waste your time hiding behind a façade of erratic behavior and filth."

That sounded a little more heroic than my general internal dialogue, but I figured I'd let that go. "So you decided not to care about what people thought, either? Is that what this is about?"

He nodded. "You got it. I'm not going to hide behind the hair and the clothes and the dirt. I'm going to get myself cleaned up. I'm going to get this house cleaned up. I'm going to finish my degree."

"Then what?" I asked, almost breathless at the transformation I was witnessing.

"I think I might want to teach." He leaned back and took a deep breath, settling his shoulders.

I perched across from him on the edge of an armchair that seemed to not have any really big chunks of detritus on it. "That's wonderful, Jasper. I had no idea."

"I'm not sure I did before you came to talk to me in jail." He shook his head. "I thought I knew what I was doing. I thought I knew what I was all about. I was so wrong. You didn't preach at me. You didn't lecture me. You just set an example I couldn't ignore."

I don't think I'd ever considered myself a shining example before. In fact, I'm pretty sure most people thought of me as a terrible warning. "I don't know what to say, Jasper."

"Nothing to say. It's all on me and all I've got is 'thank you.'" He balanced his elbows on his knees. "But I don't think you came to talk to me about personal transformation. What brought you down to my neck of the woods?"

I pulled the sachet out of my bag. "When you stopped by Coco's that . . . well, that night, did you see a basket of these on the back porch?"

He took the sachet from me. "Yeah. There was a little basket of them right in front of the door. I checked them out in case they were food. Coco left stuff every now and then."

"Did you take them? Do you still have them?" That would be one mystery solved, although figuring out where Sprocket got it was still beyond me.

He shook his head. "They weren't food or money, Rebecca. I left them where they were. I didn't think they were for me." He seemed sad, like he kind of wished the sachets had been for him.

"But you saw them there at nine thirty?" Speaking of Sprocket, I tugged his leash to get his nose out of one of the boxes. He was going to have to get therapy for his klepto-mania.

"Absolutely. I remember sniffing them. Lavender's so soothing." He handed the sachet back to me.

It wasn't doing much to soothe me now. Whoever took those sachets had been on Coco's back porch in between the time Jasper left and the time I went into Coco's shop the next morning. The person most likely to have been there during that time was the person who had faked the break-in, and the person most likely to do that was the person who had killed Coco in the first place.

I thanked Jasper and told him to let me know if there was anything else I could do to help on his new journey of per-sonal transformation. He hugged me. I stiffened as he put his arms around me and then remembered that it wasn't the same filthy, smelly Jasper I'd known all these years. This Jasper smelled a little like bay rum.

As Sprocket and I walked back toward downtown Grand Lake, I tried to remember everyone who Sprocket had stolen stuff from in the past weeks. There'd been the baby's woolly sheep toy. There'd been Leslie Stephens. Aw, hell, it could have been stolen from anybody who'd been in the store. He'd tried to take something from Jasper just now and he'd had his nose in Jessica's purse. I pulled the sachet back out of my pocket and stared at it.

By the time I got back to the shop, we were in full fudge lockdown. Susanna and I hustled as hard as we could, but a line still stretched out the door. I even pressed Sam into service when he came by, probably looking to eat whatever mistakes I'd made in the kitchen that day. He had, after all, even eaten the popcorn breakfast bars with the raisins in them. He hadn't liked them, but he'd eaten them.

I didn't even recognize some of the people who came through. I felt like I had at least seen the faces of pretty much everyone in Grand Lake, but there were men and women coming through the store who I'd never seen before.

"Where are all these people coming from?" I whispered to Susanna as we rushed past each other behind the counter.

"You don't know?" She cut off a wedge of the new caramel popcorn fudge and wrapped it in wax paper.

"I know a lot of stuff. I know all the state capitals. I know to turn a screw to the right to tighten it and that Pluto is no longer a planet, but I do not know where these crowds are coming from." I took the wedge of fudge and boxed it.

"You're blowing up on Twitter." Susanna rang up the fudge while I got another box ready.

"I am? I'm not even on Twitter." Or Facebook. Or Instagram. Or Tumblr. Or Pinterest.

"Totally. Hashtag foodgasm. Hashtag fudge. Hashtag GrandLake. I don't remember all of them. I'll show you after the rush." She took another order and cut off another hunk of fudge. "And tomorrow, we're getting you on Twitter."

"Foodgasm?" Well, at least I was giving someone some kind of gasm.

The rush ended at about four thirty again. I had no idea what the psychology was there, but I'd figure it out eventually. Or I'd accept it and hire another counter person. Susanna showed me what was happening on Twitter. With Sam's help, we tried to trace it back and followed the train of Retweets and favorites back to a food critic at the *Toledo Times* who had Tweeted a picture of Coco Pop Fudge with the caption: Best thing to hit Ohio since the Rock and Roll Hall of Fame.

"I didn't even know a food critic had been to POPS." I put my feet up on one of the kitchen chairs. I'd been on my feet that day almost as long as I used to be when I was a student. My feet were a lot older now, though. They hurt.

"I'm not sure she was. She said someone gave her the fudge as a gift. Someone she calls LSteph." Sam peered at his laptop.

As in Leslie Stephens? "Who's LSteph to the food critic?"

He shrugged. "Girlfriend, I think."

I guess I'd have to forgive Leslie Stephens for serving me papers if she also served my fudge to a food critic. Antoine had no idea what he'd started.

I was still thinking about Antoine and Leslie Stephens when I finally got home. I glanced at the clock. It was eight o'clock here. I'd missed Friday night dinner. But it would only be six o'clock in California. Antoine would be elbow deep in cooking at L'Oiseau Gris. He'd be overseeing the kitchen and the serving staff. He'd be tasting and chopping and fixing the disasters that happened pretty much every night in a busy kitchen. It would be a terrible time to call him. He would be busy and distracted. I picked up my cell phone and dialed.

He answered on the second ring. I knew he would. "Rebecca, is everything all right?"

"I cannot believe you hired a private detective to follow me around." I leaned back on the couch and put my feet up on the arm, stretching out my full length. I could hear voices and a lot of clanging and banging in the background. Antoine would be on his feet for at least another five hours, and he was even older than I was.

"Ms. Stephens let me know you had, how did she say, made her?" He made it sound kind of sexy.

"Yeah. I made her." And served her fudge and coffee before she served me court papers.

He sighed. "Rebecca, darling, I was concerned for you. You would not tell me what you were doing or how you were doing so I found a way to stay informed."

This was one of the problems with Antoine. He made everything sound so reasonable, including having hired a private detective to follow his ex-wife. I was pretty sure that he actually thought it was reasonable. It was so not. "I wasn't keeping you informed because my life is none of your business. I'm not married to you anymore. Remember?"

"You will always be my business. I will always love you." I could imagine him standing in the middle of the kitchen with his hand on his heart as he said that. Chaos would be erupting around him. He would be like the eye in the center of a storm. It was actually kind of romantic. This kind of gesture was his meat and potatoes. It was exactly how he'd kept me with him for as long as he had. It was hard for a girl to resist that.

"Oh, Antoine." I didn't know what else to say.

"Come home, Rebecca. Come back to me. Your little

town is full of crazies. People are hitting little old ladies on the head. Teachers are driving into trees. You are being arrested every other day by your childhood friend. Come back to California."

Funny, the offer wasn't so tempting anymore. Not so long ago, I'd felt a twinge every time he begged me to come back, a little something inside me that knew how much easier my life could be. The twinge was gone. I think I liked being the new action-oriented me. "No, Antoine. Thank you, but no." I hung up.

Nineteen

For the past few nights, I'd been staying at the shop later and later every night, trying to keep up with the demand for the Coco Pop Fudge line. Every flavor was a huge hit. Saturday was the first night in three days that I'd managed to make it home while there was still a light on in Dan and Haley's house.

I tapped lightly at the door. Dan opened it a minute later. "Rebecca, you don't have to knock. It's kind of your house, too."

"I expect you to knock at my place," I pointed out, walking in.

"Your place is one big room. You could be naked."

He had a point. "I've been meaning to show you this." I pulled out the sachet and handed it to him.

"It'd be a nice little thing if it hadn't been chewed." Dan handed the sachet back to me and walked into the living room.

I followed him and sat down on the rocking chair that had belonged to my grandmother. The embroidered seat was getting a little faded, but it was still comfy. "Do you have anything like it down at the station?"

"You know, Huerta doesn't usually go in for potpourri. So no. This looks like an old-lady kind of thing." He sat down on the couch.

"It is an old-lady kind of thing. Annie made them for Coco." I tossed the sachet from hand to hand.

His face creased. "I get it. CB for Cordelia Bittles. That's sweet. Why would you think we had them at the station?"

I took a deep breath. "Annie said she left the sachets on Coco's back porch before she went home that night. Jasper saw them there at nine thirty. They weren't there the next morning. Jessica says she came in the front door that morning. The only person who should have them is whoever broke that back window and tried to make it look like someone broke in."

"Rebecca, you're the one who has the sachet." He looked like he was going to laugh.

I took a deep breath to calm myself. "Only one of them and that's because Sprocket stole it."

"From whom?" Now he looked more interested.

"I'm not sure. It could be anybody who came into the shop, really." The list of people I'd caught him stealing from was as long as my arm, and those were just the times I'd caught him. Where had he gotten that tennis ball, for instance? I had no idea.

"It has Coco's initials on it, Rebecca. Maybe he stole it from her." Dan stretched and yawned.

"He didn't have the chance. Coco might have already been dead when Annie left them on the back porch." My heart clenched at the thought of Coco lying there, cold and alone, for all those hours.

"So you think the murderer has been in your shop? Long

enough for Sprocket to steal something?" Dan asked, sitting upright.

It gave me chills, but it was exactly what I thought. "I guess so."

Dan shook his head. "'I guess so' isn't going to stand up in a court of law."

"Don't you want it? As evidence?" I held it out toward him.

"The D.A. will laugh me into the deepest part of Lake Erie if I try to list Sprocket as part of the chain of evidence." He reached down to pet Sprocket, who had lifted his head at the mention of his name.

"Fine," I said, taking it back and sticking it in my purse. I couldn't win these days. If I didn't hand things over to Dan, he got mad. When I did, he ignored them. "But if you see someone with one of those, you should probably arrest them."

He arched a brow. "Except you, of course."

"I was hoping that went without saying."

Dan asked, "Are you still walking to the shop in the morning?"

"Of course. Why?"

"Be careful. It's been a few days since Barbara was attacked at her store. We still don't know who's responsible." He rubbed his chin.

"I always have Sprocket with me."

Dan flopped back on the couch. "Great. Maybe he can steal a few more clues for me."

It probably says something about the state of crime in Grand Lake that Jessica's suit against me was scheduled to be heard within seventy-two hours of her filing it. We'd drawn Judge Maximilian Romero. He strode into the courtroom, robes flapping behind his six-foot-three-inch frame. He was a man of size. Not fat. Just substantial. With wild bristling eyebrows and a salt-and-pepper beard. I smiled. This boded well for me. I knew an eater when I saw one and Judge Romero was definitely a good eater. He rapped his gavel and we all sat. I didn't even look to see if there was a chair.

The gallery was full. I hadn't realized how much interest the case had generated until I walked in with Garrett and saw Samantha Freeman from the *Grand Lake Sentinel* with Glenn Becker acting as photographer. I also saw Tom Moffatt, Jasper and a host of other Grand Lake personalities.

Jessica got to go first. She always got to go first. She had been going first since the first grade when we lined up according to height. I was really getting sick of it.

Russ Meyer, Jessica's boyfriend/lawyer, stood up to make his opening argument. He'd been in Haley's class at Grand Lake High. He'd been one of those normal kids. Smart, but not so smart he was neurotic. Athletic, but not a football star. Well-liked, but not super popular. Just a nice kid trying to do the right things. Now he was a nice guy in a nice enough suit, but he so wasn't doing the right thing. I had no idea how he'd gotten involved with Jessica. "If it please the court, it is our contention that Ms. Rebecca Anderson used her position of trust with the recently deceased Cordelia Bittles to gain access to her famed and very secret fudge recipe. That recipe has been left in Ms. Bittles's will to my client, Jessica James. Ms. James is the only person who should be making any kind of fudge using that recipe.

"Recently, Ms. Anderson has begun selling a confection she calls Coco Pop Fudge at her store, POPS. We allege that the Coco Pop Fudge recipe is actually Ms. Bittles's secret Signature Fudge recipe and that Ms. Anderson is further damaging my client by using Ms. Bittles's nickname, Coco, in the name of her confection. We would like her to cease and desist in the making and selling of this fudge and to not use references to Ms. Bittles in the names of her products."

Russ sat down. Jessica stroked his arm and smiled at me.

My boyfriend/lawyer stood up. I was pretty sure Garrett's suit had not come from Men's Wearhouse. The wool was a little too soft and draped a little too well for that. His hair had style without looking like he'd just stepped out of Ray Bob's Barber Shop over on Crocus Street. He moved like a guy who ran five miles along the lake every day. In other words, my boyfriend totally trumped Jessica's boyfriend. I sat back to listen to his opening argument.

"It's true, your honor. My client is well aware of Ms. Bittles's secret recipe. She worked for Ms. Bittles when she was in high school and the two remained close friends. In fact, Ms. Bittles had written up an extensive business plan for a joint venture with Ms. Anderson that would have excluded Ms. James." Garrett picked up one of the business plan binders from a banker's box by his chair and thumped it onto the table.

Judge Romero held out his hand and Garrett carried the binder up to him. "You will note in the calendar section of the business plan, Ms. Bittles made a schedule for rolling out new products. We believe the first of those products were to be Coco Pop and Tuxedo Coco Pop Fudge."

Russ stood up. "Objection, Your Honor. What proof does my colleague have as to which products Ms. Bittles was referring?"

"Mr. Mills?" Judge Romero asked.

"I'm coming to that, Judge. If you will give me a moment. While Coco Pop and Tuxedo Coco Pop Fudge are definitely in the style of Ms. Bittles's original recipe, they have been substantially altered. What's more, Your Honor, Ms. Bittles willingly collaborated with Ms. Anderson to develop Coco Pop and Tuxedo Coco Pop."

Garrett held up my recipe notebook. "I have here the notes Ms. Anderson took in her personal recipe notebook as she and Ms. Bittles worked together on these recipes. A handwriting expert has confirmed both Ms. Anderson's and Ms. Bittles's handwriting in the notes detailing the development of Coco Pop and Tuxedo Coco Pop Fudge."

Judge Romero wiggled his meaty fingers in a come-hither gesture, and Garrett brought him my recipe notebook encased in a plastic bag like there might be DNA on it, and the business plan binder. Then he returned to the table next to me but didn't sit. "Looking through that notebook, Judge Romero, I think you will find that what Ms. Anderson is doing and plans to do at POPS truly honors Ms. Bittles unlike the plans being made by Ms. James."

Russ clambered to his feet again. "Your Honor, objection." He sounded less enthusiastic, though. "How does Mr. Mills know what my client's plans are?"

Judge Romero turned back to Garrett. "Well, Counselor?"

Garrett held another piece of paper up in the air. "I have here a sworn affidavit from Mayor Allen Thompson regarding the overtures made to him by Miss James for the sale of Ms. Bittles's shop."

Garrett didn't wait for the judge to ask him to come forward this time. He walked up to the bench and slapped it down. There was a buzz in the gallery. Apparently Jessica's plan to sell Coco's Cocoas was news to most of the town.

"I also have sworn affidavits from officers of no fewer than three chocolate companies." Garrett paused and looked around at the gallery. "Three chocolate companies who have been contacted by Ms. James to see if they were interested in purchasing and/or licensing Ms. Bittles's secret recipes for her Signature Fudge. If anyone should cease and desist, it's Ms. James. Not Ms. Anderson."

The spectators in the gallery gasped. The court reporter's head swung up, and she fixed Jessica with a glare. Coco had a lot of fans in a lot of places. No one was going to be too happy to find out what Jessica's plans were for that recipe or for the dismantling of everything that Coco had spent her whole life building.

Garrett went on. "What my esteemed colleague is failing to mention is that Ms. James's main concern with any infringement on the intellectual property represented by the Coco's Signature Fudge recipe is that she does not want it to be devalued before she sells it. She has no intent to honor Ms. Bittles's legacy. She intends to sell it to the highest bidder. She has already accepted an offer to sell Ms. Bittles's shop."

Judge Romero held up his hand to stop Garrett. "While many people of Grand Lake, myself included, would be saddened to see Coco's Cocoas closed and her recipe sold to some large conglomerate, it is well within Ms. James's rights to do so. I believe Ms. Bittles's will left the recipe and the shop to Ms. James, free and clear."

"True enough, Your Honor. While there is some evidence that Ms. Bittles was planning on changing her will in the near future, she did not get the chance to do so. The Signature Fudge recipe belongs to Ms. James."

"Anything else, Counselor?" Judge Romero asked.

Garrett dropped his head and leaned with one hand on the table and then looked up sharply, a little like that surprised groundhog on YouTube, but handsomer. "Your Honor, I think we could actually put this matter to rest very quickly with one more item. There would be no need to waste any more of the court's time."

"And that is?" Judge Romero said as he turned my notebook over in his hands.

"A taste test."

Judge Romero's eyebrows went up. "Of?"

"A side-by-side taste test of Ms. Bittles's fudge next to Ms. Anderson's fudge." Now Garrett pulled out tins of my newest offerings. "One taste will show that Ms. Anderson's confections truly honor Ms. Bittles for who she was, not what kind of price someone could get for her recipe, and do not use her exact recipe."

"With who as the arbiter of the test?" Judge Romero sat up a little straighter.

"You, Your Honor." Garrett smiled and leaned against the table.

"I'm not sure if I'm qualified," Romero said, but he leaned forward to look at Garrett more closely.

"Trust me, Your Honor. One taste will be all it takes to settle this matter." Garrett smiled. "One taste by an educated palate, that is."

Romero tilted his head and thought for a second. Then he said, "Very well. Bring me the fudge."

Russ stood. "Objection, Your Honor. We were not informed of this taste test." He said the last two words as if Garrett had suggested a relay race to settle the matter. "Where does my colleague propose to get a sample of Ms. Bittles's Signature Fudge?"

Judge Romero looked at Garrett. "Mr. Mills?"

Garrett held up one of Coco's tins. "This tin contains a sample of Ms. Bittles's Signature Fudge, which she gave to Sheriff Dan Cooper as a birthday present three weeks ago. Sheriff Cooper has graciously consented for us to use this fudge for our taste test despite the fact that he was saving it for a special occasion."

"Is Sheriff Cooper here?" Romero asked.

Dan stood up from his seat in the courtroom. "I am, Your

Honor, and I am willing to swear that this is the fudge given to me by Ms. Bittles."

"Very well. That satisfies my need for chain of evidence." Judge Romero motioned for Garrett to come up to the bench again.

Jessica pinched Russ and he leapt to his feet. "Objection, Your Honor."

Romero's giant eyebrows twitched. "On what grounds?"

Russ actually looked over at Jessica like she might have the answer. Apparently she didn't.

"Do you doubt the provenance of the fudge?" Judge Romero asked.

"No, Your Honor. I can see it is in one of Ms. Bittles's signature tins and Sheriff Cooper has always performed with the highest moral standards," Russ said.

Judge Romero leaned forward. "Do you doubt my tasting ability?"

"No, of course not, Your Honor." Russ's nose started to turn a little pink.

"Then I see no reason not to go forward." Romero relaxed back onto his seat.

Russ sat down. Jessica glared at him.

Garrett set the two tins down in front of the judge. He took a piece of Coco's Signature Chocolate Fudge, bit into it, and moaned. "Oh, Coco. You will be missed. Yes. This is how I remember her fudge. Rich. Creamy. Yet somehow light."

He took a sip of water and took a piece of the Coco Pop Fudge and bit into it. His eyebrows climbed up his forehead, which was a little like watching two very large caterpillars do a downward dog yoga move. He laughed. "How piquant! Delightful and playful. I can see how it owes something to

Coco's Signature, but it is its own thing altogether." He banged his gavel. "Case dismissed."

Jessica stood. "But, Your Honor . . ."

Judge Romero pointed his gavel at her and cut her off. "Not another word, young lady. You have wasted this court's time with this frivolous case. Go work out your personal differences with Ms. Anderson on your own time." He stood. We all stood. Then he left the courtroom.

The room erupted into applause. I turned around to stare at them. Had they been on my side that whole time? The *Sentinel* photographer snapped photos so fast it didn't even look like his finger was moving. Tom Moffat grumbled that both Jessica and I should be sent home where we belonged.

I looked around at the court reporter and the clerk and all the other people in the courtroom. Samantha from the *Sentinel* gave me a little wave. Word was going to be all around Grand Lake in a matter of hours.

I had been vindicated. In a court of law, no less. I turned and threw my arms around Garrett. Which was when I saw Antoine stride into the courtroom as if it was the kitchen of L'Oiseau Gris.

I turned to ice in Garrett's arms. He must have felt it. "What's wrong? We won. You know that, right?" he asked.

I nodded against his shoulder. "Yes, but my ex-husband just walked into the courtroom."

"Awkward," Garrett sang sotto voce into my ear.

I pulled away and pulled my blouse straight. I stepped around Garrett and said, "Hello, Antoine. What exactly are you doing here?" I held out my hand.

Antoine took my hand and pulled me toward him. "I am here to take you home, Rebecca. Enough is enough."

"Uh, fella, I think you need to let the lady go." Garrett tapped Antoine on the shoulder.

Antoine glanced over at Garrett, his expression imperious. "And you are?"

"My name is Garrett Mills. I'm Ms. Anderson's attorney and her . . ." And that was where he faltered. I didn't blame him. I didn't exactly know what he was besides my lawyer, either. I did know he was a damn fine kisser and often smelled really good in a non-kitcheny way and that he was smart and funny and had a low tolerance for vegetables coming out toddler nostrils. What the exact nature of our relationship was? I thought it was too early to tell.

"My friend, Antoine. He's my friend. Now let me go, please." I kept my voice cool and steady. The last thing you should do with Antoine was match him passion for passion. That way lay mutually assured destruction. He was like a ballistic missile of passion.

"Fine." Antoine released me. "Can we go somewhere to talk? I am serious about taking you home."

"Antoine, I am home. Grand Lake is home." I backed up so I was standing next to Garrett.

"How can a place that doubts your integrity as a chef be home to you?" Antoine grabbed my hand and started pulling me toward the door. "They have dragged you in front of a judge. It's humiliating. Ridiculous! *C'est fou!*"

To stay in television shape, Antoine works out almost as much as he cooks. He tugged and I sailed along after him. I tried to plant my feet and pull back, but I couldn't get a purchase on the slick courtroom floor. Whose idea had it been for me to wear heels?

Garrett positioned himself between Antoine and the door, forcing Antoine to stop. "I said that you needed to get your hands off the lady." His voice was low and menacing.

"This is between Rebecca and myself." Antoine waved his hand. "Please get out of our way. We have much to discuss."

"I don't think she wants to discuss anything with you." Garrett didn't budge.

"It's okay, Garrett. I'll go. I'll call you later." I didn't really want to go, but I didn't really want more of a scene than we'd already had.

Garrett shook his head and squared his shoulders. "It is not okay. You're not going anywhere with him. Not while I'm here to stop it."

Antoine looked back and forth between us. "Have I been replaced already, Rebecca? With someone so prosaic as a lawyer?"

"Prosaic?" Garrett shook his head. "I'd rather be prosaic than narcissistic." Garrett had that one pegged.

"And I would rather be extraordinary than stuck in some Podunk town in the middle of one of the flyover states." Antoine lifted his chin.

Garrett laughed. "Then go off and be extraordinary somewhere else."

"Not without Rebecca. You don't understand." Antoine turned toward me, his tone going from belligerent to beseeching. "I have not developed a single new recipe since you left me. Not one. You were my muse. Come back to me. I will do whatever you want. You can have a popcorn shop right next to L'Oiseau Gris. You can have two popcorn shops. Three. Whatever you want."

"I don't want a popcorn shop next to L'Oiseau Gris," I said, although that was a pretty sweet piece of real estate. I bet I could sell a lot of popcorn balls to tipsy people out on wine-tasting adventures. That wasn't the point, though. "I want to be here."

Antoine's face had begun to turn an interesting purple color. "Where you are accused of crimes you did not commit? Arrested on a regular basis? Attacked? Reviled?"

It seemed harder to defend when he put it that way.

"Yes. That's what she wants. She likes being reviled. It makes her feel alive. Now let her go." Garrett tried to push in between Antoine and me.

Antoine pushed him back. "Not until I speak to her in private. Get out of my way, shyster."

"Shyster? Glorified onion chopper." Garrett squared his shoulders and glared.

"Ambulance chaser!" Antoine yelled, head reared back.

Garrett leaned in and half-whispered, "Jacques Pépin imitator!"

Apparently that was too much for Antoine. I wasn't surprised. Antoine hated Jacques Pépin. He let go of my arm and took a swing at Garrett. Garrett took the punch directly on the chin, stumbled backward and then came up swinging himself.

He'd blacked both of Antoine's eyes before the security guards were able to separate them.

Twenty

"Thanks for going my bail," Garrett said as we walked out of the police station.

"It would have been unseemly for Dan to do it," I pointed out. "Can't have law enforcement playing favorites and all that."

"I also appreciate you testifying that I didn't take the first swing." He rubbed the swelling bruise on his jaw.

"That didn't seem to impress Judge Romero too much. Good thing I had another batch of fudge with me or you might have been spending the night in lockdown." I'd also promised to bring over some of the caramel fudge tomorrow. I didn't mind. Judge Romero was an appreciative audience.

"You talk pretty tough for a cook." He put his arm around my waist and pulled me against him.

"Well, I've been arrested a time or two now. I know how things are in the slammer." I smiled up at him. "Can I buy you lunch, Counselor?"

"Sure. I wouldn't mind a little sustenance." He steered

me onto Main Street and we walked to Bob's Diner. The lunch crowd had cleared, so we were able to get a booth right away. Megan brought us both cups of coffee without being asked and plunked menus down in front of us.

"Is it true what you said?" Megan asked as she tried to top off my still-full coffee cup. I was so not going to drink that stuff. I was pleased to see that Garrett took one sip and then set his cup down. "In court?"

"About what?" I'd said a lot of stuff lately.

"About Jessica selling Coco's recipe to some big chocolate company." She set the coffee carafe down and rearranged the salt and pepper shakers on the table.

"Absolutely one hundred percent true." I'd been ready to swear to it in a court of law. I might as well be ready to swear to it in Bob's Diner.

Megan shook her head. "Coco's probably spinning in her grave. She'd rather have burned that recipe than sold it."

That was true. "I know."

"And she's already sold the shop?" Megan asked.

"As good as." Main Street wouldn't be the same, but maybe Barbara was right. Maybe we'd all forget eventually.

"You know, maybe that Jessica isn't as sweet and nice as everybody always says." Megan picked up the coffee carafe.

I scratched my head. "Possibly not."

Megan went on to the next table and Garrett said, "I'm surprised you're not doing a happy dance in your seat."

"I'm doing it in my head." I smiled.

"So now that you've got what you've always wanted, are you going to let up?" He poured cream and sugar into his coffee and took another sip. By the way his mouth twisted, it hadn't helped.

"What have I always wanted?" I asked.

He smiled. "For the town to be on your side instead of Jessica's."

I considered that for a moment. "It's not all I've ever wanted, but I'm liking it so far."

"Fine, but step carefully, Rebecca. She's littler than you, but she's still got a nasty bite."

I knew that better than anyone.

If anything, the afternoon Coco Pop Fudge crowd had grown that day. I pressed Sam into service, otherwise he was taking up space where customers could stand, and his feet are huge. He had to easily take up the same square footage as two small customers. Way better to have him behind the counter being useful than in front of it, getting in the way.

Amid the usual midwestern polite call and response of "hellos" and "how are yous," "thank yous" and "fines," I heard the occasional "I always wondered about that Jessica" and "Coco would be so proud of you."

Then as the crowd began to thin, Jessica barged in. Her hair was tangled around her face. Mascara dripped down her cheeks. She swayed in the doorway and staggered the rest of the way into the shop.

Everyone got quiet in a hurry.

She pointed a shaky finger at me. "You have no right. No right! No right to do this." She gestured around POPS.

"The judge says that I do, Jessica." I came out from behind the counter. "Do you need a ride home?"

"I don't care what that stupid fat judge says. What does he know? I know who was always here for Coco, and it wasn't you, Rebecca. You weren't here when she had her knee replaced. You weren't here the winter she got pneumonia. You weren't the one who shoveled her sidewalks in the winter and helped her carry in her groceries. You were off in California finding yourself, marrying a rich husband and then deciding that still wasn't good enough for you." She grabbed hold of one of the ice cream parlor chairs for balance.

"I was the one who was here. Coco's legacy should be mine. Her will—the only will that counts—says it's mine. But you have to go and ruin everything with some new thing you say that she was going to make with you. You ruin everything. You always do." With that she made a slow circle and staggered back out of the shop.

"Was Ms. Jessica drunk?" Susanna whispered to me as I went back behind the counter feeling chastened.

"I think so."

"So was she really drunk when she had that car accident, too? Was it maybe not cough medicine?" Sam asked.

I shrugged. I'd done enough damage to Jessica that day. It was starting not to feel so much like a victory.

Garrett had been right about the mornings getting darker and colder. Sprocket and I needed lights now to walk into POPS in the morning. I had a headlamp for me and a little blinking collar light for Sprocket. Not exactly high style, but it was better than tripping and falling in the dark. We probably wouldn't be walking much longer. As soon as snow started to fly we were driving. I could get a treadmill for the apartment so I could walk off all the tastes and wee bites I ended up taking each day.

I pulled my keys out of my pocket as we walked up to the door. For a second, I thought I saw movement in the window. Nothing much. Just a dark patch moving against the general blackness of the interior. I stopped and waited, watching the window again. Nothing. I must have imagined it. I opened the door and let Sprocket in first and followed him. I took two steps into the shop and stopped. Sprocket growled. I could have sworn I smelled almonds. Then something smacked down on top of my head and everything went black.

I woke lying facedown on my Versailles tile floor. Sprocket was howling and Annie was talking. She was giving someone the address of the shop.

"What happened?" I asked, trying to push myself up and then deciding that wasn't such a good idea as my stomach lurched.

"You were attacked." Annie crouched down next to me. "The ambulance is on its way. So is Dan."

"Who would attack me?" Sprocket came over and licked my face.

"Based on the fact that your back window is bashed in, I'm guessing it's the same person who attacked Coco and Barbara." She patted my back.

I managed to push myself up into a sitting position without barfing. "That doesn't make any sense. I don't fit the profile."

"You're a female shop owner," Annie pointed out. She took her shawl off and wrapped it around me.

"I'm under seventy," I countered, trying to stop the shaking that had started.

She shrugged. "Maybe the age thing was a coincidence." Then she went into the kitchen to get some ice to hold against my head.

My head hurt too much to argue. I knew there was more, but the pounding in my brain was keeping thoughts from forming. Apparently my head isn't anywhere near as hard as Huerta's or Allen Thompson's. Once Dan and the paramedics arrived, there was no point in thinking at all. Everyone had too many questions and they seemed to all be asking them at once.

"Jesus, Rebecca, are you okay?" Dan asked, crouching down next to me.

"I think so." I reached out and took his arm. It was nice to have something solid to hang on to. I tried to get up, but the room swam in front of my eyes.

The paramedic who was poking and prodding me and asking questions about drug allergies shook his head and held me down. "You have to be careful with head injuries. We're taking you in to be thoroughly checked over. Let the professionals decide if you're okay or not."

That actually sounded like a good idea. "Will you take Sprocket?" I asked Dan.

"I'll take him home to Haley and Evan. She's going to want to know what happened anyway, and I don't want her to hear it from someone else." Dan patted Sprocket on the head.

That also sounded like a good idea. She'd be upset enough as it was. If she heard it from someone else there'd truly be hell to pay.

"Did you see anything? Hear anything?" Dan asked as the paramedics helped me onto the gurney.

I tried to remember. "There was a shape. Something in the window. I don't know. I thought I saw it and then I thought I imagined it. I walked in and then pow." I touched the top of my head. Everything started to swim again.

"That's where you were hit? On top of your head?" Dan asked, peering over at the top of my head.

"That's where it hurts." I could feel a knot forming up there, too.

"Were you bent over or something?" He looked from me to the door.

"No. I was walking into the store. Why?" I looked over at the door to see if there was something there.

"Think about it, Rebecca. You're five foot ten. For someone to hit you on top of the head like that, they'd have to be close to seven foot tall." Dan stood up and put his hands on his hips.

"Or standing on something," Annie said, pointing to one of my ice cream parlor chairs that was nowhere near the table it went to. She stood next to Dan, staring at the scene.

The paramedics slid the gurney into the ambulance. "We need to take her to be checked out now. You can come by the hospital to ask her questions later."

I waved good-bye as the doors shut, and closed my eyes for the ride.

"You're the lady who showed up at the other lady's store when that lady got hit on the head, aren't you?" the dark-haired paramedic asked.

It took me a few seconds to parse out that sentence. "You mean Barbara? From the antique store?"

"Yeah. You showed up as we were taking her to the ambulance," he said as he wrapped a blood pressure cuff around my arm. "Weird that you both got hit on the head at your stores."

I could have thought of several other words besides *weird* to describe it if my head hadn't hurt so much. "Totally."

"She smelled like nuts," he observed. He sniffed my head. "You smell like almonds."

"Are you saying I have something in my hair?" My hand

flew up again, but it didn't do much good since he'd already put the oxygen sensor on my index finger.

"No. I'm saying you smell a little like almonds." He started an IV line.

"Barbara smelled like something, too?"

"Yeah. Although she smelled a little more chocolatey."

"Lucky her."

"Yeah." He sighed. "I really like chocolate."

Haley was at the emergency room when I got there. I wasn't quite sure how she managed to beat the ambulance, but never underestimate a big sister.

"Where's Evan?" I asked.

"Dan's taking him to preschool. I can only stay for a little bit, but I wanted to see that you were okay for myself." She brushed the hair off my forehead. "Don't scare me like that again, okay?"

"I didn't mean to. I really didn't plan on anyone smacking me on the head." I lifted my hand to touch the bump on my head, but Haley stopped it.

"I know you didn't plan it. I just think you're poking around too much and may have upset someone." She bit her lip. "Someone besides Dan."

"Yeah, I get that." She had a point.

After checking me out and declaring I had a mild concussion, Dr. Tanaka shuffled me off into the corner of the emergency room for observation. Haley left to pick up Evan at preschool.

A few hours later, Dr. Tanaka seemed satisfied. She said if I didn't do anything crazy and could find someone who would stay with me, she'd let me go home. One of the volunteers brought me a magazine to read while I waited, but the words kept blurring. Dr. Tanaka said that would pass in a few hours or perhaps a few days or maybe it was weeks? I was having trouble paying attention.

According to Nurse Jing Jing, I was also having trouble sitting still. She kept shooing me back into my corner. "You are getting in the way of the actual sick people, Rebecca. Lie down. Be quiet."

"I'm bored." I had tried to count the ceiling tiles above me, but the blurred-vision thing wasn't helping with that, either. Plus, I kept forgetting which number I was on.

"I know you're bored." She smiled at me and patted my hand as she led me back to my corner. "But I don't care. You're in my way. Lie down. Stay out of trouble or I will bonk you over the head, too."

She was a little mean for someone who looked that cute and wore scrubs decorated with Hello Kitty. Appearances were so deceiving. Dan finally came by about two hours into my forced incarceration behind curtain number three.

"Oh, thank God, you're here. Get me out of this place." I grabbed his hand. "I'm going to die."

His face grew alarmed. "They told me it was a mild concussion. That shouldn't be life-threatening."

"It's not the concussion. It's the boredom. I don't have anything to do." I pulled myself to a sitting position using his arm. "Take me home."

He shook his head and peeled my fingers off his arm. "Can't you lie quietly for a little bit until they know you're okay?"

"No, she can't," Jing Jing called from the nurse's station. "Take her home. She's driving me nuts."

"You heard the woman. Take me home." I looked around for my shoes and jacket.

"Who's staying with her?" Jing Jing asked. "She has to have someone watch her for the rest of the day."

"Is Haley home?" I asked, not caring one whit that my tone was whiney.

Dan shook his head. I had a momentary pang of jealousy that he could do that without shooting pains through his head. "Evan has Gymboree in Amherst today. She won't be home for a couple of hours. What about Annie?"

"She has a wedding coming up that she's prepping for." This wasn't good. I was afraid Jing Jing might really bonk me over the head if I kept annoying her, and I wasn't sure I could stop myself from annoying her if I stayed there.

"I'll stay with her." Garrett peeked around the curtain.

Jing Jing yelled, "We have a winner."

"When did you get here?" I asked.

"Just now. I had to shuffle some appointments around. I can take her home." Garrett clapped Dan on the back. "You can go back to work."

"Don't you have work to do?" Dan asked.

Garrett lifted the briefcase he carried. "I brought some stuff I can work on at her place."

"Good luck with that." Jing Jing walked over to my bed. "She's super needy."

"I'll take my chances," Garrett said.

"Then I'll get the paperwork filled out." She walked away on her squeaky nurse shoes.

"I suppose it was naïve to think that this would stop with Coco and Barbara," Dan said. "I was hoping that whoever it was had moved on."

I leaned over to tie my shoes, but got a horrible head rush and sat back up. "I still don't think I fit the profile. I'm not over seventy and Allen doesn't want to buy my shop."

"Maybe we don't understand what the profile is," Garrett observed as he tied my shoes. "Maybe Barbara's and Coco's ages had nothing to do with it. What else do they all have in common?"

"All women. All shop owners. All single." Dan counted similarities off on his fingers.

"Both Coco and Barbara could have gotten married," I said.

"How do you know?"

"Barbara told me. Tom Moffat asked both of them to marry him at some point." I shut my eyes to wish the throbbing in my head to lessen.

"Who's Tom Moffat?" Garrett asked.

"The guy in the park who's always complaining about women," Dan said. "One of Jasper's panhandling buddies."

"The guy in the courtroom today who said both Jessica and Rebecca should be sent home?" Garrett helped me on with my jacket.

I looked up at Dan. "He comes by nearly every evening to get the leftover popcorn. He has been since Jasper was arrested."

Dan held up his hands. "Let's not get ahead of ourselves. Tom's been spouting off about women, Nessie, and contrails since we were in high school. How hard was that blow to your head?"

"Hard enough to seriously hurt me, Dan. You'll talk to him, right?" I asked.

He gave me a look.

"Fine. Go do your law enforcement business all on your own. Was anything taken from POPS?" I asked Dan.

"You'll have to come in and look around. Did you leave any money in the register?" Dan asked.

"No. I put it in the safe every night."

"Good girl." He looked from Garrett to me. "Nothing

was really taken from Barbara's. The only things taken from Coco's were used to frame Jasper. Whoever's doing this doesn't want stuff."

I sensed a shift in the mood of the emergency room. There were fewer beeps, less rustling. It was like the weird stillness that happens before a tornado tears through the town. Then I saw him. Antoine. I should have known he wouldn't leave quietly.

"I can take over from here," he said, trying to shoulder Garrett aside. "I am her husband. I will take her home."

"You're not my husband anymore, Antoine. We're divorced. Remember?" I said.

"What's going on in here?" Jing Jing shouldered her way in now, too. Then she looked up at Antoine. "Hey! You're the guy from the grocery store. Man, I love your Alfredo. It's the bomb."

Antoine smiled. "Thank you. Thank you so much."

"But you can't take her home," Jing Jing said.

"Why not?"

"She said you're not her husband so you can't be back here." She actually started to push him. I was liking Jing Jing more and more every second.

"What about him?" Antoine gestured to Garrett. "And him?" He pointed at Dan.

"Her lawyer and law enforcement." Jing Jing shrugged. "They both have reasons to be here. You? Not so much. Time to go." She took his arm and tried to guide him out of the bay.

Antoine didn't budge. "Not without my wife."

"Antoine," I said, my head starting to throb again. "Please go."

Dan put his hand on my arm. "I've got this one, Bec."

In one smooth move, he had Antoine's right arm twisted up behind his back and was marching him out of the emergency room.

"Well, that's take care of," Garrett said cheerfully. "And without me being arrested, too."

"It's not over, though." If anything, putting obstacles in Antoine's path made him more determined. I used to think that was sexy. I don't know what was wrong with me.

Jing Jing shook her head. "How come so many men are fighting over you? Don't they know what a pain in the neck you are?"

"It's one of her charms," Garrett said and helped me into the wheelchair to leave. "Let's get you home before you get twin disturbing-the-peace citations from the hospital and your house. Jing Jing is ready to kill you and your dog is howling nonstop."

Twenty-one

I could hear Sprocket howling from two blocks away. "What did Dan do to him?" I asked Garrett.

Garrett steered his Lincoln Navigator onto my street. "I believe he put him in the backyard with food and water."

"Why is he howling like that?" I strained forward against the seat belt to try to see my dog.

Garrett pulled into the driveway. "He's your dog. You were hurt. He doesn't know where you are or if you're okay. He's worried about you."

Awwww. My dog loved me. But ohhhhh that racket he was making was making my head throb. I opened the gate and called to him. "It's okay, buddy. I'm here."

It was like flicking a switch. He went silent, and then he was a quivering, whimpering, face-licking bundle of fur (well, hair actually, since poodles don't have fur). "It's okay, big guy," I kept repeating as I knelt down next to him. "Calm down. It's okay."

Garrett leaned against his car, a funny look on his face. "I know how he feels."

"Dan has been locking you in the backyard? Dude, you have thumbs. You can totally undo the gate." I rested my head against Sprocket's neck.

Garrett snorted. "No. I know what it feels like to be worried about you and to not be able to do much."

I looked up at him. "You worry about me?"

"At this point, I think the whole town worries about you." He held out his hand to help me to my feet.

"The whole town worries about what I might do. That's entirely different than worrying about me." I stumbled a little as I stood up and he caught me against himself. I was suddenly way too aware of the breadth of his chest and the hard muscles beneath his dress shirt.

He shook his head and turned me toward the stairs to the apartment. "Whatever you say, Rebecca. I don't think you see Grand Lake any clearer than it sees you, though."

We went up to the apartment and I put on hot water for tea. Garrett watched as I first warmed the pot and then added the boiling water. "You do have a knack for making everything into a production. You could have microwaved a mug of water and dropped in a tea bag."

"Taste the tea first and then complain about my methods." I poured milk into the bottom of a teacup and then added the tea.

He took a sip. "Fine. It's better. Do you think you could sit down now, though? I'm supposed to be watching you while you rest, not while you make tea for Her Majesty."

I curled up in my favorite spot on the couch with my own cup of tea. "So what do we do now?"

Before he could answer, there was a knock at the door.

Garrett answered it. Jessica walked into my little apartment. "Hi, Garrett," she said. "I didn't know you'd be here."

"I'm staying with Rebecca for the afternoon. The doctor didn't want her to be alone. What exactly are you doing here, Jessica?" He didn't sound like his usual amiable self. He sounded a mite testy. I found that remarkably satisfying.

She held out a pink box. "I heard about what happened. I made these for Rebecca." She cleared her throat. "I'm, uh, also sorry about my little outburst at POPS. I've been having kind of a tough time."

She really did look pathetic. I motioned for her to come in and she handed me the box. She looked around at my apartment. "Ever heard of beige, Rebecca?"

Sprocket stood up from where he'd been lying next to me on the floor and growled a little deep in his throat. I was glad there was someone out there who was willing to defend my interior decorating. I patted his head and he settled back down.

I set the box Jessica had handed me down on the coffee table and opened it. It was filled with little round sandwich cookies. I picked one up. "Macarons, Jessica? Did you make these?"

She nodded.

I was impressed. Macarons are seriously difficult. In fact, I'm not sure there's a more difficult cookie out there to make. Just about everything can go wrong with a macaron. There can be air pockets. The feet can be uneven. The almond flour can be too chunky. The surface can get sticky instead of glossy. They can be mushy. I took one out and took a bite. It was everything I could do not to spit it out in my hand. From what I could taste, pretty much everything that could go wrong did go wrong. That's a lot of wrong for one tiny cookie. I mumbled through the mouthful of crumbs and goo, "Thanks. When did you have time to make these, Jessica? Macarons take hours."

"You're welcome." She shifted from foot to foot. "I'm, uh, not sleeping too well these days. I'd rather keep busy than stare at the ceiling for hours."

Having spent hours staring at the ceiling in the emergency room while being terrorized by a tiny Filipina, I could understand.

"Pretty scary what's going on in town right now. It doesn't feel safe anywhere." Jessica looked at the floor.

"No. It doesn't."

"I heard you think Tom Moffat might have something to do with it." She came over and perched on the edge of one of the armchairs, setting her purse down on the floor.

"Where'd you hear that?" Garrett asked sharply.

She shrugged. "I stopped by the hospital with the cookies first. Jing Jing told me you'd been released, but she also told me what you'd said to Sheriff Cooper about Tom."

Was there no privacy anywhere? "If there's anybody out there who seems to have a grudge against women, it's him," I said.

Jessica nodded. "He's everywhere, too. He would have known about Jasper going into the alley for the popcorn. They were good friends."

I reached down to pet Sprocket and realized he wasn't by my side anymore. He was next to Jessica's purse with his nose deeply in it. "Sprocket! Get out of there!"

He lifted his head and trotted over to his bed in the corner. Jessica grabbed her bag. "Again with your dog? You need to train that thing."

"Sorry," I said. "He's going through a phase."

"Well, hurry him through it." She stood and went to the door.

Seeing Sprocket with his nose in her purse reminded me of the lavender sachet. I got it from the drawer in the kitchen where I'd stashed it. "Jessica, have you seen anything like this around?" I held out the sachet to her.

She looked at it, but didn't take it from my hand. "What is it and why does it look like it's been slobbered on?"

"It's one of the sachets Annie made for Coco. She left them on the back porch that evening. Somehow Sprocket got hold of one of them. Have you seen any others?"

"Where?"

I tried to keep the impatience from my voice. "Anywhere. Jasper says he saw them on the back porch that night around nine thirty before the window was broken, but they weren't there the next day."

"So?" Now she sounded impatient. And annoyed.

"And it seems like whoever took them might know something about what happened."

"So we're to look for an unknown person carrying lavender sachets, and that will be our murderer?" She should carry a bowl to catch all the disdain that dripped off her voice.

"Never mind." I put it back in the drawer, feeling a little stupid. "I won't keep you any longer."

Jessica let herself out. "See you around."

It almost sounded like a threat.

The next day I stopped by the fire department. I walked in through the open bay. "Hello?" My voice echoed off the concrete in the high-ceilinged space.

A young man came out from behind one of the ambulances. "Can I help you?"

"I'm looking for a paramedic."

He grinned. "Well, you've come to the right place. Did you have an idea of what size or shape paramedic you might want?"

I was old enough to be this broad-shouldered young man's . . . aunt. Yeah, let's say aunt. But he was making me blush. "I was actually looking for the paramedic who helped take me to the hospital yesterday."

"Ah. Come on back to the office. If you know where you were, I should be able to find out who gave you a ride." He stopped and turned back to me. "You're not suing us, are you?"

I held up the box of Coco Pop Fudge I'd brought. "No. I'm involved in enough court cases already. Actually I wanted to say thank you."

"And you brought baked goods, too?" he asked.

"You bet." You could get in almost anywhere if you brought baked goods.

He grinned. "You sure I didn't take you?"

I laughed. "Pretty sure. He had dark hair." My flirty friend here was totally a blond.

I followed him into the office. He got behind the computer and tapped a few buttons. "You want Eric Gladstone."

"I don't suppose he's here." That would be too much to hope for.

"I'll check." He went out into the bay and bellowed, "Gladstone! You here? Someone wants to give you treats!"

Apparently I was not the only one who responded to tragedy by bringing food. My paramedic came out from the back room, wiping his hands on a rag as he walked. "Ah," he said. "The popcorn lady."

"Yes. That's me." I held out the box. "I don't remember

a lot of what happened, but I do remember you saying that you liked chocolate."

He took the box and opened it. "Is this that popcorn fudge that everyone's been talking about?"

I blushed again. "Well, I guess I am a bit of a Twitter sensation."

He took a bite and his knees bent a bit. "Whoa. I can see why. Thanks." He started to walk away.

"Wait, Eric. I had a question," I called to his back.

"Shoot." He turned back around.

"Did you say something about Barbara smelling like chocolate and me smelling like almonds when you were taking me to the hospital?" It all seemed a little fuzzy, but I was almost sure that hadn't been a delusion.

He nodded. "Yeah. I noticed the chocolate smell because, well, I love the stuff." He held up the wedge of fudge he had in his hand. "The almond thing reminded me of my grandma. She loved that liqueur, the one that's made out of almonds. Almost smells like maraschino cherries."

"Amaretto?" I suggested.

"That one. Yeah." He smiled and nodded. "She could sure get toasted on that stuff."

"I don't suppose you were on the scene for Coco Bittles, were you?" I asked.

He nodded his head. "Yeah. I was. I'm on graveyard and we're a pretty small department."

"Did you smell anything on her? Any chocolate or almond or anything like that?" Maybe there was some kind of olfactory connection that could help figure this out before all the lady shop owners of Grand Lake had concussions.

He shook his head. "No. But she'd been gone awhile when we got there. Eight or ten hours, easy. I've got a darn good sniffer, but I don't think anybody's that good."

"Thanks. I appreciate you talking to me."

"I appreciate the fudge. This stuff is amazing."

So much for the idea that the chocolate and almond smells would connect all three of us.

I made it to POPS to open for the breakfast crowd the next day. I'd been worried that my on again/off again hours would have chased away my regulars, but there were about five of them waiting when I unlocked at seven thirty. Janet Barry brought me a little teddy bear holding a "Get Well Soon" heart. She brought a smaller one for Sprocket, who took it from her fingers like a nurse removing a splinter. She gave him a pat.

Brandy Johnson and Olive Hicks brought me a bouquet of flowers.

"Aww, you guys," I said. "Coffee's on the house for everybody!"

"I was real sorry to hear about you being attacked," Olive said. "But I was kind of glad at the same time."

I stopped mid-pour. I wasn't sure I wanted to give free coffee to someone who wanted me to be bonked on the head hard enough to knock me out. "You wanted me to be attacked?"

She shuffled her feet. "No, of course not. But now we know for sure that you're not the one who killed Coco, aren't we? Least that's what everyone's saying."

I hadn't realized the jury was still out on that, but rather than pour hot coffee over her head, I decided instead to smile and say, "I was always sure."

She laughed. I gave her her coffee and didn't even spit in it.

The afternoon fudge line was no different. People handed me cards and flowers and little stuffed animals along with their money as they paid for their Coco Pop Fudge. Lots of people told me that they never thought for an instant that I would hurt Coco.

Lots of people had clearly entertained the idea, or they wouldn't have felt it necessary to tell me they hadn't.

While I appreciated the support, I still worried about the idea that there was someone out there with a grudge against the women shop owners of Grand Lake. Worried enough that I had Sam come with me as I took the garbage out to the Dumpster.

He took the bags from me as we walked down the steps of the back porch.

"Thanks, Sam." I stayed by the porch railing as he tossed the bags up and into the bins. I was glad of the chance to stand still. My head had started to throb again and I was looking forward to getting home and curling up on the couch with Sprocket.

"Off to youth group?" I asked as we walked back into the kitchen

Sam shook his head. "You didn't hear?"

"Hear what?" I looked around to see what still needed to be done. Pots and pans had been washed and dried. The floor had been swept. Garbage was out. I sat down at the table.

"Ms. Jessica was asked to step down. We can't meet until we have a new advisor. I guess they don't want to turn a bunch of kids loose in the church with no adult supervision." He sat down across from me and started to play with the salt and pepper shakers.

That was definitely news to me. "Why did they ask her to step down?"

He shrugged. "I think it was that whole car accident thing and then coming in here and yelling at you in front of everybody. People are saying she'd been drinking. They want whoever is advising the youth group to set a good example for us."

And apparently drunk driving at six thirty in the morning didn't count as setting a good example.

"She's not teaching at the preschool, either." Susanna came in and sat down next to Sam. "Mrs. Santos is substituting for her until they make a decision."

Poor Jessica. I never thought those two words would cross my mind together at the same time, but here they were now.

"Reverend Lee said everything was up in the air pending an investigation." Sam nodded gravely.

All these years, I'd wanted everyone to see Jessica as I saw her. Somehow it didn't feel so good once it happened. I knew what it felt like to have everyone look at you with suspicion. It didn't feel good. I didn't want anyone—even someone I didn't like very much—to have to feel that way.

I shut out the lights in the kitchen. Susanna and Sam went out the front door. I flipped the sign on the door from Open to Closed and followed them. As I locked the front door, a huge bang went off behind me.

Instinctively, I crouched in the doorway, arms around Sprocket to protect him. I looked up to see bursting colors in the air over Main Street. Fireworks.

Feeling stupid, I straightened up. Another barrage of fireworks went up. Giant red and blue blossoms of color against the twilight sky. Delicate white arcs of light crossing in front of them. "Ooh," I said. I swear it must be a reflex.

Then the music started. Van Morrison's "Moondance." Possibly the sexiest song ever. I looked around. People stood stock-still on the sidewalk, staring up at the sky at the fireworks, smiling at the music.

Then he was there. Antoine came striding toward me, his

arms full of calla lilies, my favorite flower. He handed me the flowers, and then, in front of everyone, with fireworks going off behind his head and Van Morrison saying it was a fantabulous night to make romance, he sank to one knee. "Rebecca, my love, my muse, my everything. Marry me. Marry me again."

Everyone on the sidewalk burst into applause.

Except me.

Twenty-two

"What the hell?" I whispered to Antoine.

He knelt there before me, his beautiful blue eyes swollen and bruised. "Come home with me, Rebecca. Come back to me. Be with me. Love me." His voice was far from whispery. He knew how to project for an audience and he was using his knowledge. He wanted everyone to hear what he was saying to me.

I swayed on my feet, but not in my heart. Of course he would do it like this, with a huge audience. Of course he would make it over-the-top romantic. Of course he would put me in a ridiculous and uncomfortable spot. If I said no right now in front of all these people I'd look like the meanest girl ever. I'd just gotten the town on my side for the first time since forever. I didn't want to lose them that fast.

I leaned down so it would look like I was kissing Antoine and whispered into his lips, "I am going to kill you."

The whole town cheered. At least, it felt like that.

* * *

After Antoine's way-over-the-top PDA, I'd managed to get home and lock the door with him on one side and me on the other. I'd taken the phone off the hook and stayed inside. I was incredibly relieved to find my porch empty the next morning when I got up.

I was generally the first person on our block of stores to open up. Annie didn't have a breakfast crowd for flowers, although she sometimes came in early to get orders ready. Plus, apparently that whole gardening thing made people get all in sync with nature and sunrises and all that. Lake Erie Collectables never opened before ten. Barbara contended that garage salers got up early, but antique collectors slept in.

Because it was getting darker every morning and what with the whole being smacked on the head with something heavy and hard, I'd started driving to the store in the morning. On Friday, I came in the back and started the breakfast bars. I was getting ready to open my doors at seven thirty when I heard the screaming.

My first thought was, "Not again." I knew the second the words popped into my head that they weren't admirable. But there it was.

I ran to the front door and threw it open. Janet Barry was there with her land cruiser of a stroller, pointing at the doorway of Coco's and screaming. I ran to where she was pointing. Jessica was collapsed in a heap in the doorway. I ran back into the shop and called 911.

Sheila Kim answered. "911. What's your emergency?"

Sheila had been one year behind me in high school. We'd shared a few bleary mornings back in the day. "Sheila, it's

Rebecca Anderson over at POPS. There's been another attack."

"Another one?"

"Yes. Jessica James has been attacked at Coco's Cocoas."

There was a pause. "Not by you, right?"

"No, Sheila. Not by me. Could you send someone? Fast? I think she's unconscious." There was no other way that a person could stay asleep with Janet screaming like that, especially now that the baby and the toddler had both joined in. The noise was deafening and showed no sign of stopping. I wasn't sure which one of them to slap.

"On it, Rebecca."

I went back out and ushered Janet and her kids in. "Sit. Eat whatever you want. There's coffee in the kitchen." Then I ran back out to be with Jessica. She was coming to as I got to her.

"What happened?" she asked groggily.

"You were attacked, Jessica. Don't move too much. The ambulance is on its way." I could already hear the sirens coming. "What were you doing here so early?"

"I wanted to pick up some things." She tried to sit up again and grabbed the back of her head.

I put my arm around her to support her.

She glared at me. "Why are you being nice to me?"

"Because the milk of human kindness runs in my veins, Jessica. What did you think I'd do? Leave you here in the doorway?" I knew the last time I'd helped Jessica hadn't worked out so well, but this time I wasn't going to drag her anywhere. I was going to sit with her until the ambulance came. Nothing more.

"Maybe."

I rolled my eyes and almost got up and left her for saying

that. I wouldn't give her the satisfaction, though. Instead I took off my scarf and wrapped it around her because she'd started shivering.

"Jessica?" I asked.

"What do you want, Rebecca?" She sounded weary.

"Did you happen to smell anything right before you were attacked?" I'd smelled almonds. Barbara had smelled hazelnuts. I'd never know if Coco had smelled anything.

"What do you mean?" Jessica asked.

"I'm not sure, but did you maybe smell some kind of spice or nut or something?"

"Right now the only nut I smell is you." She shut her eyes.

I really, really almost snatched my scarf back for that one. Luckily, Eric Gladstone arrived right then and moved me aside before I could find something to smack Jessica on the head with myself.

Eric had taken Jessica to the hospital, but had left all her stuff in Coco's Cocoa's doorway. I took her bag with me into POPS. Once my morning rush was over, I closed the shop and left a note on the front door saying that I'd be back by two, and drove over to the hospital.

When I walked into the emergency room, Nurse Jing Jing said, "Thank goodness you're here. Are you taking her home?"

"Taking who home?"

"The little one. Jessica. The one who got hit on the head like you." She pointed at one of the bays. "Eric said you were the one who called 911."

Jessica sat propped up in the hospital bed, looking for all the world like a little china doll. Her hair wasn't even mussed. "Isn't someone else coming for her? I was only bringing her bag."

Jing Jing shook her head. "She called about five different people. No one will come. The boyfriend dumped her. Something about using him for free legal help. The preschool principal is teaching for her. Nobody wants her."

"Well, I don't want her, either." I couldn't imagine that Jessica would want me to be the one to take her home. The thought of it made my head start to ache again.

"Yeah, but you're here and I need the bed. I'll sign her out to you." She pulled out a chart and starting making notes on it. "She's really no trouble. Not like you, and you had people fighting to take you home. There's no accounting for taste, I guess."

I was going to protest, but decided it wouldn't kill me to give Jessica a ride home. "Do I have to stay with her?" There were limits to exactly how much human kindness milk was running in my veins.

Jing Jing shook her head. "No. No concussion. She didn't get hit as hard as you did. Whoever hit you really gave you a wallop. Hers was more like a love tap. Hardly even a bruise. Are you sure she was unconscious when you found her?"

"She sure looked unconscious to me." She hadn't even twitched when I first ran up to her.

"Whatever." Jing Jing squeaked over to Jessica. "Your ride is here."

"My what?" She looked up and saw me. Her facial expression told me she was about as thrilled to have me give her a ride as I was to give her one. Then it changed to resignation. "Fine. I'll get dressed."

I pulled the car around. I coaxed Sprocket into the back and helped Jessica into the car once Jing Jing wheeled her out.

Sprocket growled as Jessica got into the car. "Of course you have the beast with you."

"He's not a beast. You and Allen Thompson are seriously the only people he growls at." I buckled my seat belt. "Where do you live?"

Jessica stared at me. "You don't know?"

"Why should I know, Jessica? It's not like you ever invited me over for tea." Although she apparently knew where I lived despite me not inviting her to my place.

She snorted. "Good point. I'm on Marigold Avenue. The seven-hundred block."

That I could work with. I glanced in the rearview mirror. Sprocket had his nose in Jessica's bag again. I snapped my fingers at him, hoping Jessica wouldn't notice. For once, she didn't. When we got to her house, his nose was in my bag. I made sure he wasn't eating any of the fudge I'd packed in a tin in there and then got out to help her out of the car, but she rolled her eyes at me. "I'll be fine," she said. "I don't understand it. You get hit on the head and people are fighting over who gets to take you home. You get proposed to in front of the entire town. Everyone leaves me to rot in the emergency room by myself. I don't know how you do it."

My jaw nearly dropped. "I didn't ask for any of those things."

She glared at me. "That only makes it worse."

"I'm sorry, Jessica." That I really meant.

"Whatever. I mean, thank you." Then she was gone, and I felt like I could breathe again.

I stopped at Garrett's office to drop off the fudge and because he'd pretty much promised me a date once the cease-and-desist thing was over. It was over and I still hadn't gotten my date. Coco Pop Fudge had made him declare undying love for me before. I thought maybe it might at least get me dinner and a movie.

When I walked in, Pearl looked at me and narrowed her eyes. She hit the intercom button. "It's her."

Her tone was totally different than her singsongy "She's here" the last time. Before I could ask why, Garrett was in his doorway. "What do you need, Rebecca?" His tone was short and curt.

I drew back. "I, uh, brought you some Tuxedo Coco Pop Fudge." I held out the package.

He looked at the package and then looked back at me. "Thank you, but I'm not hungry. Did you have a legal problem?"

Amazingly, at the moment, I did not. "No."

He turned and went back into his office, shutting the door behind him with a click. I turned to Pearl. "What's eating him?"

Pearl pursed her lips and then said, "It's not nice to toy with people, Rebecca. Mr. Garrett's a good lawyer and a good man."

Did she think I was going to hold the package of fudge out to him and then snatch it back when he reached for it? "How am I toying with him?"

Pearl rolled her eyes. She tapped on her keyboard for a second or two and then turned the monitor to face me. It displayed the *Grand Lake Sentinel* website. Most of the page was dominated by a photo of Antoine on his knee before me and me bending down to give him what looked like a kiss on the lips. Fireworks were going off behind us.

"That is not what it looks like," I protested.

"Prove it," Pearl said.

I turned around and pounded on Garrett's office door. "That photo is not what it looks like," I shouted.

Nothing happened, so I knocked again. Harder.

This time the door opened. Garrett leaned against the frame, arms crossed loosely over his chest. "I'm listening."

"What I actually was doing was telling him I was going to kill him."

"Kill. Kiss. The words are pretty similar," Pearl said behind me.

I turned. "You're not helping."

She shrugged. "Who said I was on your side?"

I shot her what I hoped was a death-ray look and turned back to Garrett. "You know what he's like. You've met him. He's infuriating and will do anything to get his way. If you oppose him directly, it blows up in your face. I did what I had to do to get away from him without making more of a scene than he was already making."

Garrett rubbed his jaw where the bruise from Antoine's punch was still visible. "He is hard to derail once he gets on track."

"Impossible," I said. "I was married to the man for more than a decade. Believe me. I know. Plus there were all those people watching."

"Ah." Garrett nodded. "The people. Gotta worry about what the people think."

"Yes. I do. You were the one who kept telling me about that whole court-of-public-opinion thing."

"And that was the moment you suddenly decided to start taking my advice?" He leaned in toward me.

I leaned a little toward him. Our faces were very close. "Maybe."

"Where'd you sleep last night?" he asked, looking deep into my eyes.

"In my bed in my apartment." Did my voice sound breathy? It sounded kind of breathy.

"Where did he sleep?" His lips were almost touching mine. His voice sounded a little growly.

"How the hell should I know?" I asked.

"Good answer," he said. Then he kissed me.

I almost didn't notice the sound of Pearl's camera clicking behind us.

As nice as that kiss was, I needed to get back to the shop. Fudge lines were already starting to form out front. I slipped around the back so I'd have a few seconds to compose myself before opening up to the onslaught.

The crowd seemed to have doubled since the day before. After the fifth person congratulated me and asked me when I'd be moving back to Napa, I started to catch on.

Everyone thought their days of Coco Pop Fudge were numbered. That having accepted Antoine's crazy public proposal, I'd be closing up shop. I kept repeating that there was nothing to congratulate me for and that I had no intention of leaving Grand Lake in the near future except for vacations.

It was like trying to ladle out soup with a thimble.

Susanna and Sam showed up as soon as school let out and took over the front counter as I still had my usual Friday afternoon special orders to deal with. It was good to be out of full view. I collapsed into a kitchen chair and gave myself a second to breathe. It became a second to have a little bit of a cry instead. Not those big gut-wrenching boohoos that a girl sometimes needs in times of great stress, just a little weepiness in recognition of having managed to have gotten myself into a difficult spot without ever meaning to do the wrong thing.

Story of my freaking life.

The other story? Getting on with it. Which is what I did.

Crying wasn't going to get the six popcorn buckets and five popcorn ball orders made and ready for pickup.

Once again, cooking became my salvation. Antoine, Garrett, Barbara, Jessica, Coco, Annie, Allen. They all receded into the background while texture and flavor and the balance between salty and sweet took front-and-center stage and danced for me like the beautiful ballerinas they were.

Before I knew it, Sam and Susanna were helping me sweep up and haul out the garbage. "Sit down, Miss Rebecca," Susanna said. "You look exhausted."

I was. Owning a shop, starting a business, moving, it had all been exhausting. It would continue being exhausting for some time to come. With the money that I'd had to use to pay back Jessica gone, it would be months before I could afford to hire more help. I'd be at POPS seven days a week for the foreseeable future. I'd be in the kitchen making popcorn bars and popcorn balls and Coco Pop Fudge. I'd be out front at the counter, smiling and taking people's money. I'd be looking for new ways to keep the business coming in. Totally exhausting. But also exhilarating. And satisfying.

Sam and Susanna said good night and headed out arm in arm, Susanna smiling up at him as he whispered something funny in her ear.

As many times as I'd told Antoine no, as many checks as I'd ripped up and sent back to him, I still let him call me and text me. Every time I picked up the phone and heard that French accent or got a text where he said I was beautiful, I was sucked right back into his orbit. And that was all I would ever be around Antoine. Another piece of rock in orbit around a glorious sun. I might be a favorite rock, but I'd still be a rock.

I texted him a message that said, "**Go home.**" Then I selected Antoine's number from my contact list and blocked it.

As I dropped my phone back into my purse, I felt something soft and silky. The lavender sachet. One of the sachets Annie had made for Coco and left on her back porch. One of the sweet-smelling little packets that Coco would never see or hold or smell. I held it to my nose and breathed in the soothing lavender.

And sneezed. Nothing was really working out as planned that day.

I was about to drop it back into my purse when I remembered that it was supposed to be in a drawer in my apartment kitchen. I held it out in my hand and stared at it. Sprocket trotted over to me. "Where'd you get this?" I asked him. "Who did you steal this little thing from?"

Sprocket sniffed it and growled.

Sprocket has always been more of a lover than a fighter. I like to think he's too dignified to get into scrapes with other dogs, but it's possible that he's a chickenshit. Whatever his motivations, there were only two people he growled at who I could think of: Jessica James and Allen Thompson.

I'd been around only one of them that day. Only one of them had been in my car. Sprocket had only had his nose in one of their bags.

The lavender sachets that Annie had left on Coco's back porch were in Jessica's bag. There was only one way they could have gotten there. They could only have gotten there if Jessica had picked them up from the back porch of Coco's Cocoas after Jasper left that night and before I came charging through in the morning.

Which meant Jessica was the one who had shattered the window and faked the break-in. Which meant Jessica was the one who had pushed Coco hard enough to make her stumble backward and hit her head.

Perhaps the stricken face, the drinking and everything else was guilt instead of grief?

As I stared at the little lavender square in my hand, things started clicking into place. I smelled almonds right before I was attacked. Jessica had to have been making the macarons—one of whose chief ingredients was almond flour—before the attack. They took hours to make. She had to have been making them long before she showed up to give the box to me the next day. Barbara had smelled hazelnuts. The next day Jessica had brought her the time-consuming Nutella-stuffed cookies. Nutella was made with hazelnuts.

Sprocket had growled as we walked into POPS right before someone hit me on the head. Sprocket only growled at Jessica and Allen. Whoever had hit me had had to stand on a chair to smack me over the head. Jessica was ten inches shorter than me.

While I'd found Coco's to-do-list notepad, I'd never found the actual to-do list. If I was going to get rid of a list like that, I'd burn it. Jessica's fingers had been burned and bandaged when she'd gotten to the youth group ice cream social, the social she'd left with plenty of time to get back to Coco's shop, fake the break-in and then set up Jasper.

Could the cookie deliveries to Jasper be because she felt guilty for framing him? Were the cookies for me and Barbara offerings made from guilt over hurting us?

Although, who had hit Jessica over the head, then? Could it be possible she'd done it herself? Nurse Jing Jing had said it wasn't much of an injury. Could Jessica have faked being unconscious? It wouldn't be much of an act after years of faking being nice.

I picked up the phone and called Garrett's office. I got

Pearl's voice telling me the office was closed for the day, but I could leave a message. I tried his cell and got his voicemail. I glanced at the clock. Five thirty. I knew precisely where Garrett would be. He'd be running along the lake.

I snapped on Sprocket's leash. "Let's go, boy. We've got some 'splaining to do." I hoped Garrett would help me explain it all to Dan.

Twenty-three

Sprocket and I got to the lake. There was only one car in the parking lot. I did a double take. It was Coco's white Buick. Goose bumps prickled my skin. As I walked on, I saw the door of the lighthouse was open. Of course, it was Friday. The historical society would be meeting. Jessica would be setting up. She must be driving the Buick since she wrecked her Civic.

I looked around. No Garrett in sight. He hadn't made it to the lighthouse yet. He'd be here soon enough, though. I looked down at Sprocket. "How about we ask Jessica some questions, boy?"

He growled. I took that as a yes. We walked to the lighthouse and stepped through the open door into the dim interior. Jessica turned around as we walked in. "What do you want now, Rebecca?" she asked.

"I wanted to ask you about this, Jessica." I held out the sachet. I pulled back on Sprocket's leash to get him to sit. His growl had gone from something low and soft to something loud and frightening, a sound I'd never heard from him before.

"You showed me that before, Rebecca. I told you I didn't know anything about it." She continued setting out food on the folding table.

"This isn't the same one, Jessica. The one I showed you is back in my kitchen. This is another one. Another one that I think Sprocket might have taken from your purse." I took another step into the lighthouse.

She stopped rearranging the cookies on the platters and turned around. "Oh, that," she said. She reached into her purse and took out a gun. I felt like time stopped. I'd been expecting her to pull out another sachet. Or a tissue. Or a cookie. But a gun? I didn't know what to do. Unfortunately, Sprocket thought he did. He lunged at Jessica and she shot him.

For a second, I couldn't move. I couldn't believe what I'd just seen. Tiny little Jessica holding a perfectly tiny but lethal-looking gun.

I lunged at her, too, but she swung the gun around to point it at me. "Uh-uh, Rebecca. You stay right where you are."

I knelt next to Sprocket, trying to staunch the bleeding at his shoulder with my hands. There was so much of it so fast. "You shot my dog!"

"You threw out my Snickerdoodle!" she shouted back.

"What?" I pulled off my jacket and pressed it against the wound. Sprocket whimpered at the pressure.

"The Snickerdoodles I took Jasper. You took one bite and threw out the rest. You might as well have thrown it in my face. You practically spit out my Nutella-stuffed cookie that I brought Barbara, and don't think I didn't see your face when you bit into my macaron." Her eyes were wild.

I looked up and stared at her, trying to connect what she

was saying. "You're going to kill me and my dog because I didn't want to eat cookies that hadn't been made properly?"

"Oh, you and your fancy cooking education." She started talking in a singsong voice. "This is proper. That is right. This is wrong. That's not good enough. Judge much, Rebecca?"

That stung. I did judge. I judged Jessica all the time and Jessica always came up wanting. It was reason enough to hate me, but it damn sure wasn't reason enough to kill Coco. "That's why you did it? That's why you killed Coco? Because I don't like the way you bake?"

She rolled her eyes and sighed. "Don't be an idiot, Rebecca. Although that's your fault, too, you know?"

I clamped my mouth shut, not sure if I could say anything without the hot rush of tears that had flooded into my eyes spilling out, and I didn't feel like giving Jessica the satisfaction. When I finally spoke, my voice came out low and menacing. "How could it possibly be my fault that you killed your aunt, Jessica? How?"

"It was that damn business plan. That had you and your fancy cooking-school ways written all over it. I went to see Coco and I saw her to-do list. Item number four, Rebecca. Item number four was change her will. She was going to give you the fudge recipe. All I'd get was the stupid store. I didn't mean for Aunt Coco to fall. It was only a little push . . ." Jessica's face crumpled.

I took my chance and lunged forward to try to get the gun, hoping my longer arm length would give me an advantage.

It didn't.

Jessica drew back and smacked me upside the head with the gun. I reeled to the side, stunned.

"Stay back, Rebecca. Stay back or I swear to God I'll shoot." Her voice shook, but her hand was steady.

"And say what? That a stranger shot me?" She couldn't possibly think she would get away with shooting me in cold blood in the Grand Lake Lighthouse.

"Why not? Everyone thinks that Coco's murderer is still roaming free. Why couldn't it be the same person? You ever so conveniently cast doubt on Tom Moffat the other day. Maybe he did it. I sincerely doubt he has an alibi."

I almost smacked myself on the head this time. "It is the same person, Jessica. It's you. You're the murderer and you would be the one who shot me. Everyone would be right except the part about it being Tom Moffat."

Jessica made a noise of disgust in her throat. "I cannot believe you're arguing that kind of stupid detail with me at a time like this. You never can see the big picture."

I was about to point out that it didn't seem like I'd have any other time to argue with her, what with the whole part where she was about to shoot me like she'd shot my dog, when I saw him. Just outside the lighthouse door. Just a little flash of well-muscled thigh.

Jessica was still talking. "You know, Jasper's arrest was your fault, too. Dan would never have gone over there if you hadn't said he was going to pick up your stale, nasty popcorn."

"You planted evidence at his house. You framed him, Jessica. That's why Dan arrested him." I edged a little more toward the center of the lighthouse so Jessica would adjust and her back would be more toward the door.

"I only planted the evidence as a precaution. Then I felt terrible. That's why I had to break into Barbara's place so it would look like whoever broke into Coco's was still on the loose and Dan would know it couldn't be Jasper." She edged a step or two toward the door.

"Jessica, you were the one who broke into Coco's. You

were still on the loose. You didn't need to make it look that way. It was that way." Jessica never had been one to take responsibility for her own actions, but this was ridiculous.

"You know what I mean!" she shouted.

And that's when he came barreling into the lighthouse. Except it was the wrong he. It wasn't Garrett, here to save my hide. It was Antoine.

"Rebecca, why will you not answer my calls?" Antoine said, not even noticing Jessica or the gun. If he'd ever been that focused on me before, we'd probably still be married.

"Seriously, Rebecca?" Jessica said. "Now you're going to make me kill Antoine Belanger, too?"

"Kill who?" Antoine swiveled, now fully taking in the situation. "Why is this little person pointing a gun at you, *chérie*?"

"She killed Coco," I explained. "It was an accident. Everything that's happened since has been her trying to cover it up." I turned back to Jessica. "Drop the gun, Jessica. If you explain, everyone will understand. You didn't mean to hurt Coco, and afterward you panicked. No one will blame you."

"Everyone will blame me!" she shrieked. "That's your fault, too! Why did you have to tell them all I was selling the shop and the recipe? You turned the whole town against me."

"Uh, because you filed a lawsuit against me. I was defending myself." The turning the town against her had been an added bonus, one that I wasn't nearly as pleased with as I thought I'd be. "Think of it as my way of biting your knee."

"I lost everything, Rebecca. Everything. Everyone's whispering behind my back. Everyone's talking about me." She stamped her foot.

"Sucks, doesn't it?" I said wryly.

If Jessica recognized the irony of how often she'd gotten

the town to turn against me, she wasn't acknowledging it. "Yes. Yes, it does."

She looked back and forth between Antoine and me. "This will be better, though. This can be a lover's quarrel. Antoine shoots you and then commits suicide."

"What?" Antoine squawked. "I do what?"

"You first, Rebecca." She brought the gun around toward me again, legs apart, both hands on the gun. She looked like she'd practiced.

"Jessica, wait," I said.

Antoine took that moment to bolt for the lighthouse door. Jessica turned toward the movement and as Antoine high-tailed it out of the way, Garrett barreled in and tackled Jessica to the floor. Her hand released the gun as it hit the ground and it skittered away.

I collapsed onto my bleeding dog in relief.

Antoine did one thing right. He called 911. Dan was at the lighthouse almost before Garrett and Jessica hit the ground. Eric Gladstone was approximately two minutes behind him. There were a couple of minutes of confusion because I was covered in blood. Once I explained it was Sprocket's and not mine, things went a lot more smoothly. It wasn't exactly standard operating procedure, but Eric took Sprocket to the emergency vet hospital in his ambulance with me riding shotgun.

I didn't even get to thank Garrett for saving my life. Eric hustled us out of there that fast.

Sprocket's wound was what the vet called a through and through. It passed through Sprocket's body without hitting any major organs. He had a bad night and the recuperation would not be a picnic for any of us, but he was going to live.

Even so, it was almost noon the next day before I got home. I dragged myself up the stairs to the garage apartment, took a shower then lay down on the bed and let myself have a good long cry.

Sometimes a good cry is the only remedy.

Jessica was in custody. No one would be preying on the women shop owners of Grand Lake anymore, unless you counted Tom Moffat's occasional verbal attacks. After being hit on the head and almost shot, I didn't count it. Sticks and stones and all that. He could yell at me all he wanted.

I didn't open POPS for a few days. I knew it wasn't smart business. It doesn't do to disappoint regulars. Still, I didn't have the heart to go back right away. Plus, Sprocket needed me. He was healing well, but a gunshot wound is a gunshot wound. Seeing him in pain without understanding why was one more reason that I didn't think I'd ever be able to forgive Jessica.

Then, of course, there was the press. It wasn't every day there was a shooting in a historic lighthouse involving a celebrity chef, an officer of the court, a standard poodle and a fudge recipe. According to Dan, there were probably at least ten different news outlets with vans and cameras and giant microphones camped in front of the store. To Dan's relief, I listened to him and used his advice as one more excuse to stay home. A few days of no story and they took their curiosity and their resources elsewhere.

The days were up, though. It was time to go back. Sprocket had healed to the point that he could walk down the stairs from the granny flat. Have I mentioned how much fun it is to carry a fifty-pound dog up and down even one flight of steps? Probably not, because it was really no fun at all.

There was no way he could make the walk. Besides, I was still having a little trouble walking anywhere in the dark without hyperventilating. So I loaded him into the car and we drove through the darkened streets of Grand Lake. I parked in the alley. The back window of Coco's shop had been repaired. It looked like it was waiting for her to show up and open for the day. I wasn't sure which was worse: seeing it boarded up and looking deserted or seeing it look so expectant.

Both sucked. Grand Lake without Coco sucked. The fact that I was more than a small part of the reason that she'd never open Coco's Cocoas again made my heart hurt.

I went in anyway. What else was there to do? I turned on the lights and let the kitchen soothe me. I started coffee and fresh popcorn. I measured and stirred and chopped and combined. I stopped to taste test because Jessica had been right all those years ago with the chocolate mousse.

There was butter and salt and honey. The water boiled, the steam condensed, the ingredients greeted one another and mingled like good friends at a reunion. This was what Coco had given me. Work that made all my senses sing, as it had done for her. I went out to the front of the shop, ready to see an empty sidewalk when I flipped the Closed sign to Open and turned on the lights.

Instead, Janet with her double stroller stood there looking anxious and tired. "You're opening?" she asked.

I nodded.

"Is there coffee?"

I smiled and held the door open for her.

A few minutes later, Annie poked her head in. "You opened!"

I nodded and poured her coffee.

Ten minutes after that, Eric Gladstone and another

paramedic showed up wanting post-shift breakfast bars. Apparently they go as well with beer as they do with coffee.

It started like that. A trickle of customers when I opened the doors. The trickle became more of a stream at about nine. When coffee-break time hit at ten, the stream grew that much more. When I finally hit a lull at lunchtime, I realized I'd better get the fudge ready for the afternoon. When that was done, I collapsed onto a chair in the kitchen only to be confronted by the binder that contained the business plan Coco had mapped out for the two of us.

Annie slipped in the back door and sat down across from me.

"I'm not sure I can do this," I said.

"Of course you can," she said.

I tapped the binder. "If I hadn't come back, she wouldn't have written this and she'd still be alive."

"I don't think that's the only way to look at this." Annie pulled the business plan over and started leafing through the pages. She sighed. "Damn, she made a nice pie chart, didn't she?"

"What other way is there to look at it?"

"You revitalized her. You put a skip back in her step. She always loved her shop, but she'd gotten bored and tired. You brought excitement back."

"And that excitement got her killed." If Coco hadn't gotten that spring back in her step, would Jessica have even noticed the business plan that pushed her over the edge?

"No. Jessica got her killed." Annie leaned back in her chair, fixing me with those bright blue eyes.

"Because Jessica was jealous. Of me." Try as I might, I couldn't seem to get away from it. Jessica had told me it was my fault that Coco was dead, and even though I knew she was crazy, I could see her point.

"No, because Jessica is an entitled little brat and always has been. That's not your fault." Annie shut the binder and smoothed her hands over the front. "I'm not saying what happened wasn't tragic. You're not the only one who's going to miss Coco."

"I know that." I covered her hand with mine. "Even Jessica misses her. You can see it on her face."

It had been hard to tell what Jessica was more upset about when she was arraigned: Coco's death or the fact that she'd been caught. When Judge Romero asked if she had anything to say, she'd stood and talked about the example Coco had set for how business should be done in a small town and how to lead a life of dignity. She'd talked about her grief at losing the person who'd been both a mentor and a friend. She'd talked about what a loss Coco's death was to the community.

"I know," Annie said. "Everything she said about Coco was absolutely right. Yet somehow she missed the fact that she was the one who ended it all."

I picked up a popcorn bar and took a bite. "It just goes to show you, even in the craziest bowl of popcorn, there's often still a kernel of truth."

RECIPES

BREAKFAST BARS

4 cups popcorn
⅜ cup brown sugar
⅙ cup honey
1 tablespoon butter
½ cup dried fruit
½ cup nuts or seeds

Or seriously, get crazy with it. I love dried cranberries and white chocolate chips together. Coconut with slivered almonds is pretty awesome, too. Pack those puppies with everything you like and call it good!

Line a square pan with parchment paper. Mix together all ingredients. Press into prepared pan. Let sit for 10 to 15 minutes. Turn out onto cutting board. Cut into bars.

POPCORN BALLS

3 ½ ounces marshmallow crème
Kahlúa (or vanilla if you prefer, or really any kind of
    liqueur)
4 cups popcorn

Heat the marshmallow crème in the microwave. I recommend using 50 percent power for 30 seconds. Keep going with 30-second increments until crème is easy to stir. Stir in Kahlúa. Fold in popcorn. Grease your hands and form into balls. Allow the balls to sit on wax or parchment paper while you make the chocolate glaze.

CHOCOLATE GLAZE
3 tablespoons cocoa
2 tablespoons butter
1 cup powdered sugar
3 tablespoons milk

Combine all ingredients in a saucepan. Whisk together over low heat until combined. Don't let this glaze sit. It hardens relatively quickly. You can reconstitute it by adding a little milk and heating again, but it won't be quite the same.

Dip the popcorn balls in the glaze. Let sit until the glaze hardens.

POPCORN FUDGE

¼ cup butter
¼ cup brown sugar

4 teaspoons corn syrup
½ teaspoon baking soda
1 teaspoon vanilla
4 cups popped corn
1 ¼ cups sweetened condensed milk
2 cups chocolate chips
½ teaspoon salt
⅛ teaspoon cayenne

Preheat oven to 250 degrees.

Combine butter, brown sugar and corn syrup in a saucepan. Bring to a boil while stirring. Then hands off for four minutes! Seriously, let it do its thing. At the end of the four minutes, add in baking soda and vanilla, then pour the caramel sauce over the popcorn and combine well. You'll have to use your hands, so grease 'em up and get in there.

Spread popcorn out on a baking sheet. Bake for 30 minutes to an hour at 250 degrees. Check it every 15 minutes to avoid burning. The caramel corn should be light and crispy.

Once the popcorn is out of the oven, start making the fudge layer.

Line a square pan with foil. Combine sweetened condensed milk and chocolate chips either in a double boiler or in the microwave. Either way, stir often. When everything is melted and mixed together, add in salt and cayenne. Pour into prepared pan. Press caramel corn into the fudge. Refrigerate for two hours. Turn out onto a cutting board and cut into squares.

Keep reading for a special preview of
Kristi Abbott's next Popcorn Shop Mystery . . .

Pop Goes the Murder

Coming soon from Berkley Prime Crime!

I knocked on the hotel room door. No one answered. I glanced at my watch. Seven forty-five in the morning. I was right on time. The fact that I'd had to dump the hectic breakfast crowd on Susanna and Sam to be on time for this meeting didn't irritate me at all. Now that it appeared that the person who had insisted she could only make time to talk to me from seven forty-five to eight fifteen on Wednesday morning wasn't answering her door, I didn't feel like the top of my head was about to explode like a can of dulce de leche left to steam too long. No. Of course not.

I knocked again. I'd never really liked Melanie, not from the first moment Antoine Belanger had hired her. Everyone thought it was about jealousy, but if it was, it wasn't because I was jealous of Melanie. I'd been fine with Antoine needing an assistant. I'd been fine when he hired a young and frankly quite good-looking woman. I'd even been fine when I'd realized that she pretty much looked like a younger, slightly prettier version of me, from her curly, sandy brown hair to her slightly too-long feet. I'd just gotten an odd vibe off Melanie. A vibe I recognized. A you're-in-my-way vibe.

I knocked a third time. Hard. This time, the door swung open. Melanie must not have latched it all the way. "Melanie?" I called. "It's Rebecca. I'm here for our meeting."

The meeting you called.

I wasn't even all that thrilled about the reason for the meeting. A few months before, my ex-husband, Antoine, had walked in on someone threatening to shoot me and had run the other way faster than a soufflé can fall. While he kept explaining to me that he'd been running to get help, we both knew the truth. He was a big fat French chicken. He was also, however, a big fat French chicken with a seriously influential television show. A show that was watched by tens of thousands of people across the nation. A show that had launched Antoine's successful line of pasta sauces.

A show that could launch my little gourmet popcorn shop into the stratosphere.

To make up for leaving me to be gunned down in the lighthouse where my father had proposed to my mother, Antoine had offered to feature my breakfast bars and popcorn fudge on his television show.

Antoine somehow thought this might win me back, but I'd been done with him since before he'd left me staring down the very black, cold tunnel of a gun. Now I was beyond done. So done you couldn't even stick a fork in me. The starstruck culinary school student who had run off with the man who taught her to make a béchamel sauce that could make gods weep existed no longer. In her place was a grown-ass woman who still knew it was stupid to turn down free publicity, even when it came from her ex-husband.

I walked into the hotel room, Sprocket at my side. Having

my dog with me made me feel brave. "Melanie," I called again. "I'm here for the meeting."

The bed was made. Clothes were strewn across the couch in the sitting area. Papers covered the desk. The bathroom door was ajar.

The first feeling of unease climbed up my spine. I ignored it. I watched way too many psychological thrillers. I was being dramatic. Apparently Sprocket had watched too many movies with me. He whined and then growled low in his throat. I knocked lightly on the bathroom door. It swung open.

Melanie floated in the bathtub, sightless eyes staring at the ceiling. A big, black blow-dryer plugged into the wall floated in the tub with her.

Apparently our meeting was going to be indefinitely postponed.

Sheriff Dan Cooper, my bestie and brother-in-law all rolled into one handsome, broad-shouldered package, crouched down next to me where I sat slumped against the wall in the hallway. "You okay?"

I looked up at him. "Define okay."

He knocked his hat back a little on his head. "Are you going to barf or faint?"

I did a quick mental scan. "No, but I might have nightmares." I buried my nose in Sprocket's fur.

"That's Sprocket's problem. Not mine." He patted my shoulder. "Do you think you can answer some questions?"

I nodded. "Is there any chance that I could have some coffee while I do?" I felt ridiculously cold. Plus I'd sort of been counting on having coffee at the breakfast meeting that was now very clearly not going to happen. I was fairly certain that I'd remember more of what I'd seen with some caffeine in my system.

"Sure. We can go down to the coffee shop in the lobby."

"I meant real coffee." I wasn't sure what the Grand Lake Café used to make the fluid they sold as coffee—I suspected liquid from wringing out dirty rags—but I was fairly certain it had never come from a bean.

"I don't think this is the moment to be snobby about your coffee." Dan stood and extended a hand down to help me up.

"I'm probably in shock. I can't think of a more important moment to be sure to have good coffee." I took his hand and let him heave me to my feet.

He gestured for me to walk in front of him down the hall. "Maybe they can make you some tea."

"I doubt it." Trust me. The number of restaurants in America that can make a decent cuppa is fewer than hen's teeth, and hens have absolutely no teeth whatsoever. I walked anyway.

The Grand Lake Café was a typical hotel-lobby coffee shop. Not quite a diner. Not quite a restaurant. Not quite anything, really, but a place where desperate travelers could at least get enough sustenance to maintain life. I didn't recognize the waitress on duty. She looked young. Maybe nineteen or twenty, and like she might be pretty out of the horrid mustard-colored uniform she wore. It was weird to actually run into someone in town whom I didn't know somehow. My footsteps balked as we crossed the threshold.

"Sorry, Bec. You're going to have to slum it. I can't leave here right now and I need to know what you saw." He shook his head. "Again."

We sat down in the café with Sprocket under the table. The waitress gave him a pointed look, but Dan smiled up at her. "He's kind of like a service dog at the moment," he said.

"As long as you're the one telling the Health Department that," she said with a shrug.

Dan asked her to bring a cup of coffee and a pot of Earl Grey. Sure enough, she showed up with a white mug full of a tannish, greasy-looking liquid and a do-it-yourself assembly kit of a tea bag, a mug and a pot of tepid water.

I sighed and poured the water over the tea bag. Aromatic oils were not released. I could tell. Dan took a sip of his coffee and winced.

"Told you so." The satisfaction of being right did little to make me feel better at the moment.

"I'll suffer in the line of duty," he said. "Now what were you doing in Melanie Fitzgerald's hotel room?"

I sighed, sipped at my weak, tepid tea and explained about the meeting, about how we were going to go over the logistics, the shooting schedule, the cooking scenes in the kitchen.

Dan rubbed his face. "I knew there would be trouble the second you told me Antoine was coming to town with his crew."

Dan had never been exactly what I'd call an Antoine fan. First of all, Antoine tended to appeal to women more. They loved that hint of French accent, the piercing blue eyes, the blond hair, the quick grin, the way he threw his head back when he laughed . . . basically all the reasons I fell in love with him. He had legions of female fans, many of a certain age. They called themselves the Belanger Bunnies. They had Facebook groups, Twitter hashtags, YouTube channels, Tumblrs, Pinterest boards. Well, everything. So Dan wasn't exactly Antoine's usual demographic. I thought if you asked Dan to tweet he'd tell you he never did that in public.

Second, my marriage to Antoine had represented the moment when Dan realized I was never coming back to Grand

Lake. Or at least, he thought I'd never come back. With my marriage, my life had taken a turn that set me firmly on a path that did not include little resort towns on Lake Erie.

Boy, had he been wrong about that! I had come running back full speed after my divorce. Somehow, though, Dan still harbored ill will toward my charismatic ex.

"I'm not sure you can blame him for this one, Dan." Which was when it occurred to me to wonder who should be blamed. Who was responsible? Or was anyone to blame at all? Maybe I was a little in shock.

"I know. How well did you know Melanie?" Dan asked, taking his little notepad out of his breast pocket.

I shrugged. "She's been Antoine's assistant for years. He relies on her for everything."

Dan arched a brow at me. "Everything?"

"Get your mind out of the gutter, Cooper. Seriously, do you think about my sister with that brain?" Men. Need I say more?

He grinned slightly wolfishly. "Actually I do. But that's beside the point. Was Melanie Antoine's lover?"

"I can't say what they are and aren't to each other now, but I don't think she was Antoine's lover when Antoine and I were married." I suspected it wasn't for lack of trying on her part, but that was another story. I also suspected that Melanie had had something to do with the last big fight Antoine and I had. She had been the assistant who packed up everything in our hotel room in Minneapolis while I was seeing a play at the Guthrie and whisked Antoine off to a last-minute TV spot in Florida, leaving me behind without even a change of underpants in Minnesota in January.

But I wasn't bitter. Not me.

"What do you know about her personal life?" Dan asked.

I leaned back and shut my eyes, but nothing much came to me. "Not a whole lot," I said, straightening up and looking at Dan. "I think there was a boyfriend in the picture back in the day, but that was over two years ago now. They could have broken up or gotten married. I wouldn't exactly be on the list of people Melanie would have notified about it. She wasn't wearing a ring, if that helps any."

"Yeah. I see your point." Dan chewed on the end of his pen. "Let's talk about the crime scene."

I took a big gulp of my tea. I didn't want to think too hard about the crime scene. It was bad enough as it was. The fact that it brought back memories of another time I'd had to describe a crime scene to Dan didn't help. The last time it had been my dear friend and mentor Coco Bittles who had lain dead at the center of the scene. I still saw her lifeless body slumped against her antique credenza as I fell asleep some nights. I knew he had to do his job, though. "Okay."

He touched my hand lightly. He knew this was hard for me. "Tell me about when you first entered the room."

"The door swung open on its own when I knocked." I shut my eyes to try to picture it all. "The room was kind of a mess. She had clothes strewn across the couch and bed and shoes all over the floor."

The bed had been made, too. I tried to picture the clothes on it. Dresses. Some jeans with a silky top. My head came up. "Dress-up clothes. Not everyday clothes. Like maybe she was getting ready for a date or something." My hand flew to my mouth. "Do you mean she was lying there dead in that tub all night?"

Dan's lips tightened. "I have to wait for the medical examiner to make that determination, Rebecca. She may have been, though."

Poor Melanie. Floating like that all night, waiting for someone to find her. I tried to choke back a sob and made a weird little whimpering sound instead.

"You okay?" Dan asked. "Do you need a break?"

I shook my head. It would be better to get this over with. Then maybe I wouldn't have to think about poor Melanie floating in the bathtub like an extra poached egg no one needed for eggs Benedict. "What else do you want to know?"

"Did you see anyone in the hallway or the elevator as you were going up to her room?" His pen was poised over the notepad.

"No." I was sorry to disappoint him, but there didn't seem to be much point in making up sinister strangers hiding in stairwells.

"In the lobby?" He sounded hopeful.

I was about to shoot that down when I remembered something. "I think I saw Lucy coming in here, into the café."

"Lucy?" Dan arched a brow at me.

"One of the production assistants. They're all staying here at the hotel." Hardly significant, but he asked. A television show employee getting coffee in the morning didn't seem like it would be a big break.

"Did you touch anything at the crime scene?" Dan asked, looking at me pointedly.

I'd known this question was coming. I'd known what I was—or more to the point, wasn't—supposed to do. After all, hadn't I been yelled at enough for straightening Coco's skirt after she died so the entire town wouldn't see her knickers? It couldn't be helped, though. Only a woman who did not have the milk of human kindness in her latte could have left Melanie like that, floating naked in the tub to be ogled and photographed and gossiped about. "I covered her with a towel." I said it really softly in the hopes that Dan would let it go quietly.

I was disappointed. He slapped the table so hard our mugs jumped. Coffee and Earl Grey sloshed all over the fake wood. "I knew it! The second I saw that towel I knew it. It's a crime scene, Rebecca. A. Crime. Scene. You're not supposed to touch anything. You know that."

"I wanted to grant her that much dignity. Lord knows she won't have much else." I grabbed some napkins to soak up the spills. "No woman could have left her uncovered."

"You said the same thing about Coco." His lips were set in a grim line.

I shrugged. "The circumstances were similar in a lot of ways."

He shook his head. "Did you touch anything else?" he asked.

"Nothing." I thought back over my trip through the hotel room. "Definitely nothing."

Dan made a note. "Did you notice anything else? Anything out of the ordinary? Anything that didn't seem quite right?"

Like it or not, every time I shut my eyes, the whole scene flooded back in high relief, every detail distinct and sharp. Melanie. The bathtub. The bathmat. The towels. The blow-dryer.

Wait. The blow-dryer. I sat up straight.

"What?" Dan asked. "What are you remembering?"

"That blow-dryer isn't Melanie's."

Dan leaned back in his chair and crossed his arms over his chest. "You don't know if she's married, but you know what kind of blow-dryer she uses?"

I ignored the blatant skepticism in his voice. "Melanie had curly hair like mine."

"So?"

"No self-respecting curly-haired woman would use a blow-dryer without a diffuser if she used one at all, and Melanie respected herself plenty. Trust me. That was not her blow-dryer."

He shrugged. "So it was the hotel's."

Oh. I hadn't thought of that. Still . . . "Why was it plugged in then? She wouldn't have used it."

"I don't know, Rebecca." He sighed. "Honestly, you know as much as I do at this point."

"What do you think happened?"

Dan sighed again. "I have no idea at this point, Rebecca." He leaned forward to look me right in the eye. "And if I did, I wouldn't tell you. You are a witness. In fact, you're barely that. You're just the person who found the body. This has nothing to do with you, and there is absolutely no reason for you to get involved in any way. Understood?" His eyes had gone laser-beam bright and a muscle twitched in his jawline.

I leaned back, slightly affronted. "I know. This isn't like what happened with Coco."

He leaned even farther forward. If this kept up he'd be in my lap, and then the gossips of Grand Lake would really have something to talk about. "There was no reason for you to get involved the way you did with what happened to Coco either, Rebecca. You're a civilian. Not a detective. Not a police officer. You're a chef. Stick to the kitchen."

I'll admit it, that stung a bit. I got it. I had almost gotten myself killed, but I was also pretty certain that Coco's killer would never have been caught if I hadn't intervened.

Sometimes it takes a chef to sniff out what's rotten in a kitchen.

ABOUT THE AUTHOR

Kernel of Truth is Kristi's first book with Berkley Prime Crime. She has been obsessed with popcorn ever since she first tasted the caramel-cashew popcorn at Garrett's in Chicago. If you've never had it, you might want to hop on a plane and go now. Seriously, it's that good.

Kristi lives in northern California, although she was born in Ohio like the heroine of *Kernel of Truth*. She loves snack food, crocheting, her kids, and her man, not necessarily in that order.